MURDEROUS
MISTRAL

MURDEROUS MISTRAL

CAY RADEMACHER

TRANSLATED FROM THE GERMAN BY PETER MILLAR

MINOTAUR BOOKS ✖ NEW YORK

MURDEROUS MISTRAL. Copyright © 2015 by Cay Rademacher. Translation copyright © 2017 by Peter Millar. All rights reserved. Printed in the United States of America. For information, address St. Martin's Press, 175 Fifth Avenue, New York, N.Y. 10010.

www.minotaurbooks.com

Designed by Omar Chapa

The Library of Congress has cataloged the hardcover edition as follows:

Names: Rademacher, Cay, author. | Millar, Peter, translator.
Title: Murderous mistral : a Provence mystery / Cay Rademacher ; translated from the German by Peter Millar.
Other titles: Mörderischer Mistral. English
Description: First U.S. edition. | New York : Minotaur Books, 2017.
Identifiers: LCCN 2017022285 | ISBN 9781250110701 (hardcover) | ISBN 9781250110718 (ebook)
Subjects: LCSH: Murder—Investigation—France—Provence—Fiction. | Private investigators—France—Provence—Fiction. | GSAFD: Mystery fiction.
Classification: LCC PT2678.A238 M6713 2017 | DDC 833/.92—dc23
LC record available at https://lccn.loc.gov/2017022285

ISBN 978-1-250-19804-4 (trade paperback)

Our books may be purchased in bulk for promotional, educational, or business use. Please contact your local bookseller or the Macmillan Corporate and Premium Sales Department at 1-800-221-7945, extension 5442, or by email at MacmillanSpecialMarkets@macmillan.com.

First published in Germany by Dumont Buchverlag Gmbh under the title *Mörderischer Mistral: Ein Provence-Krimi mit Capitaine Roger Blanc*

First Minotaur Books Paperback Edition: October 2018

10 9 8 7 6 5 4 3 2 1

It is noon; the day itself stands at a point of balance.

–Albert Camus

MURDEROUS MISTRAL

An Old House in Provence

Roger Blanc kicked at a stone, startling a black scorpion underneath it. The creature was as long as his thumb and its curved stinger rose threateningly. Within seconds it had scuttled away under the gravel. Welcome home, Blanc thought.

He was a captain in a special unit of the Paris gendarmerie, in his early forties, with pale blue eyes, and he wore a black T-shirt, jeans, and shabby sneakers. He was an expert detective who had solved so many cases it seemed almost supernatural to his colleagues. He lived in an apartment high above the sixteenth arrondissement, and was married to a wonderful woman. Or had been. Until 11:30 A.M. last Friday. Now it was 9:00 on Monday morning and his career was in the trash can. There were already photos of his apartment in the real estate agent's window and his wife was in the arms of her lover. He'd known weeks that had started better.

The sun shone mercilessly down on a ruin of yellowy-brown stone more than five hundred miles south of Paris. The hamlet of Sainte-Françoise-la-Vallée was so tiny that it had taken his Nokia cell phone's maps app nearly a whole minute to plan a route here from the capital. Provence. It sounded wonderful until you zoomed in on the map. Sainte-Françoise was so far south it almost bordered the Étang de Berre. Weren't there oil tankers and refineries down there somewhere? In any case it wasn't far from Marseille, and that meant drugs and corruption and the scorn of headquarters back in Paris.

Blanc had inherited the dilapidated house in the Midi from an uncle ten years ago. He had only been here once before and that must have been back when he was just four or five years old. He had only a few images in his head: a tiny room, wooden shutters on the windows, closed to keep out the heat. Rays of sunshine that fell through the wooden slats and spread across the tiled floor like a yellow fan. But his main memory was much clearer: his uncle putting down a glass of rosé wine in front of him. He had been gasping with thirst and downed it in one, only later noticing the bitter taste of the alcohol.

Blanc hadn't been back to his uncle's since. Years later he had nonetheless paid the inheritance tax without thinking, simply because he couldn't be bothered to go to the trouble of selling a house he cared nothing for. In any case he was always too busy. He could probably see that changing now. The house was a lot smaller than he remembered. And in worse condition.

In the eighteenth century it had been home to an olive oil press in the Touloubre valley, a two-story house leaning against a sixty-foot-high cliff face like some tired hiker. The walls were made of roughly rectangular hewn stone, as thick as the walls of a castle. The roof tiles were a reddish ochre, some of them broken, others having slid out of place. Wild vines sprawled over the walls, the iron grids on the windows, and the wooden front door. Once upon a time it had been painted blue, but now the paint had peeled and weathered to a pale gray. The shutters hung from their hinges at oblique angles like ragged sails. In the stream that ran around the little patch of land, bottle-green water flowed over stones covered in moss, dragonflies hovering in the reflected light like miniature helicopters. Around the house were flowering thistles and other bushes Blanc didn't know the names of. At one corner to the rear an ancient oleander grew as high as the gable, releasing an intoxicating perfume from its green leaves and bloodred flowers. It was already so hot that the cicadas were clicking away in the trees.

Blanc weighed the blacksmith-made key in his hand: It was as heavy as a hammer, a piece that any local museum would have been proud to display. He used his Opinel knife to clear away the vine growth around the lock and inserted the key. It took a few minutes and all his strength to get the rusty mechanism to work. At least nobody had broken in, he thought, taking a deep breath of the aromatic air outside before venturing into the murky interior.

It had the cool of some ancient ruin, and a dusty smell somewhere between sand and old paper. Nobody had ever cleared the house out. Blanc had walked into a time capsule: a kitchen with yellow marble worktops and an ancient enamel sink with a dulled bronze faucet. Five non-matching chairs stood around a wooden table that once had been painted white but was now chipped and scratched. Blanc entered the living room: a little table from the 1960s, a fireplace of soot-coated stone, and a sofa on which lay the desiccated corpse of a bat. In the bedroom he came across a mahogany wardrobe from the Empire period, which would have cost a fortune in Paris. Next to it was the iron frame of a double bed. No mattress. (That was where his uncle had died, Blanc recalled.) In the bathroom stood an enormous bathtub with cast iron feet in the shape of fierce lions, encrusted in dirt, and lying in it three open wine bottles, the contents of which had long since evaporated.

Blanc decided not to take the stone stairs up to the next floor. He went back into the hallway, where a gray telephone with a dial stood on a little shelf. He lifted the receiver. The line was dead. What else had he expected? He opened the fuse box next to it, hesitated for a second, then pulled down the main switch. He expected to hear a series of bangs as ancient fuses blew, to see sparks and smell the stench of melted cables. Instead a little living room lamp lit up, giving a yellowish light through the dust on the bulb. So, there was still electricity. He suddenly remembered that every summer he got a bill from the electricity company that he never understood, but paid it all the same. Now he realized what it related to. Blanc pulled out his cell phone. No reception. Probably because of the cliff that held up the rear of the house. Some advantages then, he thought.

Blanc went back out again. He was still exhausted from his last row with Geneviève, from the long overnight journey down from Paris, from the heat, and from the task ahead of turning this wreck into an inhabitable house again. All his possessions were in his old green Renault Espace. He and Geneviève had bought the car when the children were still small: It was spacious but unfortunately was prone to go on strike as often as the trade union members who made it. His wife—his ex-wife—had left him the car. He wondered what sort of car her new man drove, then told himself not to be an idiot.

"Hey," an aggressive voice yelled from somewhere on the

other bank of the Touloubre river. "This shack isn't for sale. It belongs to some idiot from Paris."

"I'm the idiot from Paris," Blanc called back. He spotted a white-haired but not very old man sitting on a dented green tractor, scowling at him suspiciously from the opposite bank. Behind him was a dirty white-plastered house of an ill-defined shape, surrounded by rusty iron scaffolding but with no wooden planking. Somewhere in the distance a goat was bleating. Had to be a farmhouse, Blanc reckoned. "I'm the new inhabitant too," he said in a more friendly voice. The last thing he needed was to be on bad terms with his neighbor. The man on the tractor was small and wiry, like a bantamweight boxer. "If you're renovating, you can't extend it," he growled, "The *commune* won't allow it."

His voice was tinged by the yellow Gitane that hung from his mouth the whole time he was speaking.

"I'm not intending to build a hotel," Blanc reassured him, muttering *connard*—idiot—under his breath.

The neighbor shouted something incomprehensible in the direction of his house, where there was obviously someone Blanc couldn't see. Then he roared off on the tractor.

Blanc bent his nearly six-foot-six frame double and dived into the Espace, fumbling around amidst the piles of stuff on the passenger seat. A sports bag fell into the foot well, notebooks and CDs tumbling out of it. He wasn't the most dexterous of men; his arms and legs were too long and somehow always got in the way. Finally he found his faded blue baseball cap with NOVA SCOTIA printed on it. He had been born up north, where people apologized to strangers if they went two

days without rain. He didn't want to meet his new colleagues
with his nose peeling.

New colleagues . . . It was July 1 and every decent French-
man was in lazy summer holiday mood. But he had to turn up
at his new workplace. *"Merde,"* he cursed, thumping the steering wheel, *"merde, merde, merde!"*

At 11:30 A.M. on Friday he had been called in to the gendarmerie
headquarters, a bland new functional building in the rue Claude
Bernard in Issy-les-Moulineaux, outside Paris's Périphérique
inner ring road. Monsieur Jean-Charles Vialaron-Allègre had
summoned him—a graduate of the top civil service college, a
member of parliament, a ministerial deputy in the ministry of
the interior, and one of those men in the ruling party whose in-
satiable ambition would only be satisfied when he moved into
the Élysée presidential palace. His office was kitted out in the
same easy-clean luxury as the Air France first-class lounge
at Roissy Airport. The minister of state was fifty years old,
slim, his thinning gray hair glued to the dome of his head with
pomade, his tailored suit of the sort that was extremely expensive but at the same time not in the least flashy. He had a Charles
de Gaulle nose and when he walked his head nodded back-
ward and forward on his long neck so that the captain thought
he resembled a ponderous heron.

Blanc stood in Vialaron-Allègre's office, swaying with fa-
tigue. He hadn't had a day off in two months, and the few hours
of sleep he had managed had as often as not been at his desk in
the gendarmerie station, with the rubber mouse mat in front of
his monitor as a pillow. That was the price he had had to pay

(the only price, he thought at the time) to convict a former trade minister before the man could get rid of all the incriminating documents. It had been an old story but it hadn't exceeded the statute of limitations. Back in the nineties France had sold power station turbines to the Ivory Coast. The African state's government had paid millions of francs for them, but the money hadn't ended up in the state coffers nor those of the constructors, but in bank accounts in Liechtenstein. It had ended up financing the minister's campaign to be elected mayor of Bordeaux, which he had hoped would be a cozy sinecure for his old age.

No politician likes a policeman who uncovers corruption, in case every new scandal brings the ax closer to his own head. On the other hand the former minister had been one of the heavyweights in the rival party to that of the minister of state, and there were once again elections on the horizon. That made it more important than ever to appear incorruptible. Blanc therefore had hopes he might be promoted; commandant of the gendarmerie, perhaps. At his age, that would be something.

"Congratulations," said Vialaron-Allègre, "you're moving on." His voice sounded like chalk on a blackboard.

In his tired and optimistic state, it took a few seconds for the meaning of the minister's words to explode in his head: "Where to?" He realized himself that he was spluttering as if he'd been punched in the kidneys. Paris was the center of the world—at least for any policeman with ambition. Especially for a northerner like him who never ever wanted to be reminded of the damp and dreary place he came from. He had longed to escape the grimy terrace houses and shut-down steelworks, where the only people who still had jobs were those that worked at the unemployment insurance offices, where life consisted of beer and cigarettes and nothing more.

"To the south."

Blanc's mind was reeling. The Midi. Mafia. The provinces. The asshole of the world. The graveyard of any career. "You're freezing me out?"

The minister of state raised his hands. "Freezing you out? In the warmest part of France? I should think not."

What have you got to hide? Blanc asked himself. Was Vialaron-Allègre involved in the turbine engine corruption? What position had he held back then? Was he already in parliament? Which committee had he sat on? But it was too late: For millions of French the south was a dream. Insofar as they might be remotely interested, the voters would think the reassignment of Roger Blanc was a reward for exposing corruption, rather than a punishment. Very subtle. "When?" he asked, trying to keep the expression on his face under control.

"Right away. You start Monday morning. In the gendarmerie of a place called Gadet. A bit different from Paris, eh, *mon Capitaine*? I believe you own a house nearby."

It took Blanc what seemed like an eternity before he understood what the minister of state was talking about. How did he know that? Blanc himself hadn't thought of the wreck he had inherited for years, and had never mentioned it to any of his colleagues. "In that case I'll clear my desk and take my files with me," he muttered. It was meant as a threat, a last defiant gesture, a warning: I've got stuff on you, just you wait.

But if the minister of state was discomfited he didn't show it. He gave a token smile, his small gray eyes looking Blanc up and down. "I imagine we'll meet often," he said, shaking his hand formally. As Blanc reached the door he called after him, "I'm sure your wife will be pleased at the move to Provence." It sounded snide, but it took Blanc more than an hour to realize what he really meant.

Blanc entered the address of the Gadet gendarmerie into his smartphone. The app pulled up a rural road, a few curves, a roundabout, barely a mile and a half in all. He turned the key in the ignition and on the third attempt the Espace finally burst into life. He shoved the Fredericks Goldman Jones CD Geneviève had bought him after their first week together into the player and drove off toward the big, dilapidated gate to his property. At least he wouldn't be stuck in a traffic jam like he would have been in Paris at this time of the morning. But just twenty yards on he had to slam on the brakes. In front of him stood three whitish gray horses, peering disinterestedly through the windshield.

Blanc honked his horn. One of the horses whinnied. He honked again. The horses turned their rear ends to him. Blanc wondered if he should just try to drive around them. But his Renault was so ramshackle that he feared it would come off second best if he went up against them. He extracted the Nokia from its in-car holder and zoomed in on the map. This minor road was the only way to get to Gadet. He rolled the window down and shouted angrily at the horses: "I'm going to make sausage meat out of you."

"For sausage meat you want donkey, not Camargue horses."

Blanc spun round in his seat. Next to the passenger window stood a horse that was a good head taller than the other three, with a woman on its back. She had to have come across the field. Blanc put her at about forty years old, with thick black hair tied back in a ponytail, her skin so brown from long hours in the sun that it would probably never lose the color. She was wearing moccasins, jeans, and an old white T-shirt with a red heart and the words DON DU SANG. Blood Donor.

"*Pardon*, sometimes my daughter forgets to close the gates." She nodded toward a meadow on the other side of the road, half hidden behind a row of tall cypress trees. Next to it was a house in reddish stone with yellow oleander blooming in front of it and bougainvillea cascading down from a wrought-iron balcony on the first floor.

"I guess we're neighbors then." Blanc introduced himself and climbed out of the car, leaving the engine running, just in case it wouldn't start again.

She sprang down from the horse as lightly as a gymnast and said, "Paulette Aybalen."

He shook her hand and nodded toward the ruin behind him. "I've got to do something with that heap of stones."

"It will be nice to have someone living there again. Is it your holiday home?"

She's seen the number plate, he thought to himself, the "75" that indicated Paris, and down here probably "idiot." She'd think the worst. Best to tell her the truth. "I've been posted down here," he said. "*Gendarmerie.*"

She hesitated a second, ever so slightly distrustful, the way everybody reacted at first when he told them his job. "Well, you certainly won't get bored down here," she said in the end.

"I'll split my time between work and renovating this place. I've already had a few tips."

Paulette's smile faded. "Serge," she said. "Serge Douchy."

"A man who speaks his mind."

"Serge runs around the place like a drunk tramp, his sheep-dogs bark all night, his goat herd stinks to high heaven, his grubby little house doesn't have planning permission, he uses an asthmatic old diesel pump to siphon off water from the Touloubre and an antique flintlock to shoot anything with feathers or fur. Apart from that he's okay."

"That was more or less my opinion of him too."

"Hmm, you really are an expert." Paulette was smiling again. "I'll get the horses back into their meadow before they end up at the butcher's."

Blanc looked at her and took a deep breath. There was a scent in the air. "What's the smell around here?" he asked.

"'It was there that I first saw dark green bushes like dwarf olive trees sprouting up among the wild herbs,'" she replied. "It's a quotation," she said, when she noticed the confused expression on his face. "From Marcel Pagnol. He reacted the same way as you when he first went out into the countryside in Provence. The scent overwhelmed him. It's wild thyme. It grows beneath the trees everywhere around here. It's very good for you, very flavorful."

Blanc, who had for the past few years subsisted mainly on croissants and soggy baguettes, had no idea what thyme tasted like or looked like, just nodded so as not to appear a complete idiot.

"I'll come by and give your wife a few recipes," Paulette said, realizing he hadn't a clue what she was talking about.

"You'll have to mail them to her. My wife is in Paris."

Paulette Aybalen didn't reply, just swung herself back into

the saddle. The other three horses had meanwhile trotted back into the meadow. Blanc had no idea what secret sign their mistress had given them. "Then I'll bring the recipes round and give them to you. We'll run into one another quite often."

"I promise never to mention horsemeat sausage again." Blanc got back behind the wheel and put his foot down gently on the gas so as not to frighten the animals. In the rearview mirror he saw the horsewoman watching him.

The air above the narrow asphalt roads shimmered. On the radio an announcer was warning of the risk of forest fires and reminding listeners not to drop cigarette butts or glass in the countryside. It sounded like a threat. On either side of the road the land was as brown and crusty as dry bread. He passed by a little drystone wall, with the gray-green leaves of young olive trees on the other side, along with the ruin of a building that might once have been a stable or even a little homestead. Beyond that was a slope with pine trees and oaks growing on it, and then a little dip in the land with rows of vines.

A dented white van was coming toward him, much too fast. The road was so narrow that he had to swerve the Renault onto the sandy shoulder in order to avoid being rammed. Blanc cursed and the Espace bounced up and down as he crunched over the stones. The glove compartment fell open and an old toy car fell out, a green Opel Rekord. Blanc had never been able to throw out the Majorette and Matchbox cars he had collected as a child. He didn't display them in glass cases like nostalgic collectors did; they just lay around here, there, and everywhere, coming to light in the most surprising places, then vanishing again for a bit. Like this old Opel. A present from his father.

He had been a cop too, but was long dead: out in the patrol car one evening when he hit an oil slick on a bend and the old Renault 4 that the gendarmerie used in those days had hit a tree and collapsed in on itself like a tin can. His mother had always been a heavy smoker, and just after her fortieth birthday the doctor had found a shadow on her lungs in an X-ray and had calmly given her the bad news. Two pathetic deaths in one year had left Blanc an orphan in his teens.

He had gone on to study law in Paris because he wanted to join the police after taking his master's at the École des Officiers de la Gendarmerie Nationale in Melun. In his second week at the university he had gotten to know Geneviève. She was a first-term history of art student. She was small and dark-haired. He was big and blond. She came from the Languedoc, he came from the north; she talked constantly, he was strong and silent; she thought Éric Rohmer's movies were the best in the world, they had the same effect on him as valium. She smoked Marlboros, he hated cigarettes; she liked painting late into the evening, he got up early to study. They had absolutely nothing in common. They were the perfect couple.

The children came along quickly, a long time before they got married, something they only did later, for form's sake. Then all of a sudden Eric was twenty-one years old and studying biochemistry in Montreal because the job opportunities in France were so poor. And Astrid was twenty and working as an event manager in Paris, though Blanc hadn't the faintest idea what sort of a job that might be. It obviously wasn't much of one, because his daughter's bank account was a black hole. He had taken living with Geneviève as much for granted as breathing, with the result that the bloodhound famed for his

sensitive nose hadn't had a clue she'd been seeing someone else
for a year. Minister of State Vialaron-Allègre must have known
though on Friday morning when he transferred him to the
ends of the earth. Maybe he had even known how Geneviève
would react? Gendarmes were soldiers who behaved by military rules: An order was an order! Even if it was an order to
be gone from Paris within two days. When Blanc had come
back from Issy, still in shock, his wife had listened to what he
had to say and then announced that she would be staying in
Paris, that she had been meaning to have a serious talk with
him for some time and now the moment had arrived. Then she
had packed her bag. Blanc had slept no more than four hours
since then, and felt like a boxer in the twelfth round.

He noticed red and yellow shapes in the forest to his left.
There were big fire engines parked in the shadow of the pine
trees, firemen in full kit who'd just taken their helmets off. A few
of them were sitting at a wooden picnic table having breakfast,
others were dozing on top of the engines. It appeared that in
the Midi the fire service didn't keep watch from their fire stations but out in the middle of the threatened forests. Clever. He
would pay a few euros himself if he could take a snooze in the
pine woods right now.

A bit farther on he parked the Espace between two pine
trees and got changed. T-shirt, jeans, and shoes were all thrown
carelessly onto the backseat as he donned a uniform for the first
time in ages and strapped on his gun belt. Gendarmes could
usually choose whether to turn up for work in uniform or plain
clothes. In recent years he had usually worn all-black clothing
so that his plain clothes still looked somewhat like a uniform.
For his first day at a new post, however, he thought it was

better to turn up in full kit: The uniform reflected the authority of the state and added just that little bit of magic. Then finally he put on the narrow blue gendarme's cap. A lot of his colleagues had protested when the old *képi* had been abolished in 2011 but Blanc had always felt like an extra in one of those old Louis de Funès comedy movies. He put his foot down on the gas.

At the next crossroads he saw a tall plastered wall to his right with a graveyard and little chapel behind it. It was the road leading in to Gadet. Little brightly colored houses on either side, a modest church in the center, shady plane trees, four bars, tables on the sidewalk, the scent of *café* and croissants in the air. The morning customers—farmers, older men in rustic clothing, young guys with motorbikes parked between the chairs, stared after him as he drove by. Two *boulangeries*, a butcher's shop, a tiny Casino supermarket, a *bar-tabac*. At least he wouldn't go hungry here. He wondered what newspapers there were. There was a modern athletic field next to the river—a sign said it was the Touloubre. Post office on his left, opposite the *mairie*, the town hall, which looked like a little castle hibernating in the summer sunshine. He would have to wait until August 15 to register his new address and change the plates on his car.

Then finally, the gendarmerie. A two-story flat-roofed concrete building with rows of dark, shuttered windows and a steel door. It was one of those UFOs from the seventies that didn't age gracefully like the traditional buildings but just decayed. There were marks of dog piss at the corners. He noticed a movement behind a curtain near the entrance. Blanc parked the Espace next to a patrol car and took a deep breath.

At the desk a young, overweight gendarme with dark sweat

marks on his light blue uniform shirt looked him up and down. Blanc introduced himself and showed him his police ID card.

"Ah," the gendarme grunted, evidently not feeling the need to give his own name. The badge on his uniform shirt read CORPORAL BARESSI. "The boss is upstairs," he said, waving one fleshy hand toward a staircase at the back of the room. "He knows you're coming. He was told you'd been posted here," Baressi added as Blanc was just about to climb the stairs.

"When did he hear?"

"Thursday evening."

That means they knew down here I was coming even before I did, Blanc thought angrily. The staircase reeked of strong detergent that was giving him a headache. On the floor above was a corridor with orange-painted metal doors on either side, some of them open, others closed, along with a pin board with torn duty rosters on it, faded wanted posters, circulars from the ministry in Paris, a few police photos and random notices. The coffee machine was out of order, probably had been for a long time, judging by the layer of dust. Cigarette smoke wafted from one of the open doors. At the end of the corridor was one door bigger than the others, closed, with a bronze name plate: COM-MANDANT NICOLAS NKOULOU. *"Merde alors,"* Blanc whispered, and knocked on the door.

He opened the door into the most well-organized office he had ever seen: The light-colored desk with a leather blotter and a black computer monitor looked like something out of a furniture catalog. Against the wall stood a bookcase with fastidiously labeled files, the window facing the door covered with an immaculately pleated off-white blind. There was a gold-framed certificate on the desk, but no private photos, no souvenirs, no knickknacks, not even a coffee cup.

Enthroned on the leather office chair was the youngest commandant Blanc had ever come across. Nicolas Nkoulou was in his midthirties at most, with an unlined face that made him look even younger. His skin was as black as ebony, his crinkled hair cut so short that it looked like his head was encased in a thin helmet. He wore elegant gold-rimmed glasses. His blue uniform shirt was so bright it almost hurt Blanc's eyes. He wore dark blue summer pants, immaculately pressed. Polished leather shoes.

"So, Paris sent you down here," Nkoulou said, getting to his feet with what seemed to be immense effort.

Blanc looked at his new boss and thought he could hardly have done worse. Brilliant. Ambitious. This one wants to get to Issy, he thought, all the way to the top. He's afraid I'm going to stick like bird shit to his impeccable reputation.

"Reporting for duty, *mon Commandant*," he said, wondering whether he ought to give him a military salute, reach out to shake his hand, or do neither. In the end he left his arms hanging where they were.

"I believe you're an expert on corruption?"

Blanc nodded.

"Down here in Provence, everybody's corrupt."

Blanc nodded.

"But they don't get caught."

Blanc stopped nodding.

Nkoulou cleared his throat. "I'll introduce you to your colleagues," he said without enthusiasm.

Blanc followed the commandant from office to office; a row of names and faces, a little guy with a broken nose and massive shoulders, a character with wire-rimmed glasses that might have been modern when he was at school. An overweight brunette, with lips that were way too red and a Gauloise between them, pushed the crumpled pack over toward him. Blanc, whose mother had been consumed by cancer, declined. She made such a face that it wouldn't have taken an expert psychiatrist to guess what she was thinking. Two dark-haired men who might have been brothers and gave each other an ironic look when he came in. A young female officer with long brown hair who barely looked up from her mouse mat when he was introduced. At the end of the corridor, the office farthest away from Nkoulou's, were two oak-veneered desks, with two computers, the oldest Blanc had ever seen in a gendarmerie station, gray boxes, the only ones that still had flickering bulky monitors on them, rather than flat screens.

"Welcome to your new home," the commandant said wearily. "Your partner is Lieutenant Marius Tonon." He gave a look of disgust at the croissant crumbs on the desk before adding, "No idea where he might be."

"Has he been without a partner for long?"

Nkoulou shrugged. "Don't let yourself be misled by the office gossip."

"I haven't heard any office gossip."

"You'll hear whispers in your ear soon enough, believe me: 'Tonon is a bad-luck charm.' Provincial superstition. I've been in charge of this station for a year and nothing bad has happened. But I can't persuade anybody to go out on a job with Tonon. So I'm glad to have somebody from Paris. A free spirit."

Blanc wasn't sure if it was meant to be an insult or a compliment. "We'll get on fine," he replied.

Just at that moment entered a man of about fifty who must have had to wear insoles to meet the five-foot, ten-inch minimum height requirement for the gendarmerie. He had strong hands with a coat of black hair on the back like huge paws, a body that stretched his crumpled suit, a blob of a reddish violet nose, and thinning, tousled black hair. He trailed behind him an aroma that Blanc at first thought reminded him of cheap aftershave until a memory from his childhood hit him like a hammer: rosé wine. "Lieutenant" was normally a rank people reached in their midtwenties. If it was still your rank thirty years later, then something had gone wrong. Blanc was certain there must be something after all to the office gossip. He shook the man's hairy paw and introduced himself.

"A colleague from up north will be good for us," Tonon said. His voice was pleasantly deep. The sort of voice that could calm a hysterical witness or get a confession out of a suspect, Blanc found himself thinking.

He smiled. "Parisians don't normally think of themselves as from 'up north.'"

"As far as we're concerned anything north of Lyon is Scandinavia." He nodded at the empty desk. "In the afternoons the sun coming through the window means you can't see anything on the screen. It's better to go and think things through down at the café." He laughed.

Nkoulou gave a wry grin. "I'm afraid you're going to have to give the café a miss, *mon Lieutenant*. I'm giving you and Blanc here a routine case. So that you can get to know one another a bit. It's in the ZGN."

"ZGN?"

"*Zone de responsabilité propre de la gendarmerie nationale.* The ninety-five percent of French soil that we are responsible for rather than the *Police nationale.* You really have been in the capital too long, *mon Capitaine.*" It was true that in Paris the old, traditional, ridiculous separation between the gendarmerie and *Police nationale* had become meaningless: Down here the gendarmerie were responsible for rural areas while the police were in charge of the cities. Blanc was going to have to get used to working in the sticks.

"What do you call a routine case?"

"A corpse, found on a garbage heap."

"You call that routine?"

"You're a provincial gendarme now. When we first get a report like that, I assume all we're supposed to do is to cordon off the scene. There are a few things that our colleagues from Marseille will then take over. ZPN. *Zone de responsabilité propre de la Police nationale.*" He once again gave a humorless smile. "But judge for yourself. Corporal Baressi has put the details together. You can't go wrong."

Blanc nodded.

"He likes using acronyms," Blanc whispered as his boss left the office.

"He can use more than that on his underlings, just you wait," Tonon warned.

Back downstairs Baressi handed over a sheet of paper. "Dead body found on garbage heap near Coudoux," he mumbled. "Right on the A7. A sanitation worker found him and called the emergency line, seventeen. He was still glowing." The corporal coughed.

"The sanitation worker?" Tonon asked.

"The corpse, it had been burnt. But that's probably not what killed him. The colleagues from traffic police were the first to get to the scene; they were already on the autoroute when the report came in. They said there were bullets everywhere. From a Kalashnikov."

"Bon," Tonon said matter-of-factly, and took the report.

"Good?" Blanc stared at him. "What's good about it?"

"We'll be back here in time for lunch. The little restaurant in Gadet isn't bad."

"Somebody's just been executed with an automatic weapon. We're going to be there for hours, at this garbage dump."

The lieutenant raised his hands. "In Marseille a Kalashnikov is as common as an Opinel penknife. You can get one for a thousand euros, and even for half that price, though most of them are pretty useless. The dealers spend half their time shooting each other with them. No need to worry. The garbage dump is on the A7 leading directly to Marseille. Commandant Nkoulou was right. We secure the crime scene and wait for our city colleagues. It'll be one of their usual customers. They'll take over the case. And we can go and have lunch."

Baressi threw Blanc a set of car keys. "Great," he muttered to himself, throwing open the steel door. "I always wanted to see a Provence garbage dump."

Tonon pointed to the patrol car. "That's our Mégane," the lieutenant said, squeezing himself into the passenger seat of the blue station wagon. Blanc didn't like the big blue lettering of GENDARMERIE on the doors, the white stripes, the red and white reflectors, the blue light. In Paris they had only ever used unmarked cars. He found the position of the seat and rear-view mirror awkward for his height, but eventually turned the key in the ignition. "I assume you know the way, Lieutenant Tonon?" he said, using the polite form, "*vous*," for "you."

"I may only be a lieutenant, but I am the elder and I suggest it might be easier if we address each other by first name. I'm Marius, by the way. After all, we're going to be seeing more of each other than our wives."

"That's for sure," Blanc mumbled.

"Head to the rotary, then follow the signs to Lançon. After that I'll navigate. It'll take us fifteen minutes."

Blanc was a lone wolf by instinct. It was true that police always worked in teams, sometimes just three or four on a case, sometimes up to a hundred. He knew that and accepted it. Nonetheless he had a habit of going for cases he could work on alone: He would follow a suspect for hours, days if need be. He would retreat to his office, go through his crammed note-book, and think it all through. Right now, sitting next to this blubbery colleague reeking of rosé wine on the way to visit a burnt corpse, he didn't exactly feel in his element.

"The commandant is very young," he said vaguely, to break the silence. He drove carefully, but unlike in Paris nobody cut him off or honked at him: They recognized the police car.

"Nkoulou is already at his desk when I get there in the morn-ing and he's still at that perfectly tidy desk when I leave in the evening. He loves rules and regulations, hard work, punctual-ity. He'd drive even a German mad. A few of us have opened a betting book. If you want, you can join in. Whoever is first to find out if Nkoulou has a girlfriend takes the pot."

"A man with no private life. Does he have a social life connected to work, or does he spend all day every day locked in his office?"

"He goes out shooting, target practice. He was the best shot in his year, allegedly."

Blanc felt the metal of the Sig-Sauer SP 2022 stuck in his holster at his back, against all regulations for carrying an official weapon. As a young cop he had shot in panic at a thief doing a runner. The guy had spent a week hovering between life and death. In the end he had come through, and Blanc had gotten his first official praise for neutralizing a sought-after criminal. But he never wanted to go through a week like that again. Never since had he drawn his weapon on duty, and he only went to the shooting range when it was his turn each year to keep in training.

Tonon directed him through an industrial estate on the outskirts of Gadet, past a swimming pool installation service that had a huge ready-made pool standing up on its side, like some vision in a surreal dream. Then they were driving through fields again, past the straw-covered roof of a pottery stall selling lacquered vases, terrine pots, and little pottery cicadas, then a village. Blanc turned onto *route départementale* 19 past a cemetery with an ancient chapel leaning to one side. Then, suddenly, several hundred feet below the level of the road, a gray strip appeared, which at first Blanc took to be a wide river: the autoroute. The A7 sliced its way through rocky gray hills, with the *route départementale* running parallel to the broad asphalt highway for over half a mile, cars, camper vans, and trucks roaring past on their left, leaving black diesel fumes in their wake. Blanc closed the window. It wasn't just pollution that he smelled, but something rotten. Ripped plastic bags fluttered in the pine branches of the trees shadowing the road to their right, seagulls circling around them.

"That's the garbage dump," Tonon said, clutching a gold medallion hanging around his neck. Blanc gave him a look. "Saint Geneviève, our patron saint," he explained.

"Ours?"

"The patron saint of the gendarmerie. Aren't you a Catholic?"

"I managed to turn up at the church on time for my children's first communion," Blanc replied. His wife would have had a laugh at that: Geneviève as the patron saint of policemen. His ex-wife, he reminded himself. "Are you afraid of something?" he asked his colleague.

"I'm afraid of throwing up. I've never seen somebody burnt to death before. He might look like a Moroccan mutton *méchoui*, and that would ruin my appetite."

"Do you always think about food?"

"You have to get your priorities straight."

Blanc turned through a gate in a ten-foot-high wire fence onto an unsurfaced track. He cursed beneath his breath as an oncoming green garbage truck forced him to one side, into a cloud of diesel, dirt, and dust. Once upon a time, this had probably been a valley between two rocky crags, but the dip was now almost completely full of garbage. Bulldozers were pushing mountains of trash here and there, with seagulls wheeling furiously in the air around them. To either side thick sheets of black plastic bulged out, the edge of an artificial barrier spread along the ground to prevent the dirt sinking down toward the water table. The air stank of rotting vegetables and meat that had gone off.

"It's always worse in summer," Tonon apologized. "Half of the garbage in all Provence gets dumped here." He nodded toward a patrol car and a motorbike of the highway police parked in between two inconspicuous white delivery trucks with plastic signs behind their windscreens proclaiming TECH-NICIENS D'INVESTIGATION CRIMINELLE.

"Crime scene people from Marseille?"

"No, from Salon, the nearest unit. They're good people, take their time. Of course they don't have as much on their hands as the guys from Marseille."

Blanc climbed out and shook hands with the corporal and a young, tanned official from the public prosecutor's office. They had nothing else to do but stand there in the heat and the stench, watching the crime scene people about their job. They were wearing full-body protective kits with NTECH on the back, booties, gloves, masks. He wondered how they survived in this heat.

The body had been found on the edge of the parking area, behind a great open container used for waste metal. Blanc recognized the skeleton of a sprung mattress and the frame of a bicycle sticking up out of it. The crime scene people had not gone directly over to the body, but were working their way toward it in a curved path from the rear. One of them was taking photographs. Two of the white-clad forms were kneeling down next to what looked like a tree trunk turned to charcoal. Blanc got wind of a smell of a different kind: roast meat, and melted fat.

"Who found him?" he asked the corporal.

The policeman nodded toward a figure in green overalls, sitting in the shade of a stunted pine tree, being handed a bottle of water by a very young policewoman. "He's a garbage truck driver. He's still getting over the shock." He smiled sarcastically.

Blanc said nothing, just walked over to the man, Tonon following him. They both kneeled down next to him. Blanc got out a notebook and a pencil, badly chewed at one end. "Do you mind if I ask a few questions? Or would you prefer I waited a while?" the captain asked.

The truck driver, a young Arab, shook his head. "Let's get it over with," he said, trying bravely to smile.

"Your name, please?"

"Mourad Ghoul."

"When and how did you come across the body of the victim?"

"I drive that thing over there." He pointed to a heavy vehicle with a crane and flat load-carrying area. "Once a week I load up a container with scrap metal and take it to a dealer. I was just fastening the chains to that Dumpster when I . . ." He searched for the right words. "When I saw . . . the body. I smelled it first. It was . . . still smoking."

"Was it already totally burnt?"

"I couldn't look for long. I ran straight back to the cabin, grabbed my phone, and called the cops. Then I threw up."

"Were you alone?"

"My colleagues had been driving in and out all morning, but they use the rear access ramp. This area is reserved for private individuals to dispose of their trash, but there's never anyone here this early."

"Take it easy," Blanc said, standing up. He was feeling queasy himself, from the heat, the stench, and his own exhaustion.

"Sometimes a few idiots meet up here secretly at weekends," said Tonon, getting back to his feet with remarkable agility for someone of his build. "To play paintball. Illegally."

"Paintball, on a garbage dump?"

"Seems some guys get a kick out of it. Every now and then we raid them and arrest one or two for breach of the peace."

"Well, this must have been one hell of a hot paintball."

"Maybe somebody saw what happened?"

"*Bien*, you can go out a bit later and knock on the doors of some of the guys you've arrested in the past. If we're lucky maybe one of them will have seen something."

A scratched white Jeep that clearly had a hole somewhere in its exhaust pipe trundled up. The asthmatic-sounding engine choked to a halt, causing the whole vehicle to shudder. A woman in her midthirties with long brown hair jumped out, her face half hidden behind a pair of huge sunglasses left over from the 1970s.

Tonon nodded to her and introduced her to Blanc: "Dr. Fontaine Thezan. *Médecin légiste* at Salon hospital."

Blanc shook her hand, noticing the slight but unmistakable odor of marijuana from her hair and T-shirt. He shot a quick glance at his colleague, who didn't seem to have picked up on it. "We'll have to wait a bit," he told her.

"Looks like I turned up just in time," the doctor said, nodding at the crime scene technician, who was pushing up his mask as he came toward her coughing, and said, "All yours, Madame." Blanc didn't even get a glance.

"Hmm, fencer position," Thezan murmured to herself. "Arms

bent due to muscular contraction caused by heat. Charred, blackened skull, facial eruption from extreme temperature."

Blanc had spent his most recent working years plowing through bank accounts, letters, and files. He tried to take shallow breaths of the air that reeked of burnt flesh, mixed with the stench of the garbage dump. This damn heat! In front of him lay a body with skin black as coal, its arms curved parallel to each other, the legs too, the face a distorted grimace—it looked less like a human corpse than a shop window mannequin after an arson attack: no hair, no ears, no clothes save for the buckle of a belt on its torso. There was no blood, no recognizable facial traits.

"You really don't have to look over my shoulder," Dr. Thezan said, watching him recoil in horror.

"It's just the heat," the captain replied.

"You're not from around here."

Blanc decided to ignore the remark. "Can you tell if the victim was burned alive?"

The pathologist shook her head, nodding toward holes in the charred torso. "I'm assuming those are gunshot wounds," she said. "The victim is male. I'll examine his lungs back at the lab, what's left of them, that is. But I'd be surprised to find any soot in them. I doubt he was still breathing when he was set on fire."

Tonon nodded at the dusty ground all around them, being dutifully marked up into numbered sections by the forensics people. "Cartridges, from a Kalashnikov. At least a dozen cases. And to think we're not allowed to use the firing range anymore, to save money." He shook his head. "Farid Berrhama was a fighter and drug dealer from Salon, with ambitions to become one of the big shots on the Marseille crime scene. They called him Monsieur Barbecue because if anyone got in his way he would sweep them aside and burn their remains to get rid of any evidence. We never caught him. But one day a Corsican clan spotted him in a brasserie: Eight hit men at once put a dozen bullets in his body. Now it looks like we have a Berrhama copycat on our hands."

"A drug dealer feud?" Blanc suggested.

The lieutenant pointed at the charred corpse. "This guy was probably doing coke or heroin. Or hadn't paid his bill. Or maybe ratted someone out. Or somebody else wanted to take over his patch. Basically, somebody in Marseille gets taken out by a Kalashnikov every couple of weeks."

Blanc cast his mind back to the recent scandal when one of the city's district mayors had suggested sending in the army to pacify her part of town. There was a wave of outrage, and a lot of sarcastic comments in Paris. Send the army into Marseille! President Sarkozy had made a wave of cuts that included suppressing 350 police jobs in Marseille alone. Nobody had protested about that.

"There's enough of him left to get a DNA sample," Dr. Thezan said. "And his teeth are intact. I can get an idea of his height and age from his bones. I might even be able to work out the color of his hair and eyes, and what he had last eaten. We'll get an ID on him."

"And then the boys from Marseille will take over. I'll report back to HQ," Tonon said. He was about to head back to the Renault when he came to a halt. The pathologist had taken hold of the body with her gloved hands and was carefully turning him over when she spotted something gleaming where the neck had lain on the ground. Gold. The remains of a chain, with a medallion. Blanc and the lieutenant bent down, careful not to touch anything. The medallion had a cobra engraved on it, poised to strike, with two tiny rubies set into its eyes.

"Fucking hell!" Tonon swore. "I know that cobra. We can save ourselves the bother of notifying Marseille. This guy is local."

Charges Against a Dead Man

Blanc waved over the forensics team and showed them the chain and medallion. Then he stood aside and let the specialists do their job. "Sounds as if it's a fairly unique piece of jewelry if you think it's enough for a positive ID on the corpse," he said to Tonon in a low voice.

His colleague nodded, looking somewhat distracted and glancing back toward the parking lot. "If it's who I think it is, there should be a motorcycle around here somewhere. He went everywhere on his enduro." Tonon called a few of the uniformed police officers over. It only took a few minutes before one of them waved an arm to say he had found an old Yamaha half hidden behind one of the other Dumpsters. Blanc had assumed it was being scrapped: The taillight was hanging loose, the fuel tank dented, the forks bent, the headlight shattered, the left mirror missing; other than that it was just a frame attached to a set of handlebars.

The lieutenant nodded at the bent number plate with the "13" that indicated it was local. "That's his ride. I know the number by heart." He called over one of the forensics team, who pulled his mask down over his face again, and told him to check for fingerprints.

"So, who is it?" Blanc asked.

"Charles Moréas, and Provence will be a better place without him."

"Customer of yours?"

"Wish he had been," Tonon sighed. "I've been trying to nail this guy for years. The only time we had anything concrete against him was when a speed camera caught him way above the limit on this Yamaha. But even then he didn't pay the fine. No idea what happened. I imagine the case is still languishing in somebody's filing cabinet."

"But you weren't after him for speeding."

"No." The lieutenant closed his eyes. "We were after him for murder, or at least manslaughter." He paused, took his time. "Moréas was a loner. Everybody who knew him wished he didn't. He lived on his own in a dilapidated house in the *commune* of Caillouteaux."

"Part of our area?"

"ZGN. Moréas is thirty-eight, if my memory serves me. Was, I should say. Nobody really knew how he made his money."

"Wife? Kids? Relatives?"

Tonon just laughed. "He owned a few bits of land. Here and there. Round and about—couple of fields, woodland, a hunting cabin. His parents were farmers, long dead."

"Land around here is expensive, so I've been told. Maybe he'd sold some of it and lived off the profits?"

"Moréas? Never. He would drive out on the Yamaha to one of his bits of land and spend the night there out in the open.

Any hikers who came across him soon learned to take another route in the future."

"He shot at them?"

"With a hunting rifle."

"Surely that was enough to haul him in?"

"I did. But that was that." Tonon nodded bitterly at the charred corpse, already being transferred to a stretcher by two undertakers who had just arrived in a gray van. "Some twenty years ago, when I was still a good cop, Moréas was part of a gang that specialized in highway robberies: They had a couple of souped-up cars, went out at night along the little-used local roads, and waited for cars with foreign number plates. Tourists. One of their cars would overtake them, then brake suddenly, forcing them to stop, often causing a fender-bender, which left the tourists angry, confused, and frightened. Before they could get their wits together, the second car would scream up behind them. The guys from both vehicles would drag the tourists out of their cars, steal all their baggage, and roar off. It went on for weeks and we never managed to catch them. Then things went wrong: As they were fleeing the scene they came across one female tourist who had panicked and run off. They ran into her, killed her instantly, and dragged the body along the road. I found traces of her blood. The thugs panicked, hid their own damaged car behind the trees. A few of them fled in the second car, but two of them were left behind. We found them straightaway, and this time we also had the plates of their wrecked car, which enabled us to nail the rest of them, save for one."

"Charles Moréas?"

"One of them told us Moréas had been with them, that he

was their boss, and had been at the wheel of the car that hit their victim. A couple of our guys found him a little later in his hunting cabin and arrested him. He denied everything, and the others we already had in custody said they'd never even seen him before."

"Sounds like they had an agreement."

"You can say that again. The one who ratted him out was found dead in jail not long after. In the recreation yard, with a knife between his ribs. It was put down to a prison brawl. The culprit was never identified. We were left with nothing to throw at Moréas. This was back in the days before DNA identification. We had to let him walk. I've been trying to get something on him ever since. I'll never forget seeing that tourist's blood on the tarmac."

"Seems like somebody else got to him first."

"A guy like Moréas had a lot of enemies. It's almost a pity we have to go after his killer."

By the time they were finally on the way back to the gendarmerie headquarters, it was already late morning. Blanc fiddled with the radio. Anything to keep him awake. Tonon was already singing the chorus of *"Les Amants de Paris"* before he could turn off Radio Nostalgie. Blanc stared through the windshield, unable to cope with a burnt corpse on a garbage dump and a colleague next to him singing Édith Piaf songs. He kept hoping that any moment now he would wake up back in his bed in Paris, with Geneviève next to him. This has to be some dream, he told himself, some crazy dream, just a dream. *Merde.* But he found himself driving along the *route départementale* all the way back to the police station in Gadet, without waking up.

Nkoulou looked like he was suffering from indigestion. "I've heard the reports on the radio," he said. "This was supposed to be a routine case," he added, as if they had already made a mess of it.

"It means we don't have to worry about Moréas anymore," Tonon said, hoping to cheer the boss up a bit.

Blanc said nothing. The commandant had given the most spectacular case in weeks to the two officers he trusted least. It had all gone wrong. He could hardly pull them off the case now without taking it over himself.

"You've been after that Moréas for years without catching him," he said. "I just hope you don't take as long looking for his killer."

"Moréas was a piece of shit," Blanc piped up in support of his colleague. "At least the press won't scream blue murder if we haven't put the culprit behind bars within twenty-four hours."

"You may be thick as thieves with the press up in Paris, but down here I couldn't care less."

"The politicians care," the captain replied softly.

Nkoulou leaned back in his chair. He had gotten the message. If neither the press nor the politicians paid much attention to this case, then he was in no danger. His career was in no danger. No senior civil servant, no minister was going to e-mail him or call him on the phone and ask what the hell was going on down south and who was responsible. "Take care of it," he said, with a nod to indicate the conversation was over.

"Thanks for pouring water on the fire, before I got my ass fried," Tonon whispered as they walked down the corridor.

"Stop or I'll shoot!" someone called from behind them.

It was the brunette policewoman with the iPad. Blanc had forgotten her name.

"*Ma chérie*," the lieutenant said. "Since when have you been talking to men like that? Let me introduce Second Lieutenant Fabienne Souillard," he said to Blanc, even though Nkoulou had done just the same thing several hours earlier. "She's our go-to girl when something goes wrong with the computers."

"Marius turns the printer on before his antique computer has fired up, crashes every time. He doesn't seem to get it." Fabienne Souillard was in her late twenties, fit, elegant. Even in uniform there was the scent of an expensive perfume about her. She reached out a hand to Blanc.

"Up in Paris our computer experts wear glasses and all look as if somebody's made them out of lumps of plastic hacked at with an ax."

"Yeah, but those are men," Fabienne answered, then nodded toward her office. "I've got something for you."

"Have you heard about our case?"

"You bet, everybody's really pleased you're handling it."

"Do you feel the same, Mademoiselle Souillard?" Blanc asked.

"You can use my first name," she replied. "Not even the police dogs are this polite around here."

"She's one of the good guys," the lieutenant said, groaning as he lowered himself onto a chair in front of Souillard's desk. "So, what have you got for us?"

"A case for heroes: a break-in," she said, nodding toward a filled-out victim's report lying next to her computer.

"Nkoulou has given us free rein on the other case. The break-in will have to go to somebody else," Tonon replied.

"An architect from Caillouteaux reported it, somebody broke into his house on Saturday, when he was out at work."

"That's his bad luck. It's still not our problem." The lieutenant was looking relaxed.

Fabienne rapped the report with her knuckles and said, "The architect names the suspect as one Charles Moréas. His next-door neighbor."

"That makes it our case," said Blanc, getting to his feet. "Let's go."

Tonon waved a hand dismissively. "We're not in Paris now."

"I want to take a look at this Moréas's house. And I want to talk to the architect."

"The crime scene people are already at the house. It'll be a few hours at least before they let us in, and the architect isn't going to run away. We can have lunch first."

"Lunch?"

"Here in Gadet. I told you it wasn't bad."

Before Blanc could say anything, Fabienne Souillard swung her computer screen round to face him. "I can give you all we've got so far. Then you can digest that. *Voilà*." She pointed to two mug shots of a young man, frontal and profile. "That's Moréas nearly twenty years ago. Taken when he was hauled in with respect to the highway robbery business. We have nothing newer because we've never got hold of him since."

"So I believe."

"Just under six foot tall, muscular. Still wears his hair as long as he did then."

"Except that it's gray now," Tonon added.

"Sometime after this he had a tattoo done on his left forearm. Contorted letters, no obvious meaning," Souillard continued.

"Connerie," Tonon hissed. "Nonsense: It was a 'G,' a 'T,' and an *I*. The gang had a BMW and a Volkswagen GTI, both stolen. Moréas drove the GTI. That was what he was in when he ran over that tourist and killed her. He had that tattooed on his arm the day the case against him was withdrawn for lack of evidence. He'd made us look like idiots." The lieutenant's voice was rising by the second.

"In any case the tattoo is now nothing but ashes," Blanc intervened, to calm him down.

"There was one other case against him when he didn't pay a speeding fine." Fabienne was reading from the file. "The case was due to be heard in Aix-en-Provence, but never came up. The judge was apparently too busy. His name keeps coming up in the files of our colleagues in Aix, in Salon, and our good friends down in Marseille, as a suspect in drug dealing. Probably as a courier, maybe the guy who hid the stash, but in any case small-scale stuff. Nobody ever charged him with anything. Apart from that, not much to be said. No relatives." Fabienne Souillard turned her monitor back round. "So what about it, boys, are you taking me with you? To lunch. I'm hungry."

It was only a short walk. Le Soleil was on place Jean Jaurès, a little restaurant with outside tables in the shade of plane trees, too out of the way for any of the passing tourists to spot it, too basic to feature in the Michelin Guide. The owner greeted Tonon by heartily grabbing his hand, Souillard by a kiss on each cheek, Blanc with a brief nod, part polite, part wary. New cop in town, you had to be careful. They took a table right next to the flaking trunk of a plane tree, with the green water of the Touloubre, which flowed right through the middle of Gadet, burbling behind them. Some thirty yards away a little bridge barely six feet wide crossed the little river. There were two fishermen standing there, still as statues, ignoring the hot sunshine. Glittering blue dragonflies hovered over the rolling stream.

Blanc couldn't even remember the last time he'd eaten in a restaurant without canned music in the background. He took a deep breath and felt himself physically relax. The owner brought over a menu and automatically set a carafe of rosé wine down next to Tonon.

"Do you recommend anything in particular?" Blanc asked, reluctant to admit that he hadn't a clue about Provençale cuisine.

"Everything," the lieutenant replied.

"Thanks for being specific," Fabienne laughed, taking the menu out of his hand. "I'm never that hungry at lunchtime. I'll make do with the *courgettes à la provençale*."

"I am hungry," Tonon announced, "but I don't want to struggle all afternoon with digestive problems, so I'm going for the *coquilles Saint-Jacques*."

"I'll have the same," Blanc quickly added.

The drinks came first. Fabienne Souillard had ordered an "energy drink" the color of cough medicine, Blanc a carafe of water. Tonon scowled at both their glasses. The men's scallops came on oblong plates, the white meat in light pastry scattered with parsley and grated garlic, accompanied by a ball of rice. Their colleague got two zucchini slit lengthwise and filled with garlic, olive oil, and basil. The first bite exploded in Blanc's mouth: the taste of the sea, pepper, basil, and roughly grated salt. He felt himself relaxing even further, like a warm wave flowing all the way down his back. All of a sudden his meeting with the minister of state felt like nothing more than a half-forgotten dream, not exactly pleasant but somehow belonging to another world. Like his row with Geneviève. Even the charred corpse at the garbage dump. He realized he was thinking how nice it would be never to have to leave this seat under the plane tree. And he also realized that he needed a coffee if he didn't want to drift off into a doze under the eyes of his colleagues.

A few minutes later, as they were stirring the sugar into their tiny coffee cups, Blanc turned to his young colleague and asked, "So what brings a computer specialist to Gadet?"

"The ways of bureaucracy are as undecipherable as those of God: I came out of the *Centre national de formation aux systèmes d'information et de communications de la gendarmerie* back at Roissy-sous-Bois. It might sound like a ticket straight to Paris, but the train got held up here on the way."

"Something of a culture shock?"

"To be honest, I never want to leave."

"Meet Mademoiselle Facebook," Tonon said.

"Last month a girl from Salon sent a friend request to a guy in Marseille, a young kid, still at the *lycée.* She persuaded him to come and see her. But when the kid turned up at the agreed spot in a park, a pair of the girl's friends who'd been waiting for him beat him up and stole his iPhone and his Peugeot 106. But because people leave so many traces on Facebook it wasn't exactly hard to trace the victim back to the girl, and from her to her two accomplices."

"I couldn't have done it," the lieutenant commented. "I'm not even on Facebook. How about you?"

"I am." Blanc had signed up when Facebook had still been trendy among adolescents and both his children had done so. Over time, even though he had posted unenthusiastically, he had acquired dozens of "friends," most of them work colleagues. In the forty-eight hours after his meeting with Vialaron-Allègre almost all of those colleagues had unfriended him. The only ones left were a couple of former school friends who never posted anything and three gendarmes who were on holiday and hadn't yet noticed his fall from grace. And, of course, his two kids. But Eric and Astrid had long since given up informing their father about important things in their lives. He had either been out of the house or too tired dealing with his cases to pay them much attention.

"I'm sending you a friend request," Fabienne said, holding up her phone.

"Well, that should increase my activity by a hundred percent," said Blanc, knocking back the last drops of his coffee. He watched her get up, excuse herself, and disappear into the depths of the restaurant.

"Give up," Tonon muttered sleepily.

"Watching Fabienne?"

"She's already taken."

"Can't say I'm surprised."

"A girlfriend. They live in Salon. A proper little married couple."

Blanc shot his new colleague a quick glance.

"Does that bother you? I mean, the fact that she lives with another woman?"

"No. Why should it?"

"You're a Catholic."

"I don't recall Jesus mentioning lesbians in the Sermon on the Mount. Let's just hope her wife is more faithful than mine."

"You're divorced."

"Have been forever. What about you?"

"About to be."

Tonon glanced down at his wineglass, where there was just a finger's breadth of rosé shimmering in the sunlight, and said nothing. When Fabienne rejoined them Blanc settled the bill for them all.

Their colleague went back to the police station on foot. Mindful of the carafe of rosé that Tonon had knocked back over lunch, Blanc didn't even suggest he might drive.

"The house is just around the corner from you. I believe you're staying in that shack in Sainte-Françoise-la-Vallée, from what I've heard," the lieutenant said.

"And who did you hear that from?"

"From the boss, Nkoulou. He had a phone call from Paris and enjoyed giving us all the details."

"So, I guess that makes me something of a star, locally."

"The commandant plays by the rules. As long as you keep to them, he'll leave you in peace. And as long as he leaves you in peace so will the others."

"Does he leave you in peace?"

Tonon laughed. "The rule book and I have never been the best of friends, but I get by. I enrolled at the *école de gendarmerie* in Chaumont. I got promoted to lieutenant during the World Cup. My wife left me. My kids have long grown up, left the house, and haven't spoken to me in years. But what the hell? I made it to the stadium in Marseille for the final."

Blanc just nodded. It had been the great event. *"Faites-nous rêver*—Make Us Dream." The cops had all got new uniforms; the last time they had *képi* caps. *Footix,* they called them. Some officers still cried when they remembered it.

"We were world champions in 1998," he replied.

Tonon tapped the stripes on his uniform. *"Oui.* But I've been stuck fast ever since. There was an accident, and something like that leaves skid marks in your personnel record. In any case I prefer riding as a passenger."

"I get the message." The captain thought back to Nkoulou's comment. Tonon was a Jonah. He wondered how the man drove back then. "That's the Touloubre again up ahead. My ruin is the last house before the bridge," he said.

"I know. We turn left just before we get there. Caillouteaux is at the top of the hill with a view down on the Étang de Berre pond. It has an old church, a quiet village square with a nice café, just a bit too quiet. If you cough out loud people fall out of their beds in shock."

"Moréas must have seemed like a werewolf to them."

"Nobody ever saw him in the village. There's no bar and no supermarket up there. His house is out of the way, between the pine trees at the foot of the hill. Drive slowly, the driveway is easy to miss."

Blanc stopped by a dented steel gateway hanging from two posts built into the wall. They turned into a dusty lane that stretched so far ahead into the woods that they couldn't see where it ended. Eventually they came to a clearing where a motorcycle, two cracked sinks, and a roll of wire lay rusting in the sun. Behind them stood a house made of unplastered concrete breeze blocks with PVC windows in various sizes, and a grotesque modern glass-and-aluminum door.

"Looks as if Moréas knocked his home together from a DIY store's leftovers," Blanc commented.

"You could say that: He used whatever he could steal."

One of their colleagues from the crime scene team was standing next to a truck, smoking. There was a name written in marker on his overall: HURAULT, D. David? Dominique? Damian? "You can go in," Hurault said indifferently.

"Anything of interest?"

"It's not exactly Versailles."

"Drugs?"

Hurault shook his head. "Clean. We let the dogs run loose. Not a single joint in the *cabane*. The usual amount of cash lying about, a few bills, some change in the drawers. No jewelry or anything like that. Nothing to suggest he was acting as a fence. Giant flat-screen televisions, Blu-ray player, notebook, and a video camera."

"Bound to have been stolen," Tonon muttered.

The specialist gave him an oblique glance. "If it was, it was for himself, not someone else. We're checking the serial numbers and the contents of the hard drives. We also found two cell phones, one of them clearly unused for a long time. The display was broken. We're checking all outgoing and incoming calls."

"Just a good citizen then?"

"Not that good." Hurault beckoned with one hand for them to follow him into the house. A dark entranceway, with nails hammered into the concrete to serve as coat hangers. A heavy motorcycle jacket hung from one, a motocross helmet on the other. A living/dining room with battered furniture and a grimy table. "*Voilà!*" the crime scene man said, pointing at one wall on which hung a gleaming samurai sword.

"Any traces of blood on the blade?" Blanc asked.

"The dogs didn't make a fuss. But we'll take the thing back to the lab." Then he showed them a pair of shotguns.

"I recognize those," said Tonon. "He used them to frighten off joggers and hikers."

"We'll take them along with the sword." Hurault then led them into the next room, the bedroom. A camp bed, unmade. The stale smell of unwashed clothing. A box that someone had pulled out from under the bed. In it, a Kalashnikov.

The captain smiled. "Looks like Moréas had invested in some Russian life insurance to help him sleep at night."

"That won't be the weapon used to kill him," Tonon said. "No murderer is daft enough to shove it under his victim's bed after killing him."

"We have the shells and cartridges from the scene of the murder," Hurault said. "It's the easiest thing in the world to find out if they belong together."

He led them to a sort of lean-to behind the house. In the twilight they made out a couple of pistons and air filters on a workbench, an old chain, oily shock absorbers, two red gas containers, a fender, and a set of tires with a deep tread. At the far end of the workbench there was a leather case. Blanc looked inside and whistled: crowbars, screwdrivers, lock picks, files, thin black gloves. "The neighbor who accused Moréas of breaking in wasn't exactly paranoid. Let's go and have a talk with him."

"You'll have to take the car."

"To his neighbor?"

"He also lives in a house in the woods, but there isn't a path from one to the other."

"Then we'll walk through the pine trees."

"There's a wire fence in the way, a very new, very high fence."

Blanc and Tonon drove back to the roadway and a hundred yards farther on turned into the next driveway, the Mégane trundling down a forest path, until they ended up in a world that was as far from that of Charles Moréas as the Louvre was from a scrap yard—a bungalow from the seventies, white-painted concrete, pale blue window frames, a brushed steel door. Raked gravel in front of the house, two abstract sculptures in bronze, not a green leaf to be seen. To their right was a garage that might have been a five-bedroom family house. Two metal doors were closed, the third was open, revealing a silver Range Rover. Behind the garage they could see the reddish sand of a tennis court set into the forest.

As they approached the house, a door opened and a man stepped out. Blanc put him at about sixty years old, well-spent years by the look of him. He was of athletic build, with a deep tan, his little remaining hair shaved close, a square red pair of glasses on his nose. He was wearing a yellow Lacoste shirt, linen trousers, deck shoes, and had a steel Rolex on his left wrist.

"You're late," he said by way of a greeting.

"Monsieur Le Bruchec?" Blanc asked, casually raising a hand to his cap. Either the man didn't know that the police had been turning his neighbor's house upside down for hours, or he was a very good actor.

"Lucien Le Bruchec. Please come in."

He led them down a sort of corridor that the two policemen realized ran around the exterior wall of the house, opening inwardly onto different rooms, each of which in turn was like a little house in its own right, each in turn opening via a glass sliding door onto a raked gravel interior courtyard with a swimming pool in the middle. Le Bruchec led them along until they came to a window with a bent aluminum frame.

"I came home from work at lunchtime on Saturday and found this as I walked through the house. Then I realized that as I turned into the driveway I had heard the sound of a motorcycle in the forest. I decided to take a closer look around. I had taken the Range Rover to work and left the garage open. There had been a few tennis rackets hanging on the wall and they were now gone."

"You mean you were burgled for a pair of tennis rackets?"

"Good equipment doesn't come cheap. They were worth more than a thousand euros."

Blanc gave Tonon a look and he nodded back: The lieutenant was to go out and ring the crime scene people to ask if they'd come across any sports equipment.

"What time did you return home from work?" he asked Le Bruchec.

"It must have been around three P.M."

"So a bit later you saw the marks on the window, then you walked out to take a look around, and discovered the items missing in the garage. That can't have taken too long." Blanc studied his notebook. "But you only reported it to us this morning. Why did you wait so long, Monsieur Le Bruchec?"

The architect frowned. "It sounds as if you think I'm the perpetrator rather than the victim."

"The delay is unusual."

"I wanted to sleep on it. Reporting things to the police means a lot of nuisance and time. The investigation. Maybe a trial. You have to think whether or not it's worth it all. And then yesterday was Sunday. I didn't want to spend it at the police station. So I waited until today."

"You didn't see anybody Saturday?"

"No."

"And then, after two days thinking it all over, you make a report and accuse your neighbor? I assume you have good reasons for that?"

"I've found this Moréas fellow on my land when I came home from work on two previous occasions. On one of them he was even tampering with the window."

"Whereabouts do you work? And do you always come home at the same time?"

"I'm an architect. I have my own studio in Salon. I'll give you a card. Sometimes I get home at midday, sometimes not until midnight. It just depends on what I'm working on."

"Do you work all through the summer?"

"Most of my work is in summer. Building extensions for Parisians down here, renovation work for the British, building new houses for Russians. But I shall take a holiday in August."

Tonon came back and gave a barely noticeable shake of the head.

"You live alone here?"

"My wife died six months ago. Cancer. Our daughter lives in Grenoble. Ever since I lost my wife this person has been roaming around here, knowing that during the day the house is often empty."

Tonon sighed and pulled an ancient scratched cell phone out of the pocket of his uniform. This time he didn't bother to conceal his intention. "I'll call the crime scene people, ask them to come over and see if they can get anything from the window. They might even find motorcycle tire tread marks."

"The ground around here is as hard as concrete at present," Le Bruchec said. Blanc suspected that the architect was disappointed they weren't already heading for his neighbor's house with the blue lights flashing, ready to arrest him. "What can you tell us about Monsieur Moréas?" he asked. There was no need yet to tell him the guy was dead.

The architect asked them to sit down, underneath a futuristically designed awning that covered nearly half the internal courtyard. In the background Miles Davis was playing from some hidden speakers. "Moréas is hardly a friend of mine," Le Bruchec began, cautiously. "I grew up around here and came back after I finished studying. If I had to list all the locals I know it would probably amount to the population of a small town: old school friends, the families I've worked for, politicians, builders, workmen, traders, restaurant owners. I'm a member of the local tennis club, a member of the Association for the Protection of the Touloubre. Believe me, of all the locals I know, I know none of them less than the man who lives next door to me. And believe me, I do not regret it. The man is, how shall I put it: excitable."

"Quick-tempered."

"That would be a better word. Aggressive. Not a nice man. But that's just about all I know of him."

"Did he get a lot of visitors?"

Le Bruchec made a dismissive gesture. "Our houses are far enough apart not to see or hear anything."

"Yet you describe your neighbor as aggressive. Just because you found him on your land a couple of times?"

"Twice at the house itself. I've seen him on my land a lot more often. Out in the forest. No idea what he might be looking for out there. Hunting maybe. In any case it was never exactly a pleasure running into him, especially when I pointed out he was trespassing on my land."

"Was he armed on those occasions?"

"Sometimes. With a hunting rifle. Just a few days ago I had a fence put up, because I found the whole situation disconcerting. Cost me a small fortune. And the workers who put it up said Moréas shouted at them when he saw them putting the posts in, threatened them."

"Moréas won't be threatening anybody anymore. He was murdered," Blanc told him in a calm voice, watching for the architect's reaction.

Le Bruchec leaned back in his chair. He looked more relieved than surprised, confused, somewhat embarrassed, but not in the least shocked.

"Who was it?"

"We don't know yet."

"Then whoever was messing around at my window on Saturday wasn't Moréas?"

"We can't be certain of that," the captain said carefully, getting to his feet. "Moréas was murdered on Sunday. What he might have done immediately beforehand we don't know. We will keep you informed on the investigation into the break-in."

"Are you his only neighbor?" Tonon asked.

"No, there's another house in the forest. On the neighboring land on the other side of Moréas's shack. It's owned by an artist. A German painter. A very quiet man, shy. Maybe he can tell you more than I can. Although I suspect he won't be shedding many tears either."

Five minutes later Blanc and Tonon were standing outside a carefully constructed little house. Blanc would have found it hard to tell if the house was recently built or if it had been hiding there amidst the pine trees since the Middle Ages. The door was open and in front of it stood a dented wine-colored Clio hatchback with the legs of an easel sticking out of the open rear. At just that moment a man of about forty years old came out of the dark interior of the house. Average height, thin, with long wavy hair, freckles, rimless glasses, and a reddish glowing pirate's beard. He was carrying a pair of white-framed canvases under his arms and stopped dead when he spotted the two policemen and their patrol car. He put down the canvases and wiped his hands on his tattered jeans. His face was red, but whether that was from exertion or embarrassment, Blanc couldn't tell. The captain introduced himself and his colleague.

"I'm Lukas Rheinbach," the painter replied. "What can I do for you?" His grammar was perfect but he spoke with a curious mixture of local Midi dialect and a thick German accent.

"Monsieur Rheinbach," Blanc began, not even trying to imitate the unpronounceable "ch" sound at the end of the man's name, "I'm afraid we need to ask you a few questions, because your neighbor Charles Moréas has been the victim of a crime."

"Come in," said the German, leading them into a brightly lit room that seemed to serve as living room and studio at the same time. Blanc was surprised that he hadn't asked what sort of crime his neighbor had been the victim of. They couldn't see his face, but Blanc got the impression that the German wasn't so much irritated as relieved.

"I can't tell you very much about my neighbor," the painter said at last, running his fingers through his hair. "We were hardly friends. Quite the contrary, in fact."

"Did you feel threatened by him?"

Rheinbach hesitated. "Yes," he admitted. "You could hardly walk through the woods without being afraid of him accosting you. On one occasion he nearly ran me over with his motorbike, hurtling along the forest path on the thing at top speed."

"Did you inform the gendarmerie? Did you report him? Or make a complaint to the local *commune*?"

"No. It wasn't really all that bad. And I just want to work here in peace and quiet."

"You're a painter?"

Rheinbach stared out of the window. "I suppose you could say that," he mumbled to himself.

"Pardon?" Blanc asked, disconcerted.

The German sighed. "You won't find my work in any museums or galleries," he said. "I paint pictures for puzzles."

"Pardon?" Blanc said again.

"Jigsaw puzzles. The sort of paintings that get printed onto cardboard and then split up into thousands of pieces. A courtyard in the Camargue. Romantic chapels. Cypress trees. Mont Ventoux at twilight."

"A bit like Van Gogh," Tonon suggested.

"A bit like Paul Cézanne, only a hundred and fifty years later, and about half as good." He pointed at a few cardboard boxes piled up at one end of a shelf. The front of one had a picture on it of a hilly landscape with a medieval village. Not bad, Blanc thought to himself, though I'm hardly an expert.

"German jigsaw puzzle fans love Mediterranean landscapes," Rheinbach explained. "When I was a student I knocked out landscapes to pay for my education. Today I still do the same thing to earn a living." He laughed and shook his head as if he was still surprised by himself. "At some stage I realized I had a certain degree of talent, but wasn't going to get any further. And seeing as I learned to love this landscape traveling through it as a young man, I decided to move down south here a few years ago."

"You own this house?"

"The jigsaw makers pay well, but not that well. I do own it, but when I bought it, it was little more than a heap of stones in a clearing in the forest. I rebuilt it myself, a bit like doing a jigsaw puzzle, if you like."

"You live here on your own?"

Once again that slight hesitation. "Most of the time. Every now and then I get to know someone. But the women I like don't like this house."

Blanc and Tonon asked a few more questions about Moréas, but he couldn't help them: He had never seen anyone visit him, never noticed anything suspicious, never had him attempt to break into his own house. Just the awareness of an unpleasant, somehow threatening neighbor it was best to avoid.

"Are you going somewhere?" the captain asked as they were leaving the house, nodding in the direction of the packed Clio.

"To Luberon, just for a few days. I want to paint the lavender fields around Sénanque monastery. It's one of the most popular Provence scenes. For next year's Christmas presents."

They said good-bye and along the forest track drove to the *route départementale* in silence. It was only when they reached the road that Tonon turned and said: "Excessively punctual, that German. If you ask me."

Blanc looked at him in surprise. "That Rheinbach guy didn't exactly strike me as a Prussian officer."

"But he's heading for Luberon, to paint the lavender fields, at the beginning of July. They only really come into bloom at the end of July. You'd think a painter who'd lived in Provence for years might know that."

Madame le Juge

Blanc took a left turn off the forest track. "You need a GPS," Tonon announced. "This isn't the way back to Gadet, this leads up the hill to Caillouteaux."

"That's where I'm heading."

"We've done enough today."

"It's still light."

"You're not in Paris anymore, what do you want with the little hick town up there?"

"Even if Moréas never showed his face there, it's still a *commune*, a small town. They must know him at the *mairie*. He might have applied there to set up a business, might have asked for planning permission. The town hall just has to have something relating to him. They have something about everybody."

The Mégane trundled onward up the D70A. The scent of pines and earth drifted in through the open window. The cicadas clicked incessantly. It was still so hot that the captain didn't like to let his left elbow rest on the metal of the open window. This isn't Paris. Thank you for telling me. He imagined his colleague was just hungry again—but there again maybe he was right. Who was he going to find to talk to in Provence in summer after 5 P.M.? Maybe a pigeon on a roof or rats in a cellar. *Merde.* But it was always good to act quickly; Moréas might have been an asshole, but his body had still been hot when they found it, goddammit.

After a few minutes they were already passing a few modern houses, and the tarmac under their wheels had gotten darker, smoother. And then they were passing between ancient stone houses baked in the sun, ochre with blue and green shutters on the windows, most of them closed to keep out the sun. Purple oleander grew out of walled courtyards. There was not a soul to be seen, no dogs wandering about, not even a sleeping cat. An alleyway so narrow that his side mirrors almost scratched the walls on either side. A tiny main square with a modest little fountain topped with a stone bust of Marianne, the symbol of the republic.

"Park here," Tonon grumbled. "We can walk the rest of the way."

Blanc climbed out of the car and stood in front of the little church built of yellow stone. On the pediment above the door two bells hung like a silhouette against the sky. In a niche to one side was a fine statue of the Madonna smiling a blessing to a fly that buzzed around it. At the far end of the square was a stone clock tower crowned with a wrought-iron bell house—a symbol of civic pride, money, and a finely calculated provocation, given that it rose higher toward the heavens than the church. On the side of the square opposite the alley they had come through stood a grand façade that Blanc at first took for that of a palace—until he realized that nearly all the windows, the grand entrance, and the little fountain on the façade were only painted on and the building had little other ornamentation.

"People here have money to spend on art," said Tonon, half admiring, half mocking. "You don't get the citizens of Gadet or Saint-César painting their houses like that."

"They're not getting money from tourism." Blanc walked up to a low wall between the church and the house at the end of the square, where a modern bronze sculpture stood: a winged, headless woman with her voluptuous rear end facing the horizon. Behind her, the hill Caillouteaux sat on fell away. The captain looked down at the dark squares of fields and olive groves, the little white dots of a flock of sheep, the blue shimmering hills and the mirror of the Étang de Berre in the distance, and imagined he could feel the steamy heat of the Mediterranean. "It's pretty here," he said.

Tonon stroked the statue's metal rear end. "Too small, too obscure."

"Her backside?"

"The town. This is the center of Caillouteaux and there are only three figures to be seen: a ceramic Madonna, a stone Marianne, and a headless woman with a fat ass. Not exactly the sort of women you can sit and sip a pastis with. And there's never been an artist here, except the guy who daubed his work on that house. There's no tasty odor emanating from a one-star restaurant, no antique seller with a load of overpriced local kitsch in his window. What is there here for tourists? Ah, but we are in luck. The mayor's still here." Tonon nodded toward the only other car on the square, a new white Audi Q7 that, set against the background of the unplastered walls, looked like a glass recycling bin on alloy wheels.

"They've got enough money here for things like that too," mumbled Blanc, trying in vain to recall if he'd ever seen any Parisian district mayor in a car like that. All of a sudden that old feeling came over him that he had had when he was tracking down fraudsters: the call of the hunt.

Tonon led him past a tiny restaurant. "Le Beffroy," he said. "Not one line about it in the Guide Michelin, no strangers, no Asian words on the menu. You can eat here if you get tired watching our colleagues chewing away back in Gadet. It gets to us all every now and then." They went up an alleyway and then a few stone steps. *"Voilà."*

"The offices are closed, I'm afraid," a pleasant male voice said from somewhere above them.

"Gendarmerie!" the lieutenant replied.

"Putain. Come on up."

They found the mayor in his office, which had a window opening onto the square. Beneath the obligatory bust of Marianne sat a man in his midsixties, heavy, with an angular head covered in gray bristle, and almost jet-black eyes. He got to his feet and Blanc noticed the expensive cut of his suit. There was more than just a whiff of aftershave in the air, expensive aftershave. The walls were covered in modern frescos, of young women with baskets of fruit and wheat sheaves, allegories of the twelve names given to the months of the year during the revolution. Blanc admired a gently smiling blonde labeled Mademoiselle Messidor, the name given to June and July by the revolutionaries. Frescos in the town hall, a trompe l'oeil façade on the square, a jigsaw puzzle painter in the woods. It seemed Provence was full of artists whose style would have been considered two hundred years out of date anywhere else. Then it occurred to him the one thing missing was a picture of the president of the republic. Wasn't that obligatory in public buildings?

"Monsieur Lafont," Tonon said, clearly on familiar terms with the mayor.

A powerful handshake. "Make yourselves comfortable. Can I offer you a glass of water?" Lafont had a thick Midi accent. Blanc saw him as a man who traveled around in his white Audi but the minute he got out could talk to locals as an equal. He wondered how long he had been the little king of Caillouteaux. Years probably, maybe even decades.

"So, you're the new specialist from Paris the minister of state has sent us," the mayor declared. Blanc leaned back in the visitor's seat, which was modern and very uncomfortable. The back of the chair was up against a steel filing cabinet that had obviously been placed there by someone with no feeling for either comfort or aesthetics, given that it also obscured the fresco of Mademoiselle Germinal. "You have good contacts in Paris?" he asked.

Lafont laughed. "With the Eiffel Tower mob? They only bother to talk to provincial clods like me once every five years, just before the elections." He made a dismissive gesture with a big bear's paw of a hand. "I have good contacts with the local gendarmerie stations. I have no idea who you are, *mon Capitaine*, but if they wanted to get rid of you in Paris, you can't be all bad."

Blanc allowed himself the ghost of a smile. "Let's hope you don't change your mind about me. I'm afraid I have bad news for you. Your *commune* has one citizen less."

"An accident or a crime?"

"Murder."

"Who?"

"Monsieur Charles Moréas."

Lafont clicked his tongue the way you might do when your favorite club loses an important league match. "I'm not exactly surprised that Charles has come to a sticky end. What happened to him?"

Blanc explained in a few words what they knew so far. The more he said, the more Lafont's expression darkened. "Kalashnikovs, burnt bodies, that's Marseille stuff," he exclaimed in horror. "Don't get me wrong, my family comes from Calenzana, a little mountain village in Corsica, but I grew up in Marseille, politically too. I still have lots of friends there. I was down seeing them just last weekend. They had a good laugh at my expense. My Audi was in for service and I had to take my wife's car. A red Mini, a woman's car. You wouldn't believe the ribbing they gave me." Then Lafont turned serious again: "*Bon.* That's of no interest to you. I was just trying to say that I still have a lot of connections in Marseille. But life there is . . ." He struggled to find the right word. ". . . stressful. I moved to Caillouteaux some thirty years ago, particularly for my family's sake. And for my own health. It's so quiet here, so peaceful."

"Well, it would seem now Marseille has come to you, *Monsieur le maire,*" Tonon said calmly.

Lafont got to his feet again, went over to the window, and waved the two gendarmes over. "Look over there," he said, pointing toward a poster on the wall of a house opposite: a photo of a smiling young blond woman. She might have been a singer or an actress.

"This time next year we have elections here in the *commune,*" he said. "And that is my most dangerous enemy." Blanc recognized the symbol of the Front National in the red, white, and blue of the tricolor. "That woman is clever, she knows how to handle herself. She's dangerous. You know, *mon Capitaine*, how strong the Front already is down here in the Midi. Oh yes, *le tout Paris* jokes about it all the time. But I don't want to end my political career with defeat by a ferocious right-wing extremist with a sharp tongue." He gestured vaguely out of the window. "We're planning to build a *médiathèque* on the outskirts of town: books, magazines, films, music, fast Internet access for everyone in a bright modern building. Free to everybody in the *commune*. That will keep our young people here, build a better future. Up until five minutes ago that was the main platform of my upcoming election campaign."

Blanc looked at the mayor expressionlessly. "You think the FN will use a Kalashnikov murder for propaganda purposes?"

"I don't think it, I know it. Every damn drug dealer who can't keep his trigger finger steady brings more votes for the far right. Whether it's drugs, criminals, Arabs, or murder, they link them all together. People are pleased with the idea of a *médiathèque*. But they're more afraid of criminals. And on election day, it's fear, not happiness, that decides where they put their 'x.' That's why I don't want to frighten my citizens, *mon Capitaine*, do you understand me?"

"Completely," Blanc said in a neutral voice.

"So please clear up this unpleasant business as quickly as possible, before it starts to get people scared."

"That's why we're here," said Blanc with a thin smile. "What can you tell us about Monsieur Moréas?"

A quarter of an hour later Blanc and Tonon knew that the deceased had no relatives and no friends in Caillouteaux or anywhere else. He hadn't applied for permission to build his house, but nobody had lodged a complaint about it. He had five pieces of land in the *commune:* one overgrown lot in the town itself and four pieces of woodland supposed to be for agricultural purposes. Moréas had never been in the post office, which was housed in the same building as the town hall offices, never posted anything or collected anything. He had never applied for a license or benefits, never applied for a passport, and didn't even have a landline.

"You promised the commandant that no politician would be interested in this," Tonon recalled with a laugh as they left the town hall, "and now the first politician we come across is hot as mustard over it. I'll be interested to see how Nkoulou reacts."

"What sort of politician doesn't even have a photo of the president on his wall?"

"Lafont says what he thinks. He's not very impressed by the gentlemen in Paris. In any case you see the president every day on television and in the newspapers. It's a welcome change not to have to look at his face."

Blanc stopped to look at the poster Lafont had pointed out. "What about her?" The face was just a little too rounded to be that of a model, but it seemed open and unintimidating. "She doesn't look too dangerous."

"Just be glad you're not an Arab. That's just a façade. The Front has another face too, not quite so pretty."

"Are Lafont's fears real? Could the old boy lose to a doll-face like that? Just because somebody killed an unpleasant good-for-nothing and burnt his body on a garbage heap?"

The lieutenant looked around to see if there was anybody

in the square and shook his head. "I thought you were supposed to be a corruption expert, back in Paris."

"And in Provence everyone is corrupt."

"Exactly." Tonon jerked his thumb toward the town hall. "Did you notice anything about the furniture in his office?"

"It was horrible, modern, uncomfortable. Has Lafont been bribed by some furniture chain?"

"It's a lot more subtle than that. The *mairie* was full of antiques, a desk from the Empire period, oil paintings on the wall, Louis XIV chairs, stuff like that. It's all in Monsieur Lafont's villa now. A rather big villa. One day he just had the town hall emptied. Then at the *commune*'s expense he bought all the new stuff. That vile filing cabinet only arrived last week. The frescos of the revolutionary year are to cover up the blank spaces on the wall left by the oil paintings that hung there for two hundred years before being relocated to Monsieur Lafont's living room. It was given out as 'modernization,' but everybody knows where all the old stuff is."

"Nobody complained?"

"The Gaullistes are corrupt, the socialists are corrupt. Who was there to complain?"

"The Front National?"

"On the button. Not that I think the Front aren't corrupt too. They just haven't had the opportunity yet."

"So it's not just racists who vote FN, it's everybody who has had enough of misappropriated antiques and mayors in expensive cars?"

"That's why Lafont wants to spend money on this ultramodern *médiathèque*, so they too get something out of all the money lying around here. He gets hysterical about anything that could win more votes for the Front. If we clear this case up quickly we'll have won a friend. A useful friend."

"*Merde,*" said the captain. "Now that's exactly the sort of thing we did make jokes about in Paris."

Blanc dropped his colleague off at the gendarmerie in Gadet and went into the tiny supermarket to buy food for the next few days: lots of coffee, two jars of jam, bread and *pains au chocolat* in plastic bags, plus two green bottles of Alsace beer. The owner, who was at the cash register, greeted him with extreme politeness and packed his purchases rapidly in opaque carrier bags. Blanc drove his Espace slowly back to Sainte-Françoise-la-Vallée. He had a thumping headache. It was evening and still nearly eighty-six degrees.

Parking in front of the old olive oil mill, he sat behind the wheel for a while, staring at the raw yellow stone of the walls. Home. *Merde.* Eventually he got out, closed the car door, and carried his supplies into the house. At least the ancient refrigerator came to life when he turned it on. He put the beer bottles hopefully into the freezer compartment, then went out, fetched the first bag from the minivan, and heaved it onto the kitchen table. Then the second. He sighed, changed out of his uniform into an old T-shirt and ripped jeans, opened up all the doors and the trunk of the Espace, and emptied it of everything. One hour later everything that remained of his career and his marriage was piled high on the rickety kitchen table. He threw his sleeping bag and the inflatable mattress onto the bare bedstead. Then he scrabbled around until he found the most recent photo of his children, a framed picture from when they were both still at school, just before the elder of the two graduated. He put the photo alongside his cell phone on the bedside table.

At long last it got dark outside. Blanc was so tired that he swayed on his feet. But he was too wound up to sleep. Instead he used an old brush and a few cloths to wipe away cobwebs and dust, then he piled up the horrid chairs and various other stuff next to the door. Tomorrow he would take it all to the garbage dump. He knew the way now.

In the end he sat down with the beer and some bread on the doorstep of the house. A soft breeze had arisen, as cooling as a silk handkerchief—it seemed even the cicadas were exhausted. The sun had already dropped beyond the horizon but the sky still had a surreal blue-violet tone. A single star, like a white needle point, shone in the heavens above the plane trees. One of God's bad jokes, Blanc thought.

He drank down the cool beer and leant back against the wall. He could feel the rough stone through his thin T-shirt, but at the same time it reflected the sun's warmth between his shoulder blades. He heard the buzz of an insect, then two of them, then thousands. It went on and on, for at least half an hour, like an ovation after a concert. Somewhere across the river he heard the shrill back-and-forth calls of two owls getting ready for the night's hunt. Then shadows appeared in the twilight. At first he took them for late swallows, then realized they were bats. Some of them hurtled down toward the Touloubre, clustered around those areas where the water lay more still behind stones and clumps of earth, then soared back up into the sky. They were drinking, Blanc realized. I didn't know bats drank. Never thought about it. Why?

Every breath he took was perfumed by the air. What was it the woman on horseback had told him? Thyme. He felt simultaneously drained and replete. He got to his feet with an effort, stumbled into the house and to bed, without even climbing into his sleeping bag.

His cell phone's alarm called him out of a deep, dreamless oblivion. It took Blanc a minute or so to realize where he was. When had he last slept so well? He went into the tiny bathroom with its brown tiles from the 1970s. He would need to get rid of those. Sooner or later. When he turned on the shower, rust-red water flooded out, but after a few minutes it turned clear. The old electric boiler had actually managed to warm the water overnight. He climbed out of the shower, hesitated for a few moments, then instead of his uniform put on black jeans and a black T-shirt. Then he scoured the kitchen cupboards until he found a little aluminum Italian espresso pot and set it on the hot plate until the scent of coffee rose from it. Blanc chewed on a doughy *pain au chocolat* and took a cup of bitter black coffee to the door. It was already nearly eighty degrees, he reckoned. It might be a good idea to make a patio out here. On the other side of the Touloubre he heard Serge Douchy trundling along on his tractor, making a point of ignoring him. He heard a rooster call from Douchy's farmyard. Then it was quiet again. I'm going to have to get used to this quiet, the captain thought.

When he was about to leave just a few minutes later, he suddenly came to a halt at the gate. The old stuff he had left outside the door had vanished. Douchy? Or someone else who had passed by in the dusk and spotted them? He shrugged, pulled the gate closed, even though it no longer had a working lock, climbed into the car, and set off for Gadet. At least this time there were no horses blocking the road.

It was as quiet as a church in the gendarmerie. The calendar on the desk by the door read Tuesday, July 2. Upstairs he heard Nkoulou's voice from behind his office door, obviously on the telephone. He wondered why the chief was up and about so early. Most of the other offices were empty. Even Tonon hadn't turned up yet. The only one of his colleagues to be seen was the dumpy woman who had offered him a Gauloise yesterday. He couldn't remember her name.

"Didn't you sleep well?" she asked. "You look tired."

Blanc didn't reply; he hadn't felt so rested in months. Instead he asked her what time his partner usually turned up.

"Marius usually makes it by midday," she laughed. "He put in more hours with you yesterday than he would normally do in a month. He'll be getting his strength back." She put her chubby thumb into her mouth then pulled it out, making a sound like a cork coming out of a bottle. "Cigarette?"

The captain made a point of giving her a friendly smile, turning down the offer. "I have an appointment at the pathology lab. Can you tell me how to get there?"

Five minutes later he was sitting in the patrol car, on his own, with the GPS illegally on the passenger seat, heading toward Salon-de-Provence. He knew the name from a trashy novel he had read as a teenager: the city of Nostradamus, alchemy, fortune-telling, Renaissance intrigue, and Catherine de' Medici as the spider at the center of a web of conspiracies. But instead of dark defensive walls or ornate palaces he found himself driving through anonymous suburbs, gas stations, shops offering scooters, their machines parked in a long parallel line with their front wheels on the sidewalk. Fifteen minutes later he parked the car on a hill next to a complex of square concrete buildings: the town hospital. It had a view over the whole town, and indeed there was a castle, like something out of a fairy tale, with a *donjon* tower, crenellated battlements, a gateway, and high walls. I must take a closer look, he told himself, one of these days. He asked directions from one person after another until he found himself at the entrance to the Institut Médico-Légal.

Dr. Fontaine Thezan shook his hand and gave him the once-over. Today she was wearing glasses that gave her an Audrey Hepburn air. "When were you last at an autopsy?" she asked.

Do I really look that pale? Blanc asked himself. "I've had breakfast," he replied. The smell of disinfectant was so strong that he couldn't be sure whether or not there was still a faint whiff of marijuana around the doctor.

"In any case, we've almost finished." She introduced him to her two assistants and a young policeman, and led them all into a cool, brightly lit room, where the charred corpse lay on a steel table. The chest and stomach had already been cut open and the top of the skull sawed off. The brain was sitting in a bowl next to it.

The pathologist pointed to an object in another bowl nearby, still with pieces of brain matter adhering to it. "We found one bullet in the skull," Thezan told him, "two in the lungs, one more in the upper thigh bone. There were also traces where more had gone through the chest and stomach. You'll get all the details in a written report. The brain, heart, and liver were all destroyed, and there was severe internal bleeding. You can pick whichever you like as 'cause of death.'"

"If there were still Kalashnikov bullets in the body, that means he can't have been shot at close range. If he had been, they would all have gone right through," Blanc suggested.

She led him over to another table with a spongy substance. "The lung," she said, using a pair of tweezers to point at it. "If you look here you'll see there's no soot in the bronchial passages. That means by the time his body was burnt, he was no longer breathing. We also haven't been able to find any traces of smoke absorbed by the blood."

"Any sign of alcohol or drugs?"

"We haven't got all the results from the lab yet, but his blood alcohol level was point zero one, which suggests he might have had something to drink several hours before his death. Maybe a glass of wine with lunch. Or it's vestigial from drinking the night before. We've found no traces of cocaine or anything like that."

"How was he set on fire?"

"There were traces of an accelerant on various parts of the skin. The easy assumption is that someone poured a large quantity of gasoline over the body and set it alight."

"Can you be sure that it actually is Moréas?"

"Absolutely." He could make out the pathologist smiling, even behind her face mask. "At first we tried using dental records. But it appears he'd never been to a dentist in his life, so we had nothing to check against. His fingers were so burnt that there were no prints left to take. But then we found this." She held up a shiny object made of stainless steel.

"In his body?" Blanc asked dubiously.

"An artificial left hip. Every prosthesis of this type in the world carries a serial number. Bingo! If you have the number you can identify the patient. Charles Moréas was given this hip replacement three years ago in the Timone hospital in Marseille. He'd had a serious motorbike accident and was taken there for treatment."

"Any signs that Moréas had been gagged or tied up? That he'd been knocked out? Maybe by a blow to the head?"

"Given the state of his skin, it's hard to tell if he'd been tied up any way, but I suspect not. And there's definitely no sign of a blow to the head, before the Kalashnikov salvo took him out."

"So it would appear he had no reason to think he was in danger of being shot. The killer didn't get close to him. Maybe he didn't even speak to him, just fired without warning. Then he pours the gas over him, strikes a match—*et voilà!*"

"That's speculation, and that's your job, not mine, *mon Capitaine.*"

By the time Blanc got back to the gendarmerie, Tonon still hadn't turned up. Blanc had fired up the antique computer and begun to compose a report when there was a knock on the door. It was the boss.

"You need to get over to the *juge d'instruction*," Nkoulou said, giving him a frown. He obviously didn't approve of seeing any of his staff in plain clothes.

Every criminal case in France had to be overseen by a judge. The police were theoretically just operative assistants who fulfilled the judge's instructions and sent him or her the results. Theoretically. Blanc had never liked the idea and preferred to have as little as possible to do with the judge's instructions. But rules were rules. He got up from his seat and asked, "Where do I find the judge?"

"Normally in the Palace of Justice in Aix-en-Provence.

But this judge prefers to work more closely with the gendarmerie when it's an interesting or complex case, and has an office next to mine." Nkoulou hesitated for a second, as if uncertain whether or not he should go on. "And by the way, the judge is female," he eventually managed to say. "She's supposed to be the best of the lot. If you'd like to follow me? Madame Vialaron-Allègre doesn't like to be kept waiting."

Blanc stopped in his tracks as if he had hit a wall.

"Vialaron-Allègre? Like the minister in Paris?"

"She's his wife." For a moment Blanc thought he almost detected a note of sympathy in the commandant's voice.

There was a brand-new business card on the door, heavy cardboard with embossed letters: *Aveline Vialaron-Allègre, Juge d'instruction, Aix-en-Provence.* Blanc knocked and went in. *"Madame le juge,"* he said, doing his best to sound traditionally formal. "Delighted to meet you."

"Really?" she said. "I'm surprised."

For some reason or other the captain had expected to be confronted by an imposing matron figure, a real-life version of the old film star Simone Signoret. Instead he found himself looking at a woman in her midthirties, five feet eight inches, slim, with olive skin, dark eyes, short black hair, a long nose, and long fingers. She wasn't exactly pretty but she was attractive, self-confident, elegant, frosty. Intimidating. *Merde,* he thought, regretting that he wasn't in uniform.

The judge closed a Moleskine notebook and replaced the top on a narrow, old-fashioned fountain pen.

"Please sit down."

Could it be a coincidence, Blanc wondered, his brain turning cartwheels. The minister had sent him to the district where his wife was in charge of police investigations. And he runs into her on his very first case. *She's watching me,* he decided, *waiting for me to make the first tiny mistake. He pushed me out of the Paris limelight, but that wasn't enough. He wants to kick my ass out here in the sticks. And his wife is going to help him do it. Just how did I tread on his toes?*

She lit a Gauloise. Left-handed, Blanc registered automatically. She didn't offer him one. "What have you found out so far, *mon Capitaine*?" she asked through a cloud of blue smoke.

All Blanc's senses were on maximum alert, razor sharp and pumped up with adrenaline. He noted every single hair in the strand that touched her left cheek, the smoke in her voice, the turquoise-colored Hermès scarf negligently thrown over the back of her leather chair, her pianist's fingers tapping out some unknown melody on the desk, the hint of Chanel No. 5 in the air. *Maybe she isn't aware of the connection between me and her husband,* he thought irritably. Then she said, "Well?" and he could hear both impatience and irony in her voice.

"We have a murder victim, discovered at a garbage dump."

"I know that already. That's why I'm here."

"Do you want me to start from the beginning, or should I skip to chapter three?"

She raised an eyebrow, inhaled deeply, and nodded. "I'd like to hear you tell it from the beginning."

The captain told her about the burnt body, the Kalashnikov cartridges, about Charles Moréas, his neighbor Le Bruchec's burglary accusations, and the little he knew about the deceased's miserable little life. "A man with many enemies, but no friends or relatives."

"Most murders are committed by friends or relatives."

"Not this one."

"So what, in your opinion, should we be doing now?"

"Go through the details of Moréas's past life. He somehow got involved with someone unscrupulous: A machine-gun murder and incinerated corpse are hardly the result of a tiff. This was a cold-blooded execution, and that suggests the killer was a professional."

"Are you sure you have the qualifications for an investigation like this?"

Blanc was taken aback for a minute. "What leads you to doubt my qualifications?"

Vialaron-Allègre gave him a long, hard look. "This Moréas is a creature of the Midi. He probably never got beyond the town of Orange in his entire life. And you want to go back through the details of his last thirty years when you've only been in Provence for a couple of days?"

"I haven't been in the gendarmerie for more than a couple of days."

"My husband has told me about your abilities," she said calmly. "Murders in Provence aren't exactly your specialty."

"I always appreciate the chance to learn on the job."

"Parisian arrogance isn't going to get you very far down here."

Blanc took a deep breath and leaned back in his chair. The way this conversation was going was intended to derail him. "I shall keep you fully informed of my progress at every step," he promised. "Feel free to intervene the moment you think I'm going off course."

"Très bien," Aveline Vialaron-Allègre replied, stubbing out her cigarette in a chrome ashtray. "I look forward to your next report." She didn't shake his hand as he left.

"Mon Capitaine?" Nkoulou caught him coming out and led him into his own office. Blanc made sure he closed the door behind him. He looked down at his boss's desk and remembered his colleagues' bet. What woman could put up with such a pedant?

"I had a call this morning," the commandant began, "from a local mayor."

"Monsieur Lafont from Caillouteaux?"

"It was a fairly intense conversation." Nkoulou's voice was almost shaking. "Your promise that no politicians would bother with this case has proven remarkably short-lived."

"Did he try to put pressure on you?"

"Let's just say the mayor would be relieved if we could solve this case quickly. Quickly enough for it not to overshadow the laying of the foundation stone for his new *médiathèque*."

"We're working on it, *mon Commandant*."

Nkoulou drew his lips in a smile that was part scornful, part resigned. "Leave out the plural in that sentence. You'll be doing most of the work on your own. Lieutenant Tonon hasn't even turned up yet today."

"We'll get the mayor his murderer before the diggers turn up in Caillouteaux," Blanc promised. Then he saluted and left the sterile little room.

Half an hour later Tonon turned up, his eyes bloodshot. Not a word about what he'd been up to all morning. Nor was it necessary. Nonetheless, he had brought with him, scribbled on a crumpled piece of paper, a list of all the paintball players he knew. They spent the rest of the day getting hold of them, either at work or at home—mostly at home, as many of them were unemployed. None of them had been at the garbage dump recently.

It was only that evening when they got back to the gendarmerie, both exhausted, that Tonon opened his mouth to say anything more than the bare minimum. "You need to watch out for this judge," he warned. "She's a dragon in pretty makeup."

"With good family connections."

The lieutenant made a face. "I'd like to know what makes her dote on that slippery clown. She would have done well enough without him. They say she studied in America, was offered a job in the ministry of justice, but preferred to stay here."

"How modest of her."

"You don't understand. She's from here. Midi. You can study in America and be offered a job in Paris—but if you get the chance to stay down here in the south, you take it."

"As corrupt as everyone else?"

"Whatever you do, don't try to bribe her." Tonon shook his head. "She's clean."

Blanc thought of her husband, who had put him out to pasture after he had successfully solved a corruption case, and wondered if the Vialaron-Allègres really couldn't be bought. "If she works down here and her husband is in Paris, then they can hardly see one another often. That means . . ."

"The minister takes the TGV high-speed train from Paris to Aix-en-Provence every Friday night and his good lady meets him at the station. They have a nice house here. In Caillouteaux."

"*Merde.*"

"And every now and then he stays over until Monday and visits a few local gendarmerie stations. Unannounced."

"Merde."

"A few weeks ago there was an issue with an officer and he got posted to Lorraine."

"Merde."

"Madame le juge thinks most gendarmerie officers are idiots. Maybe you can change her mind." But it didn't sound like Tonon would bet on it.

"I'm just getting to know her," Blanc muttered, climbing out of the patrol car.

When he got back to Sainte-Françoise-la-Vallée a few minutes later, there was a dented dark blue Peugeot 504 next to his front gate. Blanc braked, looking at the old Peugeot with a professionally suspicious eye. Behind the wheel sat a man of about fifty or so, who waved at him and squeezed his dumpy body out of the driver's seat. His close-cropped hair was turning from black to gray and years in the sun had made his skin as wrinkled as an antique leather couch. His black eyes gleamed under bushy brows. A farmer, Blanc reckoned. A woman of about the same age got out of the passenger side: thin as a rake, high cheekbones, gray hair tied back into a ponytail that reached halfway down her back. Hardly a farmer's wife, the captain told himself. He was curious.

He shook the man's iron-hard, calloused hand, and the woman's pianist's hand. "Micheletti," the man introduced himself. "You live in the old mill?"

Blanc nodded and gave his name. Micheletti laughed and said:

"Then call us Sylvie and Bruno. We're practically neighbors." He had a voice that growled like the engine of an antique American limo, but there was no reek of tobacco. An ex-smoker, Blanc decided, then caught himself: You don't have to be a policeman all the time.

"We saw a light on last night," Sylvie said, "for the first time in years. We're glad to see somebody living in the old oil mill again."

The narrow *route départementale* on which Blanc's house stood wound its way through Sainte-Françoise-la-Vallée. On the other side of the Touloubre, two other roads led off, both so unimportant that neither had a name. The one that led off to the right meandered some three hundred yards into the forest before coming to an end outside an old farmhouse. The other one had an asphalt surface and led to the left along the crest of the hill, flanked by old stone houses, tall and narrow, clinging to the back of the hill like a series of ancient towers placed against one another to form a wall. Beyond them the asphalt surface stopped, and the road degenerated into a dusty path leading into the pinewoods. Micheletti pointed down it. "If you go a bit farther down that way you'll come to our place. Our land comes all the way down until it touches yours. That makes us neighbors."

"We run a winery," Sylvie explained. "Domaine de Bernard."

Blanc had only ever seen a winery on a postcard: endless rows of grapevines in Bordeaux or Champagne, with châteaux or stately homes in the background. "A vineyard out here in the forest?" he said dubiously.

Bruno laughed. "You'll see for yourself. We'll invite you over." He fumbled in the car's glove box and brought out a crumpled business card with an impressive coat of arms on it. "That's our telephone number."

The captain pulled out his notebook, ripped out a page, and scribbled his own cell phone number on it. "I haven't got a landline yet," he apologized.

"That could take a while to sort out."

Blanc didn't quite know how much he ought to tell them about himself. He kept to the bare minimum. But neither Bruno nor Sylvie seemed either hesitant or overly curious when he said he was a gendarme. No questions about his family, no comments about his job. He got the feeling they were both simply glad to have a new neighbor. As they trundled off in the Peugeot he waved after them. Winemakers. That didn't sound bad, though it would be better if he knew anything about wine.

Eventually he found a place far enough from the great wall of rock that he had a signal on his phone. He sat down on a wooden chair in the evening heat and tried making the calls he needed to get a landline installed. For the next half hour he followed instructions from computer voices to enter numbers, hash keys, or stars on his keyboard, until eventually he gave up without ever having spoken to a human being. He'd try again tomorrow. Maybe.

For the very first time he went up the stairs in his house. The old staircase was badly worn. Upstairs there were three bright rooms—the last of them had to have been the one he remembered from his childhood as where the light played tricks on the walls. All the walls were papered, a brown-green floral pattern; furniture from the seventies lay around, plastic and veneer, all the drawers empty. Nails hung on the walls with lighter patches of wallpaper beneath them—somebody had obviously cleared out the place of all the pictures. Masterpieces hanging on these walls? Gold and jewelry hidden somewhere? Looking at the depressing pattern, Blanc seriously doubted it. The only thing even remotely good-looking was under his feet: The ancient floorboards had been painted a faded white chalky color. He ripped off a strip of wallpaper, revealing old ochre plaster that had been waxed over, he reckoned. All he had to do was throw out the furniture, rip off the wallpaper, clean and restore the floor (and the walls and the ceilings), scrape out the grouting in the old window frames and replace it, clean the windows, rewire the place, replace the damaged tiles on the roof— and in maybe a hundred years or so he would finally feel more or less at home here.

By now it had cooled down a little. Blanc shrugged his shoulders and began lugging the cupboards, chests of drawers, and bedsteads from the first floor downstairs and out the door. By the time he spotted the first bat, several hours later, the top floor had been emptied of furniture. He had pulled wallpaper from the walls and left it on the floor of the first room, used his shoe to remove a couple of scorpions frightened out of cracks in the walls and thrown them outside. He could feel the muscles in his arms and shoulders begin to ache; his hands were scratched and bruised and he was so thirsty his lips had gone numb. He felt great.

But as he slowly ate and drank, his self-satisfaction gradually evaporated. He was thinking of the charred corpse and wondering what he might have missed. Was there something in Moréas's criminal past that he could have overlooked? Anything in his run-down little home? Anything in what Le Bruchec, Rheinbach, or the mayor had said? Something . . . there was something he should have noticed. It was something that had never happened to him before. Maybe the minister was right when he exiled him from Paris. The Vialaron-Allègres. One an ambitious politician who had sent him down here, the other the incorruptible judge in charge of his first case on arrival. This cozy little couple have got me in their clutches. Just when I'm not exactly on top of the game.

A Row Down at the Harbor

When Blanc went to start up the Espace the next morning, the only sound from the engine was like a pebble dancing in a metal bucket.

"That's not going to happen."

Down by the gate there was an old blue Alpine with its engine ticking over. It had to be vintage. Probably worth a fortune. "Fancy giving me a tow?" he called out to the driver.

The man turned into his driveway: He was in his midfifties, average height, bald, with glasses. "That happens all the time with older Espace models," he said, sliding out of his sports seat. He shook Blanc's hand. "Jean-François Riou. We live just over there." He pointed to a house plastered in pale pink on the road leading up the hill.

A few more days like this and I'll know everybody in the village, Blanc thought to himself. In Paris he had never even heard his neighbor's voice. When they passed in the stairwell, they greeted each other with nothing but a nod. Down here in the south, people talked to one another freely—indeed it was hard to stop them.

He introduced himself in return. "Should I just tip it into the Touloubre?" he asked.

Riou shook his head. "May I?" He opened the hood and bent over the engine.

"You a mechanic?"

"Engineer. I work for Airbus Helicopters in Marignane. But in my spare time I like messing around with cars." He pulled a tool kit out of the Alpine's tiny trunk and began fiddling around with screwdrivers and wrenches in the guts of the Espace. "The killer with these is that as soon as one part gets fixed, the next goes. Appalling build quality."

Barely ten minutes later Riou turned the key in the ignition— and the old minivan growled into life. Blanc stared at him in amazement. "It started on the first try. It's never done that!"

"Loose contact on the starter. It'll happen again one of these days. It's just one of the dodgy construction errors."

"Thanks a lot for doing me the favor."

"You did me the favor, letting me fiddle around with the engine. Nothing I enjoy more." Riou climbed back into his vintage sports car and roared off.

Blanc finally got to the gendarmerie fifteen minutes later than he had intended, but nobody seemed to notice. Tonon wasn't there yet. The door to Nkoulou's office was closed, as was the door to the judge's office. There was an e-mail from Fabienne Souillard blinking on the screen of his monitor, sent from her cell phone the previous evening.

My partner and I have been discussing the case. She's from around here and knew Moréas. She has a little

dinghy down at the harbor in Saint-César, and Moréas
also had an old tub down there, a fishing boat. A wreck
according to my partner. Then she mentioned that
around noon of the day he was murdered, Moréas had
an almighty row down there. She doesn't know what it
was about, but she does know who it was with: Pascal
Fuligni. My partner's boat was at the next mooring and
she recognized him. He's a local builder. Never been in
trouble with the police, as far as I know. You can get his
address on Google. Kisses,

    Fabienne

Blanc's computer was so slow it took him several minutes
to locate Fuligni's address: a house just a few hundred yards
beyond Gadet. According to Google it was both his business and
private address. He did not have his own Web site.

Minutes later the blue patrol car's tires were rolling down
the gravel driveway of a newly built, imposing pink-plastered
villa. To the left a single-story extension rather contradicted
the swanky impression of the house. Next to the plain door of
the extension a brass plate said FULIGNI ET FILS, MAÇONNERIE
GÉNÉRALE—Fuligni and Son, General Masonry. Blanc knocked
on the door before opening it into a brightly lit office. A young
woman was playing with her smartphone behind a desk littered
with copies of *Paris Match*. After a few seconds she gave him
a bored glance, then suddenly did a double take when she saw
the police car outside.

"What can I do for you?" she asked in an East European accent, her voice trembling slightly. Blanc wondered if her identity
papers were in order. He gave her the once-over: midtwenties,

long hair dyed blond, dark eyes, lots of makeup, big bust, legs
that went on forever, obscenely short skirt. The sort of girl you
found hanging around on the corners of the dark lanes in the
Bois de Boulogne in Paris. He said hello and introduced himself. There was no reason to be impolite. "What is your name,
Mademoiselle?"

She hesitated for a second, obviously wondering whether to
use her own name. "Nastasia Constantinescu," she eventually
managed to say. "I'm Monsieur Fuligni's secretary."

"I'd like a few words with your boss."

As soon as she realized he wasn't interested in her, she gave
him a warm smile, then said, "Monsieur Fuligni is on vacation.
We only start taking orders again in August. I'm only here in
case someone calls or there's mail."

"Has your boss gone away?"

She gestured vaguely toward the house. "He always stays
at home for the summer. But his car isn't in the drive. I don't
know where he's gone. Or when he'll be back."

"Do you have his cell phone number?"

Yet again she hesitated, then handed him a business card.
"All his numbers are on there."

As Blanc was leaving the office, an old white Peugeot 306
convertible drove in, braking so hard it sent the gravel flying
from beneath its tires. The paintwork was so polished that it was
almost blinding. Behind the wheel was a woman of about fifty,
elegantly fighting off the depredations of age with discreet and
effective makeup. She had a body that suggested long hours
in the gym over the years and was wearing an elegant beige
summer dress, her hair covered with a headscarf to protect
against the wind while driving. He couldn't make out the

expression on her face behind the large sunglasses. There was a tennis bag lying on the backseat. "Madame Fuligni?" Blanc called out.

She climbed out and shook his hand. A strong handshake, his hand held just a fraction too long. "Miette Fuligni. Have I been speeding again?" She nodded at the patrol car. "Take pity on me, *mon Inspecteur.*"

She's flirting with me, Blanc thought with a smile. "I'm not an inspector and you haven't been speeding, at least not as far as I know." He told her why he was there.

"Pascal is down at the harbor with his boat," she replied, almost sounding disappointed. "In Saint-César. It's only a little harbor. Ask around when you get there. Everybody knows my husband. What's he been up to?"

"I just want to ask a few questions of Monsieur Fuligni."

"It's always worrying when policemen say things like that." She sighed and waved good-bye to him. She didn't look particularly worried.

Blanc drove along the back roads. He was gradually building a map in his head of the local roads so he wouldn't have to keep staring at the GPS on his cell phone to find his way. He turned onto the *route départementale* 16B. Pine trees and oaks on either side. Pleasantly shady. No cars, just a lone cyclist in a ridiculously bright outfit, struggling up the hill, his face getting ever redder. As he drove past, the captain noticed the words *Domaine de Bernard*, the winery belonging to the Michelettis, Bruno and Sylvie. But all he could see was trees and garigue shrubbery. It could hardly be a very big vineyard.

The road led over the brow of a hill then curved downward.

He crossed under the railway line via an old underpass hardly wide enough for two cars, then suddenly the horizon opened up ahead of him. The dimpled water of the Étang de Berre shimmering blue and silver like fish skin. A yacht was sailing along, its sails barely ruffled. A dozen little kids with tiny windsurf boards with yellow and red sails kept falling over practicing near the shore. An open fishing boat near a black buoy with a shirtless man struggling with a net. Across the lake, the wooded heights of Istres, a dark green wall with a few ancient, dilapidated villas. On his right a hill crowned with a ruin: Miramas-le-Vieux. And straight ahead Saint-César, a knot of ochre houses with pale red roofs and an imposing church tower. Steep, rocky hills enclosed the town on either side, linked at a breathtaking height by a stone bridge with a clock tower and supports soaring high above the little town.

Blanc navigated his way down the alleys, which had cars parked everywhere, even more chaotic than in Paris, he thought. Beautiful young women in summer dresses carrying white plastic bags. Old men in straw hats with baskets. Kids with water pistols. A market on the big square next to the church: pyramids of watermelons, heaps of red cherries, beans, eggplants. A line of olive oil bottles, their contents glittering gold in the sun, like polished bronze. A bakery with the door left open in the heat; the smell of fresh baguettes made him hungry. Coffee, fresh bread, a seat somewhere in the shade, to sit and watch people pass by. Later, he told himself. Later.

It wasn't hard to find the harbor: He just had to follow the alleyways toward the lake until he came to a grubby little square next to a few stone warehouses. A couple of jetties, a boatyard.

It was a harbor for fishermen. A few yards along the quayside he spotted a wall of aluminum and wood and the masts of yachts. He parked by the side of the road, as close as possible to some six-foot bushes, which provided the only shade. He only noticed too late that the bushes were covered in sharp thorns and had scratched the patrol car's paintwork. He shrugged and closed the door.

Blanc walked along the hedge until he came to a gate with an electronic code entry lock. He swung one long leg over, the sole of his shoe squeaking on the asphalt on the other side, where a few cars were parked in the hot sunshine. On his left was a tall crane, a concrete slipway, a few yachts out of the water, leaning to one side, looking sorry for themselves. A few little piers made of wood and steel jutted out into the water, with boats crammed together all along them. Little open-topped motorboats, dilapidated fiberglass yachts, new sailing boats. And out farther where the water was deeper, the heavy-weights: an elegant white motor yacht the size of a corvette, a well-kept twin-masted sailing ship, two huge catamarans, an-chored to buoys. There were people on every other one, work-ing at rigging, tinkering with outboard motors, spreading out sails, or just sitting in the sun drinking coffee. Blanc looked around. In the shade of the only tree, on the edge of the square, were two construction trailers, stacked one on top of the other, one with CAPITAINERIE written on a sun-bleached sign. The har-bormaster's office.

He climbed up the steps to the door of the upper trailer and went into the office. The room was made of steel and the walls were radiating heat. In one corner an air conditioner unit was

straining at full capacity. A bald-headed man of indistinguishable age looked up at him. "Sorry, no moorings free right now.
Not a one. In summer we're as tight as an oyster."

"I'm a gendarme."

"I'm afraid we still can't squeeze you in."

"I'm not looking for a mooring."

The man sighed. "Most people are. The door's forever opening and closing, like a railway station bathroom. Firemen and
pilots from Marignane come here looking for a few inches of
space for their little boats. Why not a policeman too?"

"I'm a landlubber. I'm here to speak to Monsieur Fuligni."

"Pascal's Mercedes is baking in the sun, so that means he's
on his yacht. First pier on the right. Walk about halfway down
and you'll find the sailor on board. The *Amzeri*. The code for the
pier gate is A4837X."

Blanc stepped out of the steaming trailer and looked
around. There was only one Mercedes among all the cars on the
square. Fuligni's business must be doing well.

He found the yacht without difficulty: a relatively new white
Beneteau 42, its massive stern squeezed between the smaller
boats on either side like a rugby player on the Métro using his
elbows to find a seat. "Monsieur Fuligni, may I come on board?"

A man in his midfifties clambered out of the depths of the
cabin in shorts and T-shirt, a pair of reading glasses on a leather
strap hanging from his neck. Dark, swept-back hair, held in
place with gel. Two-day stubble, dark eyes, medium height, slim.
The type who's strong without being muscle-bound. *"Bonjour."*
A smoker's voice, Midi accent. Surprisingly charming.

"I'd like to ask you a few questions." Blanc sat down on a

bench near the wheel. Something splashed in the water behind him. He turned around nervously.

"Just a fish," the builder reassured him. "When it's hot like this, they leap out of the water. Don't ask me why."

There was a strong smell of brackish water, but also a cool breeze. Seagulls circled in the endless sky above them. A little sailing ship glided silently toward the mouth of the harbor. He could hear the creaking of wood as the *Amzeri* gently swayed. I could get to like this, Blanc told himself. "Do you know Monsieur Charles Moréas?"

Fuligni stared at him a moment, taken aback, then nodded. "We've bumped into each other from time to time," he answered cautiously.

"Last Sunday for example?"

"Afraid I can't remember."

"You had a row. Here, at the harbor."

Fuligni smiled. A charmer, taken by surprise. "It wasn't a row, just a discussion."

"A very loud discussion."

"We're in the Midi, *mon Capitaine*. Things are normally loud. Even in the confessional box. I can't imagine anyone's complained about it. And I can't see Charles going to the police." He laughed, just slightly nervously.

"What was this discussion about?"

"Come with me. I'll show you. You'll agree with me."

The builder led him down to the end of the pier. "The water here is deeper," he said. "It's easier to get into the channel out of the harbor. Saint-César is at the end of the Étang de Berre. It's a big bathtub of brackish water. It's okay if you're a fisherman or have a tiny boat. Very tiny. But if you have a real yacht and want to take it out into the Mediterranean, you have to sail as far as the lifting bridge at Martigues and through the canal to reach the open sea. The easier it is to get out of the harbor here, the quicker you get to the bridge. Now look." He pointed to the boat at the last mooring on the pier, a wooden motorboat with a cabin. The light blue paintwork was faded, there were gashes in some of the decking, both outboard motors were rusty, and strips of weeds as long as a man's arm clung to the hull below the waterline.

"That wreck belongs to Moréas. He inherited the little fishing boat from his father. But he hasn't moved it in years." He pointed at the mooring ropes, which were green with algae. "You'd need a knife to cut that thing loose, there's no way those knots could be untied now."

"But Moréas comes down to the harbor."

"Now and then. He sits in the cabin and drinks."

Blanc thought about what the harbormaster had told him, the fat belly of the Beneteau yacht. "You want his mooring?" he suggested.

"I offered him a swap. If he wants to block up a mooring space with the corpse of a boat, then why of all spaces does he need the best in the harbor? *Merde*, I've offered the man money to change spaces. The harbormaster said he had no problems with the deal. It's been going on for years. But the man is a Corsican donkey."

"Not anymore, he's not," the captain sighed, pulling his Nokia from his pocket, and calling the gendarmerie back in Gadet. "I need the crime scene team," he told Baressi. "I want them to check out a boat in the harbor down at Saint-César." Then he turned back to Fuligni. "Moréas is dead," he told him.

"Oh no," the builder exclaimed, throwing up his hands defensively. "I didn't beat him to death just to get hold of his mooring space."

"I didn't say you did, and anyhow 'beaten' is hardly the word. Let's go back to your boat."

Sitting back on board the *Amzeri*, Blanc took a long, hard look at the man opposite. Would anybody really riddle a man with a Kalashnikov and then set his body on fire simply because he wanted his mooring space? People had been murdered for less. Fuligni looked nervous. "Was your argument on Sunday about the mooring space again?"

The builder rubbed his brow. "Yes, of course. What else would I have to discuss with someone like Moréas?"

"How much did you know about him?"

"Next to nothing. He was asocial. A man who enjoyed treading on other people's toes. It took me a long time to realize that he might just have sold the boat for drink if I hadn't been stupid enough to make an issue of the mooring. He realized that he could annoy me simply by turning up here every now and then to make sure the wreck didn't just fall to pieces. Just to prove to me that I would never get hold of his space."

"Did you ever threaten him?"

"Charles wasn't the sort of man it was wise to threaten."

Blanc recalled the Kalashnikov under his bed and the samurai sword hanging on his wall. "Did he ever threaten you?"

"Not directly, but in a way."

"Did he do so last Sunday?"

"I offered him five thousand euros. Five thousand euros, just for swapping moorings! His answer was to grin, jump back into his boat, and flip me the bird. I called him names, '*connard*,' and so forth. The sort of things people say in that situation. Then I came back to my yacht, and later went home."

"Do you have any witnesses?"

"Of our argument? Half the harbor must have heard us."

"What time was this?"

"I didn't look at my watch."

"Morning or afternoon?"

"Morning. I set out from home about nine A.M., and must have got here about a quarter past. Then I spent some time working on the yacht, maybe an hour or two. Eventually I spotted Moréas coming down the pier and went over to speak to him. It was definitely before lunch."

"Did Moréas stay long down here?"

Fuligni shook his head. "We had our exchange of opinions—don't ask me how long it lasted, but not that long. Then he disappeared belowdecks on his boat, but after half an hour at most he was off down the pier again. It was as if he had just been looking for something on board. I didn't exactly wave good-bye to him."

"What did you do after your argument? Where were you Sunday afternoon and evening?"

"Why do you need to know? Do I need an alibi? I had something to eat on the boat, then worked on my radio transmitter until it was dark. Then I went home."

"Do you have witnesses who can confirm that?"

"That I went home? My wife, of course, and . . ." He hesitated. "My secretary. She could confirm it too."

A little later three less-than-thrilled crime scene experts arrived. Blanc greeted them on the pier and took them down to Moréas's wreck of a boat. "Fits with his house," said one of them, groaning as he pulled on his white protective clothing. "I can't promise we're going to find any meaningful evidence. It's damp so close to the water. And anybody who was on the pier could have been on board."

"As long as they knew the access code at the pier gate."

"Or paddled their way across the harbor on a raft. You'll have to be very careful how you treat anything we find, if we find anything at all."

"Send me your report. Moréas wasn't on board very long on Sunday. Maybe he was looking for something, maybe he wanted to leave something here. Call me if you come across anything unusual." Blanc gave him his cell phone number. As he headed down the pier he touched the brim of his baseball cap in farewell to Fuligni, who was walking up and down the deck of his yacht, talking excitedly on his phone.

The captain drove back to Caillouteaux. There was an older middle-aged woman on duty at the town hall and she sighed theatrically at having to get up from her seat in front of a fan. Blanc had her take him to the *commune* archive, which was housed in a windowless vaulted room that had a musty smell but was relatively cool. He set to work going through land registers, meeting minutes, and official letters. If there was one thing he had learned in Paris it was that nowhere is there a better source of clues than paperwork. He was looking for any references that might link Fuligni and Moréas. Maybe they had quarreled over more than just the mooring?

Two hours later he found himself rubbing his tired eyes. Nothing. He had found a couple of references to Fuligni—he had built a kindergarten and a meeting hall for the *commune* and had renovated the town hall. Not exactly suspicious activity for a local builder. But in none of these could Blanc find anything that might be related to Moréas, whose name was conspicuous by its absence. He even came across a record of the civil wedding of Pascal and Miette Fuligni, but no reference to Moréas. It would have been interesting if perhaps the wife's maiden name had been Moréas, he thought to himself wearily. Defeatedly, he closed the files, glanced at his watch, and entered in the records book at the archive's only desk a note of the time he handed them in. Then he tiptoed out, trying not to make any noise so as not to disturb the clerk, who had dozed off in the stream of cool air from the fan. It was only when he got back out into the steaming heat of the town square that he clapped his hand to his head—and dashed back into the archive.

The records book.

He flicked through the pages. Everyone who used the archive had to enter their name and the time and date they looked through the records. There was no obligation to say why they were there or what they were looking for. Just a list of names, dates, and times. In the previous four weeks there had been nobody, except one man, exactly a week ago: Wednesday, June 26, from 10 A.M. until 4 P.M. Lukas Rheinbach.

The captain woke up the clerk and showed the record book to the bleary-eyed woman. "Can you tell me what Monsieur Rheinbach was looking for when he came in last week?"

Yawn. "It was my colleague who was on duty."

"How do I get hold of her?"

Even longer yawn. "She's on holiday. In Martinique. She'll be back in August. Then I'm off." Yawn.

Blanc left the town hall asking himself why an artist who painted pictures for jigsaw puzzles would spend an entire day sitting in this sleepy archive room, just four days before the murder of his neighbor, Charles Moréas.

Back at the gendarmerie he found Tonon, badly shaven and with his hair unkempt—a *clochard* in uniform, Blanc thought to himself. He told his colleague what he had been up to. "That could explain a few things," the lieutenant said pensively.

"You have an idea of some sort?"

"No. But it could explain why the boss has shut the door to his office. He got an unexpected call from high up and it put him in a bad mood."

"Vialaron-Allègre?"

"Maybe. You trod on Monsieur Fuligni's toes, almost accusing him of taking out Moréas. In the middle of the holidays, on his beloved yacht."

"I didn't accuse him. I questioned him."

"He's not used to that sort of thing. He's a big shot in local business. Thick as thieves with Mayor Lafont. And he belongs to the same political party as Monsieur Vialaron-Allègre . . ."

Blanc recalled Fuligni's agitated telephone conversation as he was leaving the harbor.

"You mean the builder rings his pal the mayor? And he in turn calls Paris?"

"Our local dignitaries aren't as provincial as you might think. There are invisible links that go far. I don't know what the minister might have said to Nkoulou. Maybe simply: 'Leave my friends alone!'"

"And what would *Madame le juge* say to that?"

"*Madame le juge* is a puzzle to us all. But I'm sure she'll let you know what she thinks sooner or later."

"Let's go for lunch," the captain replied.

"Now that's not the worst idea you've had," Tonon replied with a laugh.

In Le Soleil they once again got a table in the shade of the plane tree. Blanc ordered a whole bottle of mineral water; the heat was parching him. Tonon ordered a carafe of rosé the same size. "I recommend the lamb and rice," he said. "Both come from around here."

"The rice too?" the captain said in surprise, thinking of the flooded paddy fields of Asia and coolies in their round hats.

"Just beyond the Étang de Berre, you're in the Camargue, flat country, beaches for tourists, meadows for fighting bulls, ponds with flamingoes and lots of swamps full of mosquitoes. But they grow great rice there."

"*Bon*, I'll have that. I'm slowly becoming an expert."

"You need another few years of gourmet meals in the Midi for that."

"If I survive them."

"You afraid they're going to get rid of you down here?"

"Vialaron-Allègre still has me in his sights for some reason. I don't know where his wife stands, but I am certain a careerist like Nkoulou would rather see me out of here as soon as possible rather than have trouble with a minister in Paris and *juge d'instruction* here."

"As long as you do your work well, nobody can touch you."

"I thought that last week too, and now look where I am."

"It's not exactly Devil's Island." Tonon laughed again and

clapped him on the back. "And if you manage to put on a white T-shirt rather than a black one, you might not even feel the sun so much."

Blanc looked at his companion's glass, the rosé wine sparkling like some tincture from an alchemist's laboratory. "What have we got to so far?" he muttered. "We have Charles Moréas, a loner nobody knows anything about, not even how he earned a living. A man who probably had a criminal past and an even more criminal present, even if we haven't so far found any drugs or any other suspicious substances in his possession. He's had a few run-ins with the police but never been convicted. A man with no record."

Tonon snorted scornfully.

"This man," Blanc continued calmly, "had no friends, just enemies. Everyone who got to know him wished they'd seen the last of him. *Bon.* Now we find this guy riddled with holes by a Kalashnikov and incinerated on a garbage dump. Who do our investigations unearth? Lucien Le Bruchec, an architect, a cultivated man, a widower, who just happens to be a neighbor of Moréas. He accuses him of attempted burglary and stealing sport equipment. They've also had altercations in the woods belonging to their adjacent properties. But can you imagine a sixty-year-old man wielding a Kalashnikov on a garbage dump? *Bon.* Then we have the other neighbor, Lukas Rheinbach. A German artist, not exactly successful either with his art or with women. A man clearly afraid of a wild guy like Moréas. A man who in the week prior to the murder was the only one anywhere in the area who spent hours in the Caillouteaux town archives. Looking for something. But what?"

"And the day after the murder tells us he's heading for

Luberon to paint the lavender fields, even though he had to know they wouldn't be in bloom for several weeks yet," Tonon added.

"Should we go and see Madame Vialaron-Allègre? A harmless painter poking around in the archives? Who wants to paint lavender fields before they're in bloom? The two things could be pure coincidence, unrelated to anything. What could they have to do with a murder on a garbage heap? It's ridiculous. I don't even have enough to ask him to come in for questioning."

"Unlike Pascal Fuligni."

"An argument over a mooring place at the harbor. Sounds equally ridiculous at first, but if it's something that's been festering for years then it could have gotten out of control. Apart from anything else, Fuligni offered him five thousand euros for the spot. That means the object of their argument was of some value. He says he spent the whole of Sunday afternoon down at the harbor and only went home after dark. He claims two witnesses to that—his wife and his Romanian secretary. For the hours between their argument and when he got home he has no witnesses."

"Precisely the time when Moréas was probably killed."

"Possibly. We still don't have an exact time of death, and given the state of the incinerated corpse it's possible the pathologist won't be able to establish one. Sunday afternoon? Sunday evening? Certainly not before and certainly not after. That still leaves us with a big window, from about three P.M. to midnight."

"Fuligni has an alibi for half that window, but not the other half."

"Does that mean we should bring him in? After it looks like he's pulled strings reaching as far as Paris? Without anything more than what we have at present Nkoulou would pull us off the case immediately to save himself any more problems."

Blanc's phone rang. An irritated voice from the forensics team. Nothing out of the ordinary on Moréas's boat.

"So, what now?" Tonon asked.

"We're up to our necks in shit. We've got nothing."

"*Madame le juge* will be delighted."

"Go home," Tonon advised him after lunch. "The midday heat dulls the mind. You can't think properly anymore. Later this afternoon we can ask the colleagues in Marseille and Aix who've had to do with Moréas in the past. Maybe they'll have something for us."

Blanc didn't know what else to suggest. Here he was taking a midday break. His colleagues in Paris would have laughed themselves silly. But he was up a blind alley. He might as well sit down in the cool shadow of his ruin and do his thinking there. He did some shopping in the little supermarket just before it closed for lunch: tomatoes, melon, and eggplant. On the shelves he spotted several more bottles with the "Bernard" label so he bought a white and a rosé. This time the shop owner smiled as he packed up his purchases for him. In the newsagent's next door he bought a copy of *La Provence.* The murder had made the local paper's front page. Blanc skimmed the report, which was remarkably bland. Evidently the press were treating it as just another feud between drug dealers. Blanc folded the paper under his arm, hoping that he wouldn't have his investigations interrupted by any journalists. Then he picked up some baguettes from the bakery. The interior of his Espace smelled wonderful as he drove back to Sainte-Françoise-la-Vallée.

Three horses were crossing the *route départementale,* ridden by Paulette Aybalen and two teenagers. "My daughters, Agathe and Audrey," she said, jumping down from her horse when he stopped alongside them. The girls were in every way younger versions of their mother: slim, deeply tanned, with wild black hair tightly pulled back into a braid. Paulette threw the reins of her horse to the elder of the two. "Look after the animals. I'll be back shortly." Blanc nodded in acknowledgment to the girls. They smiled shyly and nodded back before clicking their tongues to set the horses into a trot.

As Paulette obviously wanted to have a chat with him, Blanc for better or worse opened the passenger door for her and drove her the last few yards home. Now that she was sitting just inches from him he realized again just how incredibly tanned she was. He wondered if she spent even as much as a few hours a day indoors. Maybe she even slept in the open? She smelled of grass, saddle leather, and horse hair.

"Have you started clearing out?" she asked. She must have seen the furniture he'd left outside the door, Blanc reckoned.

"The first step in a spectacular renovation."

She laughed. "You might need to call in a few experts for that."

"I've already got to know a builder. Monsieur Fuligni."

"Pascal? He's okay. He knows what he's doing. He's local."

"Like yourself?"

She glanced at him. "I was born in Sainte-Françoise-la-Vallée. There's nothing on earth that would ever make me move."

"Everything has a price."

"Not for me. Not for that. I even let my marriage go rather

than move. My husband found it too quiet here. He wanted to move to Marseille, and that's where he's been since. As far as I know."

Blanc didn't bother to tell her about the collapse of his own marriage. He just smiled and nodded toward his shopping on the rear seat. "Would thyme go with that?" he asked.

She glanced at him and shook her head at his lack of local knowledge. "You can just cut some thyme by the roadside whenever you want. It's best at midday because that's when there's the most oil in the leaves. Some people say you should pick your thyme only on May first: They harvest it then in huge bunches, bring it into the house, dry it, and keep it for the rest of the year. But one way or another the aroma is so intense that I only use it for meat sauces, or in a stew. But not with vegetables."

He braked as they came into Sainte-Françoise-la-Vallée, and she jumped out of the Espace outside her house. "That was almost as comfortable as on horseback," she called in farewell. "One of these days I'll teach you how to make lamb filet in garlic and thyme sauce."

Blanc turned off to his olive oil mill in a good mood. Don't get any ideas, he told himself. You don't know Paulette. And you're not even divorced yet. He took his shopping into the house, then lay down on the dry meadow in the shade of the plane trees. It was wonderfully cool, the scent of thyme in the air, a concert of cicadas in the background. He could feel himself dozing off. Then his phone rang. Tonon. "We've got a witness," the lieutenant told him. "Someone who saw one of our friends down at the garbage dump on the day of the murder."

Witnesses

Blanc leapt into the Espace and roared off. The *route départementale* was empty in the early-afternoon heat. It was only just
before he pulled into Gadet that he realized he had failed to lock
the house.

"Gaston Julien," Tonon informed him on the phone, "a
farmer from Lançon, nearly seventy years old. He read about
the incident in *La Provence* this morning and remembered
meeting somebody at the garbage dump."

"This morning? So why does he wait until lunchtime before
getting in touch with us?"

"He had to take his herd of goats out into the woods and
couldn't come in until his son turned up to take his place."

The captain sighed. "Where is he?"

"In the office next door. Nobody's using it at the moment and
the sun isn't as bad as in here."

Blanc would have guessed the man to be twenty years younger
than his age: Julien was a burly man with thick brown hair only
streaked with gray, in dusty jeans and a faded pullover. He

shook Blanc's right hand with a grip like a vise and hands as hard as iron.

"Monsieur Julien, I believe you were out at the garbage dump on Sunday. What time was that?"

"Just after lunch."

After the quarrel between Moréas and Fuligni down at the harbor, the captain thought. "You bumped into Charles Moréas there?"

"I saw him. He wasn't the sort of person you wanted to talk to."

"But you knew him?"

"I know everybody around here."

"What were you doing at the garbage dump?"

"The last mistral ripped the tar paper off my chicken coop. I loaded the pieces into the car and took them down to the dump. They were no use anymore."

"And what time would that have been?"

"Like I said, after lunch."

"So about two P.M.?"

Julien laughed. "Where do you come from? Later than that."

Blanc told himself not to lose his patience. "How much later?"

The old farmer took out his car key and, lost in thought, used it to scratch the inside of his left ear. "Three o'clock? Four o'clock? Let's say four."

"What was Moréas doing?"

"No idea. He was over by the skip, the one filled with trash. You would come across him often there, either putting something in or taking something out."

"Did you notice anything else?"

Julien had managed to extract a lump of dried wax from inside his ear and flicked it away with his finger. Blanc tried not to look. "I thought it was busy, for a Sunday," the farmer mumbled. "I mean, in summer you don't see people down at the dump much. But when I got back into the car, I had to do a U-turn because there was so much traffic. There was a little red car parked in the entrance gate, then there was Moréas's motorbike, and just as I was about to put my foot down that architect pulled up in front of me."

Blanc leaned back in his chair. "Which architect?"

"Monsieur Le Bruchec. He's normally nice enough. A local. But he seemed to be in a hurry. Hurtled past me in his four-by-four, without even saying hello. Had a trailer in tow, full of trash."

"Are you sure that it was Lucien Le Bruchec?"

"Am I sure that I'm Gaston Julien?"

"Did you see whether Monsieur Le Bruchec and Charles Moréas spoke to each other?"

"No. I put my foot down before some other *connard* arrived."

"*Merci beaucoup.*"

Tonon typed up Julien's statement and got the farmer to sign it before going back to his goats. "Strange that Monsieur Le Bruchec would appear to have forgotten to mention that," the lieutenant said.

"I think we need to jog his memory."

As they got into the patrol car, Tonon said, "By the way, I spoke on the phone with Miette Fuligni. We were at school together. She was hot stuff in those days. She was a couple of years below me, but never even gave me a glance." He got lost in his memories, then shook his head and added, "She told me her husband came home almost exactly at eight P.M. on Sunday. He interrupted her watching the headlines on the evening news."

"If what he told us is true, then he must have been in Saint-César until about a quarter to eight."

"But theoretically he would have had time to drive to the garbage dump, kill Moréas, and still get home on time. He has no alibi."

"Nor does our architect."

Tonon directed him to the town center of Salon, as they assumed Le Bruchec would be in his office. They didn't call first. Blanc wanted to take him by surprise. Yet again they found themselves on a big square shaded by plane trees, part of it covered by a roof of glass and green wrought iron, with cafés and three-story houses all around. "Place Morgan," the lieutenant said. "Used to be nice here. Great market and you could always find a parking place, except on market days."

Heavy building equipment had ripped up the tarmac, as if it was an orange that had been peeled, and even the sidewalks looked as if hand grenades had exploded on them. The façades of the houses shook with the noise of jackhammers and drills wielded by men in helmets and protective clothing. White dust irritated their eyes and throats and covered the Mégane, which Blanc left between a digger and a pile of gravel.

"They've been working on Place Morgan for three months. Everything is supposed to be better when they've finished. But one thing's sure: It won't be easy to find a parking space anymore. I'm not even sure we'll still have streetlights. These guys aren't exactly specialist electricians." Tonon nodded at a restaurant with its window broken and the plasterwork covered in soot. "When they began work, they sliced into the electric cables underground. The next day they reconnected them, but they connected the mains cable to the restaurant's electricity supply and set the freezer and oven on fire."

"I'm amazed Le Bruchec can work in all this chaos."

"Architects are used to building work and noise, and in any case his office is down a side street."

Tonon led him down a shady alleyway, and stopped outside a nineteenth-century building with a heavy wooden door almost ten feet high. On it was a brass plate that read: LE BRUCHEC, ARCHITECTE.

Two minutes later Blanc was staring at a double-barreled shotgun.

Le Bruchec had let them in himself, saying his secretary was on holiday. He led them into his studio where the weapon hung on the wall next to an enormous buffalo head.

"A trophy, from Africa," the architect said, slightly embarrassed by the look on the captain's face. "I was a keen hunter when I was young. Today I let off steam playing tennis and golf. I find it suits me better."

"Suits the animals better too, I imagine," Blanc muttered. "Monsieur Le Bruchec, why did you not tell us you had spoken to Charles Moréas just a few hours before his death?"

Le Bruchec took a deep breath and stared out of the window. "That was stupid of me," he admitted. "How did you find out? No, it doesn't matter." He sighed. "Although 'spoken to' is hardly the right expression. I said *salut* and Moréas didn't reply. That was fairly normal."

"But nonetheless you were down at the garbage dump where his incinerated body was found."

Le Bruchec held up his hands. "I didn't do it. I went there on Sunday to dump some trash left over from building the fence. I simply bumped into Moréas. It's not unusual to bump into people. I completely forgot about it afterwards."

"You claim somebody tried to break into your house on Saturday. You suspected it was Moréas. The same man you bumped into on the following day. Didn't you mention it? Accuse him? Did you not discuss it at all?"

"What, and have him beat me up at the garbage dump?" The architect shook his head. "You didn't know him, *mon Capitaine*. I was angry enough, but I didn't say anything."

"What time was it when you bumped into him?"

Le Bruchec thought for a moment. "About three or four P.M., I think."

"How long were you at the dump for?"

"It took me about ten minutes to empty the trailer. Fifteen at most."

"Were you alone? Maybe somebody who worked there helped you?"

"At weekends there are only a few people working down there, just to keep an eye on things. I unloaded the trailer on my own."

"And then?"

Le Bruchec shrugged. "Then I left. It's not the sort of place you hang about longer than necessary."

"Was Moréas still there when you left?"

The architect thought for a moment. "I didn't pay much

attention to him. He was messing around over by the Dumpster. But yes, I think he was."

Blanc remembered that the dead man's Yamaha bike had still been chained up. "Did your neighbor also have trash to dispose of?" He was wondering what Moréas might have been able to carry on a motorbike.

Le Bruchec rubbed his thumb and middle finger together. "He was scavenging. Moréas wasn't exactly the type to take his garbage down to a dump. He just left it outside his house or threw it away in the forest. I imagine he was rooting around in the Dumpster to see if there was anything of value. Old computers, phones, stuff like that. I had the impression he hung around there most of the day waiting for people like me to turn up and throw stuff away. Then he went through it to see if there was anything worth having. Like I said, a scavenger."

Blanc leaned toward Tonon and whispered, "Call the crime scene people. Have them go through the Dumpster."

The lieutenant nodded and left the studio.

"Why didn't you mention to us that you'd met Moréas?" Blanc asked when his colleague had left the room.

Le Bruchec rubbed his eyes with one hand. "When I made the complaint on Monday I didn't think it was important. What had it to do with the attempted break-in? In any case I had forgotten about it by then. Then when you told me Moréas had been killed I was shocked. I had accused him of a crime. I had bumped into him on the day he died. I thought if I admitted that you would arrest me as a suspect."

"Instead, the chance of you being arrested has dramatically increased," the captain said softly. "You have to admit that your behavior is suspicious."

"I didn't do it!" Le Bruchec insisted. "When I drove away from the damn garbage dump Moréas was still alive."

Blanc thought for a moment. Should he tell Madame Vialaron-Allègre that Le Bruchec should be arrested as a suspect? How would the *juge d'instruction* react? She was from the Midi, as was Le Bruchec. It was quite possible that they'd known one another forever. It was quite possible that she would see such a suggestion as overenthusiastic and ill considered. What proof did he have? No. He would be giving her a chance to accuse him of unprofessional behavior. An unforgivable error. Then, a quick chat with her husband and he would find himself transferred to Lorraine.

"You'll be hearing from us," he said in as friendly a tone as possible, and got to his feet.

He found his colleague outside in the shade. "So, what did you make of him?" Tonon asked, as they strolled back to the patrol car.

"Too good to be true. Le Bruchec has a motive: He felt threatened by Moréas, suspected him of attempted burglary. Le Bruchec knew Moréas visited the dump regularly—knew he searched through the Dumpster. He could have planned for them to bump into each other. He can shoot—there's proof enough hanging on his wall. He didn't tell us about the meeting. And, Le Bruchec ran into him in the window of time when we think the murder took place."

The lieutenant shook his head. "There's a catch. Our witness, Julien, said he saw Le Bruchec down there about three or four P.M., but he also said there were more people than normal around. Too many. I mean, somebody was shot dead and his body incinerated down there, but only spotted by one of the staff on Monday morning. It can't have happened in the early afternoon. Somebody would have reported it on Sunday."

"All we know from Julien is that he saw Le Bruchec down there about three or four P.M. God help us, can nobody around here remember an exact time? And we have no witnesses to say Le Bruchec left again after no more than fifteen minutes, as he claims."

"You think the architect waited until he and Moréas were there on their own, and then killed him?"

"It's a possibility we can't exclude."

"But you can't prove it."

"So what now?"

"I'm thirsty."

"I'll take you back to Gadet," Blanc promised him.

"But you won't have a glass of rosé with me?"

"The sun hasn't gone down yet."

Blanc carefully circumnavigated the diggers, their engines ticking in the heat. He thought about what Vialaron-Allègre had said to him about his lack of experience in the Midi. You don't know anybody. He felt like a European anthropologist stranded on an island in the South Pacific. All the locals invited him to join in their rituals, but he didn't understand any of them. "I need a fixer," he said aloud. "A spider in the web, someone who knows everything about everyone, including the stuff you won't find in the newspapers or official documents."

" 'Newspaper' might just be the key," Tonon said, clearly in a good mood. "Gérard Paulmier. Retired journalist who used to work at *La Provence*. Knows every family, every company, every restaurant, every politician, every farmer. Still writes a bit now and then for his old paper. But spends most of his time, allegedly, working on an oral history of the region."

"A journalist, happy to talk to the police?"

"A pensioner, with too much time on his hands. Mention anything you like to him and he'll tell you all you want to know."

"Where do I find him?"

"He has a little house in Caillouteaux."

"Want to come along?"

"I'll wait for your summarized version tomorrow."

Blanc parked the Mégane on the outskirts of Caillouteaux; the narrow alleyways were blocked with cars parked all over the place, all with the local "13" number plate. There was a lot of noise in the distance. Loudspeakers. A woman's voice. Applause. Even before he reached the church square he found himself looking at the backs of a couple hundred people. The open space was filled with people with tricolors flying above their heads, along with images of Marianne and slogans of the Front National. There was a smell of sweat and picnic food between the sunlit walls. On a podium in front of the house with the painted façade stood the blond woman he had seen smiling down from the poster opposite the town hall. The PR system had been so badly set up that her voice echoed in his ears and he could only make out a few words: "Euro . . . *austerité* . . . Marseille . . . France . . ." then last of all, "Kalashnikov." The people all around him could hardly have understood more than he did, but were listening with a sort of ill-tempered politeness. Every now and then some of them would wave their flags or shout slogans that were no more comprehensible than the words of the speaker on the podium. He felt as if he had been catapulted into some piece of theater, as an extra on the edge of a crowd scene where everyone else was simultaneously dull, conservative, and dangerous. The young workers and their girl-friends in short skirts from cheap shops, the dumpy middle-aged women, the pensioners in dark glasses with battered hats didn't exactly look as if they were going to light up flaming torches and storm the houses of their fellow citizens. But he could literally smell their anger, their sense of disappointment, and above all their fear—fear for their jobs, their savings, their children's schools, fear of the unfamiliar, the new, the threat-ening. Mayor Lafont was right. Fear was a vote-winner.

He made a detour around the town center, through empty alleyways. The sound of his cell phone startled him so much he nearly threw himself to the ground. It was one of the crime scene forensic squad: They had got back to the dump too late and the Dumpster full of old metal had been emptied. Next time, if he wanted something like that, he would do better to advise them a bit earlier.

Blanc managed to suppress a sharp reply, and just said thanks. Before long he found himself standing outside the ad-dress Tonon had given him: an old, narrow, two-story house hemmed in between two much larger buildings, like a small boy squeezed between his two bigger brothers. Blanc couldn't see a bell so he lifted the heavy bronze door knocker and let it bang with a dull thud.

A small, thin man in his midsixties with gray hair, gray eyes, and an amiable face opened the door. The captain introduced himself and explained what he was doing there: "My colleague, Lieutenant Tonon, suggested I talk to you."

"Marius still in the cops, then, is he? Managed to hold down

his job all these years, despite the old scandal? How long ago
was that? Ten years?"

The captain had no idea what the man was talking about
and mumbled something vague. Paulmier led him into a living room with plush upholstered armchairs, an overstuffed
bookcase, and a glass table. There were framed photographs
everywhere: men, women, and children all smiling out at
him, many of them from a beach, others in the mountains. In
one corner an old computer stood on a little cabinet, hum-
ming away. No sign of a television.

"You were a journalist for many years," Blanc began, slump-
ing into one of the soft armchairs and immediately wondering
if he would ever get out of it.

"I still knock out a piece most days for my old colleagues,
as a freelancer," Paulmier said.

"Then you'll know the sort of people I'm interested in,
people like Charles Moréas."

The old guy laughed. "Nobody knew Moréas. Sure, everybody on the desk had heard the name at one time or other. There
was that old story about the highway robberies and the tourist
who got killed. He got arrested, but the case was never tried.
That got the cops upset. But since then? He wasn't exactly a
headline-grabber."

"But he was a criminal?"

"Maybe, but a small fish. Thievery, if and when he got the
chance. Dealing in stolen goods, stuff like that. A veritable saint
compared with the guys from Marseille."

"Maybe he'd got involved with them."

"The dealers down there wouldn't waste five seconds of
their time on somebody like Moréas. He got more and more

weird over the years. Used to drive his enduro bike through the woods, swearing at anybody who got in his way. Lived in that *cabane* of his like a *clochard*. Apparently he'd been offered money a few times, or so I've heard, to buy that piece of land. He'd inherited it from his parents, but never sold off a single square yard, even though land down here in the Midi is worth a fortune. He could have made himself rich, without doing a stroke of work. But Moréas wasn't interested. I think he had a screw loose in the head."

"It can't have been easy being his neighbor."

"Le Bruchec? I find his architectural style too modern, but apart from that he's okay. Pillar of the establishment. Does his bit for charity. On lots of committees."

"Does well in business?"

"Very well. Ever since land down here got so expensive, only the really rich can have new houses built. Parisians, Russians, Brits. And anybody who is rich enough doesn't bother to count the cents. Nice business for an architect."

"Were Le Bruchec and Moréas enemies?"

"Le Bruchec has no enemies. Moréas had no friends."

"Do you know if Le Bruchec ever said he felt threatened by his neighbor?"

The old journalist shook his head. "No. He drinks rosé at the Gadet town festival, plays tennis with his friends, fishes in the Touloubre. Not exactly the sort of stuff you do if you're in fear for your life, is it?"

Blanc leaned back cautiously in his chair, not sure if the back would really support him. "What about Monsieur Fuligni? Did he feel threatened? He and Moréas had an argument about a mooring at the harbor in Saint-César."

"Oh, stuff and nonsense. Pascal has too much on his plate. If somebody annoys him he swears at them, and then five minutes later he's forgotten it. He built half of Caillouteaux. Him and his pal, Lafont."

"The mayor?"

"Those two have known each other for decades. In the seventies and eighties Caillouteaux was well on the way to becoming a ghost town. The fashion back then was all for steel-and-glass high-rises. Nobody wanted to live in a medieval house up in the hills. Lafont and Fuligni between them renovated lots of houses around here, or persuaded their owners to. Now you won't find an empty building here. The town's been gentrified."

"I noticed the house on the square, with the painted façade. And the naked bronze beauty."

Paulmier shook his head, and gave an embarrassed smile. "Sometimes Lafont overdoes it. But better a little too much than much too little, don't you think?"

"It must have cost a lot of money, even now—Lafont has this dream of a *médiathèque*."

"And it'll happen. The plans have been sitting in the town hall for ages. They're due to lay the foundation stone soon. Just in time for the election." He nodded toward the window: "But it'll be interesting to see how he does against the blondie from the Front."

"But where does all the money come from?" the captain pressed him.

"Midi Provence. That's the name of an organization that groups together the *communes* around the Étang de Berre. They coordinate projects that one little community couldn't manage on its own: roads, schools, buses, environmental protection, things like that. They get money from Paris and from taxes on local businesses. An annual budget of some eight million euros. That would have been five billion francs in old money," Paulmier added, as if only the old currency made any sense.

"Used for bribes?"

"No need. Midi Provence includes Berre and Fos, and they have factories, the oil tanker harbor, and the refinery. They get so much tax money from the local industries that they don't know what to do with it. Some of it goes to *communes* like Caill-outeaux. A pretty little place a long way from the horrid industry—it's a perfect model."

"Lafont is using money from an oil refinery to prettify his little town?" Blanc reckoned there had to be endless ways in which that money could be diverted elsewhere.

Paulmier saw what was on his mind and grinned. "Nobody has ever complained. There's more than enough to go round."

The captain thought back to the Front National march. "Maybe not quite enough," he muttered. But what could any of this have to do with the murder of a loner like Moréas? "Did Fuligni and Moréas argue often?"

"You mean about the mooring down at the harbor. It's something of a local legend. Half Saint-César laughed about it behind Fuligni's back. He should have known that someone like Moréas was never going to give in. But Pascal is a thickhead and stubborn as an ox. He thought his smile could win over anyone, even a *clochard* from the woods. When it failed he got furious. More out of frustrated vanity than because he really worried about the issue. Sooner or later he'll get a bigger spot for his yacht anyway, without arguing about it with Moréas."

"Did he get really furious?"

"No. Pascal shouts and curses like the builder he is. But five minutes later he'll sit down over a glass of rosé with you, and talk about the last Olympique de Marseille soccer game. After all, he doesn't have much to complain about, really." Paulmier used both hands to suggest the silhouette of an attractive woman.

"Nastasia Constantinescu?"

"There's a lot of men around here who would like to have a Romanian secretary like that, even if they don't have their own office."

"Madame Fuligni doesn't mind?"

"Oh, Miette doesn't spend too much time on her own," the journalist added, without going into details.

"Merci," Blanc said, and managed to pull himself up out of his armchair. Paulmier, who had leaped to his feet agilely, accompanied him to the door. "Funny that you should be asking so much about Moréas, though," he said as if in passing. "Just a few days ago, somebody turned up at the offices of *La Provence* and began asking my former colleagues in editorial what they knew about Moréas."

"Who?" Blanc asked, stopping dead in the doorway. He could hear the loudspeakers outside echoing ever louder in the alleyways. This time it was a man's voice, louder and more aggressive.

"His other neighbor. That German painter."

"Monsieur Rheinbach?" Blanc felt the hair on the back of his head stand on end. The German had been in the town archives, and had been in the offices of the local newspaper. Days before the murder. "What in particular did he want to know from your old colleagues?"

Paulmier shrugged his shoulders. "They didn't tell me. They sent him off with a few polite excuses—we're not an information office. I doubt he would have gotten anything about Moréas from them."

An Inquisitive Painter

Blanc got back to his old mill in late afternoon. Nobody had broken in. He fetched a chair out of the house, sat down on it in the shadow of the plane tree, and opened one of the bottles of Bernard's rosé. He approached the glass carefully, the childhood memory still haunting him. He was tempted to knock it back like medicine, get it down and over with. But he repressed the instinct and took just a tiny sip. It was cool. Refreshing. Just a little sour. He leaned back, relieved that at least he hadn't reexperienced the shock of his first taste. It was a good thirst-quencher. I must be careful, though, he told himself. Otherwise I could end up like Marius. He took another sip.

Rheinbach and Moréas. Why would the German painter have been asking questions about his neighbor? Had he heard the old stories about his car-hijacking days? Maybe something similar had happened to him. Or could there be something else behind it? Maybe a bit of blackmail between neighbors? It didn't look like the painter was making a fortune on jigsaw puzzles. Maybe he was hard up enough to think he could make some money out of Moréas by blackmailing him with details about his past? On the other hand, if the painter really was a black-mailer, it didn't make much sense for him to kill off his victim.

"I'll pay Monsieur Rheinbach a visit tomorrow," he told the wine bottle, and then put the cork back in, for fear of losing himself in one-sided conversations.

The next morning he picked up Tonon from the gendarmerie station, telling his colleague on the way to the painter's house what he had found about the research the German had been involved in. He no longer needed Tonon to navigate for him: He had memorized the route.

"You're starting to drive like a local," Tonon remarked.

Blanc remembered the story about his colleague's accident and slowed down, to the extent that a farmer in an ancient R4 behind them began honking. The two gendarmes ignored him, until eventually they turned into the painter's driveway.

"Are you sure he's at home?" the lieutenant asked. "He was off to paint the lavender fields."

"Maybe he's realized by now that they're not in bloom yet." Blanc pointed with his right hand at the Clio parked by the door.

And indeed the painter himself opened the door. "Glad to see you got back from Luberon so soon," the captain said by way of a greeting.

"I only knocked out a couple of watercolors," the German replied, giving them a querying look. "The main part of the job has still to be done."

"I see," Blanc replied, in a tone of voice that suggested he didn't believe a word of it. "Can you spare us five minutes, Monsieur Rheinbach?"

The painter led his guests, for better or worse, into his studio. Blanc noticed a half-finished bottle of rosé on the table. It was a bit early in the day for that sort of refreshment. They sat down on three hard chairs. "Monsieur Rheinbach. Why did you not tell us last time that a few days before the crime you had been at the editorial offices of *La Provence*, asking questions about your neighbor?"

The artist's face went red. "Does that make me a suspect?"

"I'm just curious."

Rheinbach began playing nervously with a tube of green oil paint, then noticed what he was doing and quickly put the tube back on a side table. "I was afraid," he said eventually, sounding ashamed of himself. "Afraid of this guy. I had only come across him a few times, happily. But a couple of times when I had been out in the woods painting flowers he had come up to me and acted threatening."

"How do you mean? Did he have a weapon? Did he insult or mock you? Something must have made you feel afraid."

"I can't quite explain it, *mon Capitaine*, I mean he didn't exactly produce a weapon or hit me or anything. When I saw him out in the woods with his hunting rifle, he ignored me. And all in all, he hardly ever said a word to me. It was really just the way he looked at me. He just stared at me, like a wolf. A predator eyeing its prey."

"Why didn't you go to the gendarmerie?"

"To complain about the way he looked at me? They'd have thought I was mad."

"So instead you went to the newspaper journalists."

"I didn't tell them anything either. I just wanted to find out who this Moréas guy really was. I wanted to know if I was living

next door to a human time bomb, or just some harmless nut-
case. That's not too unreasonable, is it?"

"So what did you find out?"

The painter let his hands fall on his lap. "Nothing. I had
Googled him, but there are hundreds of men with the same
name in France—but as far as I could tell, not one of them
was the guy next door. There is simply no trace online of a
Charles Moréas in Caillouteaux. I found that just as disconcerting. But as I couldn't think what else to do, I went down to
the newspaper offices, but the journalists wouldn't tell me anything. I had the impression they were afraid too."

Blanc leaned back and closed his eyes. The story was so
pathetic it might well be true. In which case Rheinbach's re-
searches might have been nothing more than the reaction of a
frightened man trying to protect himself. A man so afraid that
he would shoot dead the supposed "human bomb" without
warning down by the garbage dump? He would have liked to
take a look around in this house undisturbed. Maybe later.

The captain got to his feet and nodded in farewell. Just
when he reached the door, he turned back around and said:
"What were you doing in the Caillouteaux town archives on
Wednesday, June twenty-sixth?"

Tonon stared at him, surprised by the revelation. And Rheinbach, whose face had more or less regained his normal color,
went red again. "The old church," he eventually managed to
stammer. He didn't even ask why Blanc had known he had been
at the archives. "Saint-Vincent, twelfth century. I wanted to
paint it. But for that I needed to send my employers a few lines
of text that they could put on the jigsaw puzzle box. So I was
doing some research in the archive. It's part of my job."

Tonon said nothing until they were back in the car. "How did you find that out?" he asked, as soon as he had pulled shut the passenger door.

The captain tapped the tip of his nose and said, "Instinct," with a wry smile.

"Don't bullshit me."

Blanc laughed and turned the ignition key. Then he told him how he discovered the fact by accident. "Strange though, that Rheinbach needed to spend six and a half hours in the archive just for a few lines of text about an old decrepit church."

Even before they had turned off the path through the woods onto the *route départementale*, Blanc reached for the radio, called the gendarmerie, and asked for an appointment with the *juge d'instruction*. "She's working at home today, in her house in Caillouteaux," a bored voice said through the static. Corporal Baressi.

"Give me the address," the captain demanded impatiently. Why was everything down here so hard?

"Number 5, rue du Passe-Temps."

"You can't get there in the car," Tonon told him. "We can park on the square by the church and you can walk from there."

"Okay, we can walk."

"I'm staying in the car. I don't fancy a cup of coffee with *Madame le juge*."

Blanc stepped on the gas without bothering to answer. His colleague was afraid of the woman. This could become problematic. He drove up the hill to Caillouteaux and parked in the shade of the bell tower. Of Saint-Vincent church. It would make a good design for a jigsaw puzzle. If Rheinbach ever got around to painting it. Tonon took off his seat belt and made himself

comfortable in the passenger seat, pointing to a perfectly polished metallic blue Citroën C5. "Monsieur and Madame Vialaron-
Allègre's car."

"An office car?"

"Paid for by your taxes."

Rue du Passe-Temps was actually a sidewalk of polished
stone slabs, leading southwest from the square: stone-built
houses on one side, on the other a wall behind which the hill
fell sharply away toward the Étang de Berre. Blanc felt as if he
were walking along the top of an old medieval castle wall. Number 5 was an old two-story town house of brushed-clean natural
stone with dark green wooden shutters on the windows and
door. There was a modern bell in a niche next to the door with
a discreet security camera just above it. The captain shrugged
and pressed the bell.

The *juge d'instruction* herself opened the door. She was
wearing pale Pierre Cardin jeans and an ochre blouse, and a
trail of pale blue smoke rose from the cigarette between the slim
fingers of her left hand. On this occasion there was a heavy steel
diver's watch on her wrist, a model for a man that on her slim
forearm looked as brutal as a handcuff. Blanc forced himself
not to stare at it. She led him down a bright hallway, with Japa-
nese woodcuts on the walls, into an office that opened onto an
inner courtyard and a little pool with sparkling blue water.
Somewhere in the distance he could hear piano music. Chopin,
or maybe Liszt?

Aveline Vialaron-Allègre offered him a seat in an English
club armchair with aromatic leather. Her Empire-style desk of
dark wood was piled high with papers and folders.

"Have you got any further, *mon Capitaine*?"

"I've uncovered a few things that irritate me," he began. "They might be clues. Or they might be meaningless." Blanc paused. He was always careful with initial clues. Don't try to tie yourself down to one version of events, motives, or even suspects. Stay open-minded. Don't stop looking and listening too soon. It was an approach that in Paris had driven his colleagues, bosses, and even *juges d'instruction* to theatrical sighs and rolling of the eyes. The woman opposite him, however, remained calm, giving him her full attention. Against his will he had to admit that his opinion of *Madame le juge* had gone up a notch. So he told her about the building contractor, Fuligni, and his row with Moréas down at the harbor. About the architect, Le Bruchec, who had felt threatened, who was good with weapons, and who had been seen at the garbage dump with the murder victim. And about Monsieur Rheinbach and his unusual research into the life of his neighbor.

"Each one of these three men had a motive," Blanc concluded. "But none of their motives is wholly convincing. A row over a mooring place? A suspected break-in and theft of sporting equipment? The vague threat of a 'wolflike' stare? Of course people have been murdered in such circumstances. But a cold-blooded execution with an automatic weapon and subsequent immolation of the body? I just don't think any of these men are capable of that."

Aveline Vialaron-Allègre looked at him pensively. "So, a settling of scores between drug dealers?"

"Possible, but unlikely. The forensics people were in Moréas's house and on every piece of land he owned, searched his motorbike and his old boat. Our colleagues in Marseille asked around in the drug world. Nothing. Nobody mentioned Charles Moréas and nobody seemed interested in his murder."

"So, what do you intend to do now?"

Blanc was listening for traces of irony in the question, but it seemed to be perfectly serious. "I need a warrant to search Rheinbach's house."

The *juge d'instruction* leaned back and took a deep draw on her cigarette. "To look for a Kalashnikov under a jigsaw puzzle painter's bed?" Now the irony was obvious.

The captain breathed in and out. "There's something not quite right about this artist. Who runs down to the local newspaper editorial office to ask questions about their neighbor?"

"Not in itself, however, sufficient cause to make him a suspect. The man gave you an explanation. You might not believe him. *Eh bien*, that is your problem. But you can't ransack his house based on that alone."

"I'm not intending to ransack it. I just want to . . ." Blanc hesitated. To find a Kalashnikov? Absurd. Something else, something suspicious? But what? "Forget it," he said in the end, giving up.

"From everything you've told me, the clues point more toward Le Bruchec," the *juge d'instruction* replied. "After all, he was the last person seen with the victim. But I have known Lucien for half a lifetime and I was a good friend of his wife's." She shook her head. For a second her mask of cool elegance slipped and Blanc thought he could see sadness in her face. "Just to think of a man like Lucien running around with a Kalashnikov is grotesque, let alone the idea of him executing someone in cold blood. I am impressed by the thoroughness of your investigations, *mon Capitaine*, but I can't see that you've presented me with a suspect. Keep looking!"

She led him back down the hallway, opened the door, and they were looking out onto a broad panorama that stretched to the distant horizon. It was as if from the protective stone shelter of her house there was a direct view of heaven.

Blanc was impressed. "The gateway to the world."

For the first time Aveline Vialaron-Allègre smiled, if only for a fraction of a second. "Provence is a beautiful part of the country. And hard, even if it takes a little longer to realize that. And the people here are like that land they live on." This time she did shake his hand.

"You don't need to say a word," Tonon grunted sleepily when Blanc got back to the car. "Winners have a different look on their faces."

"At least *Madame le juge* heard me out," the captain said in his own defense.

"Now what?"

"We start all over again from the beginning."

"Well, that's something. She could have just brushed you off."

"Did you know that the *juge d'instruction* is friends with one of our suspects?"

"With Le Bruchec, the architect. Of course. And was even better friends with his late wife. That was one of the reasons I preferred to stay in the car rather than go see her."

Back at the station, Nkoulou called Blanc in: "Have you got

any further?" Clearly he wanted to know everything that *Madame le juge* knew. The captain suppressed his impatience and repeated what he had just told Aveline Vialaron-Allègre.

"What now?"

"I keep looking."

"I wish *Madame le juge* had granted the search warrant. We might have been able to arrest the painter."

Blanc suddenly realized what his boss was thinking: a rather reclusive artist, a foreigner, nobody would have complained if Rheinbach ended up in jail. A man with no Midi family going back generations. Case closed. Reputation improved. He realized that the *juge d'instruction* had actually been more prudent than he himself. She had foreseen how badly things might go for the painter. Parisian ruthlessness didn't quite work down here. *Merde*, the woman must have taken him for a tactless idiot.

"We'll catch the killer," he promised. "Monsieur Rheinbach isn't the only one in our sights."

"It's not very clever to have a target in your sights and not pull the trigger," Nkoulou responded.

And this man is the best shot in the gendarmerie. *Merde*, thought Blanc.

When he got back to his office he found Fabienne waiting in the hallway outside. She took him over to her computer screen. "After I found out that Fuligni had had a row with Moréas, I looked into the building contractor a bit," she began, bringing up an official-looking PDF on her screen. "This is the building contract for the *médiathèque*," she said. "Contracting client: the *commune* of Caillouteaux, with money from 'Midi

Provence'; General construction to be carried out by Pascal Fuligni. Estimated construction costs: eight million euros."

Blanc whistled through his teeth. "A big fat contract," he mumbled.

"The biggest Fuligni has ever landed."

"Are there other local building contractors who could have undertaken a job this size?"

"No, in a hamlet like Caillouteaux, Fuligni is the only one who could do something on this scale."

"In other words, if we were to take Fuligni in for questioning in a murder case, or, worse still, arrest him, then Mayor Lafont would have nobody else to bring his precious *médiathèque* into the world before the elections."

"The mayor will do whatever he has to to keep us away from his old friend."

"Merde."

"Wrong word," Fabienne said, with an ironic grin, "that's where down here we say *putain*."

" 'Whore' instead of 'shit'?"

"We have different priorities than Paris."

Blanc got up and stared out of the window. "Madame Vialaron-Allègre made it quite clear to me half an hour ago that she would protect Le Bruchec. Lafont will protect Fuligni. Poor old Rheinbach, he's got nobody looking out for him."

"Yet one more reason to arrest him?"

"One less reason."

All of a sudden Fabienne got to her feet and planted a kiss on his cheek. "We're going to make a good team," she declared. "The three upright sheriffs of Gadet."

"Two upright sheriffs, and one not always quite so upright deputy," Blanc said, casting a wry glance outside, where from Fabienne's office window they could see Tonon heading along the main street and into one of the bars.

"Marius has had problems ever since the car accident last year," she said.

The captain took his leave and went to his own office. Car accident last year? The journalist Paulmier had referred to an "old scandal," but said it was ten years ago. I'd like to know how many skeletons Tonon has in his closet, Blanc thought. Or then again, maybe I wouldn't.

Back in his house that evening, Blanc looked around the place. He had done the first bit, throwing out the junk. But the major work still lay ahead. First of all, the roof. Then the walls and the rewiring. A new kitchen. An Internet connection would be good. He wondered about the heating. It was enough to make his head spin. I could spend the rest of my life here, he thought, and this old olive oil mill would still not be finished. How do those people do it, whose perfectly groomed Midi houses get into the *Show Home* magazines Geneviève loves so much? They were mostly Parisians or English who spent no more than a few weeks a year in Provence. He decided to go out and take a walk, along the two roads that made up Sainte-Françoise-la-Vallée, and then maybe into the woods a bit. It would do him good. And maybe on the way he would stumble on a few new ideas that would help him get somewhere with the case. It had never worked in Paris, but then he never had the time for anything of the sort.

He went over the bridge, past Douchy's farmhouse, then

turned left and followed the road that went over the crest of the hill, with a dozen little houses on either side. In one garage between two buildings was Riou's Alpine. Somewhere a dog barked. The last house. The road meandered in soft curves between the fields; on one side the irrigation ditch of a wheat field murmured. Eventually Blanc came to a gate where the asphalt road came to an end. Beyond lay a sparse forest with trees some twenty to thirty feet high—pines, oaks, and shrubbery. A few outcrops of stone protruded from the sandy ochre soil like the tops of buried ruins. He went through the gate and along the forest trail. Cicadas. Heat. The scent of pine embraced him like a silk handkerchief. Ancient walls of yellowish stone flanked the hill. Hundreds of tiny white snails the size of a pinhead at the tips of the scrub, a spotted brown snake as long as a man's arm, which fled under a thornbush as he approached. A round heap of stones that looked like the remains of some collapsed building. Red and blue plastic cartridge cases lying on the ground, left by some hunter. What had he been hunting? Blanc could see neither birds nor rabbits. He felt the only creature of any size in this silent forest.

The path led ever upward, deeper into the silvery green leaves and needles and knotty stems. Eventually Blanc reached a little hill from where he could make out his olive oil mill on the other bank of the river. It looked like a little picturesque ruin. On the ground beneath him he found a little round spot of asphalt on which someone had painted "328" in white oil paint. Surprised, he began to look more carefully around him and found a little circular plaque about the size of a man's head— perhaps marking a buried water tank? He had seen television news reports about forest fires in Provence and knew that water tanks had been installed all over the place. He thought back to the firemen he had seen waiting in the shade on the edge of the road to Gadet. In an emergency they would need water supplies to fight the flames.

Beyond the hill the sandy path took him between rocks and shrubbery until it suddenly opened out on the right-hand side to reveal a valley with long rows of vines, glowing golden in the evening sun. It was a depression between two hills, about a hundred yards by a hundred yards, an enchanted valley hidden from the world by pine trees and oaks. He heard a harsh cry in the distance and made out a peacock fanning out its tail feathers. Another of the birds stalked amid the vines, dragging its train of feathers behind it, while yet a third sat on a stone wall beyond the vines like a king on a throne. At the other end of the valley, Blanc could just make out some figures in the setting sun. He squinted and saw one of them coming toward him: Sylvie Micheletti.

"You've discovered Domaine de Bernard," she called out, waving to him. A frayed straw hat covered her narrow face and long neck, her jeans had red patches from the earth, and in her hands she carried filigree pruning shears.

"I didn't expect to come across a vineyard in the middle of the forest," he admitted.

"An oasis in the desert," she laughed. "The soil is good, the sun shines all day long in the valley, while the stones and trees protect the vines from the mistral."

"And the peacocks?"

"Flowers with feathers. You just have to get used to their call."

They chatted for a few minutes. Blanc noted that she was

suntanned and happy, but beneath her mood and skin tone there was something else. Maybe sorrow, or extreme exhaustion. All the long way back his thoughts were not on his murder case, but on his neighbor in her hidden valley.

The following morning it wasn't Douchy's rooster that woke him, but the clattering of his shutters. Someone trying to break in, he thought to himself, jumping out of bed, grabbing his gun and rushing to the door. But all he found outside was an icy wind, gusting around the house, the rustling leaves on the plane trees sounding like a waterfall. The cicadas were silent. Despite it being early morning, the sky above was white. In the pure light he could make out every stone in the walls and every movement on the swirling surface of the Touloubre as clearly as if he had been on drugs.

Blanc retreated into the house. The shock of his sudden awakening and the cold had driven every iota of tiredness from his body. He pulled on a tracksuit and found his old running shoes. He intended to take the same hike he had the evening before, only this time as a jog before breakfast.

A few minutes later he was already in the forest. The wind didn't relent even for a second, ripping pine needles and leaves from the treetops and chasing them down the sandy track. The scent in the air had vanished. The sun was already shining but every drop of sweat was blown away by the wind. The rustling of the leaves was so loud that he didn't hear the horse galloping toward him through the undergrowth.

"Did the wind wake you?" asked Paulette Aybalen, from the saddle above him.

Blanc flinched in shock when he noticed her next to him,

the horse having slowed to a trot. "Is this the famed mistral?" he asked.

"The infamous mistral, we'll have it all day long—if we're lucky. Or else it could last three days. Or six, or nine. Whichever it is, it will be a multiple of three, unless it dies down after just twenty-four hours."

"Is that a fact or a superstition?"

"An old wives' tale, but it's worth heeding. I should warn you it can be dangerous to be out in the woods during the mistral. In fact it is forbidden during July and August. You're not exactly setting a good example."

"Is the wind likely to bring trees crashing down on my head?"

"No, but if a fire should break out anywhere it will race through the dry wood like a ravenous monster. The flames will be faster than you, and I don't want you to end up like the guy they found on the garbage heap."

Blanc was so surprised he nearly stumbled.

"What do you know about my investigation?"

"I read *La Provence.* Most of what they cover is Olympique de Marseille games and the most gruesome local crime stories. I believe you even interviewed Pascal about the murder."

"I didn't 'interview' Monsieur Fuligni, I only asked him a few questions. Anyway how do you know that? It wasn't in the paper."

"You sought him out in front of half the harbor at Saint-César. Something like that doesn't have to be in a newspaper for people to get wind of it. And the old boy has troubles enough."

"You mean his mooring?"

"I mean his wife."

Blanc thought of the Romanian secretary in her skimpy clothes and nodded. "Is she making his life hell?"

"She's putting cuckold's horns on his head. And with the man for whom Pascal has built loads of houses: Lucien Le Bruchec."

Blanc came to a stop, and not just because he was out of shape and the track led steeply uphill. "Those two are an item? Who else knows about it?"

Paulette laughed. "Everyone who knows them. It's been going on for quite a while. Lucien was lonely after his wife died. Miette was lonely because . . . well, you've seen Pascal's secretary, I assume. Nobody's ever too old for a little affair." She glanced at him with just a trace of a challenge in her eyes.

Blanc's mind was racing: Had Moréas found out about the affair and mocked Fuligni for it until he decided to get revenge? Or had Moréas threatened to make Bruchec's secret public, and had to be silenced? On the other hand, if Paulette Aybalen already knew and told him so openly about it, then surely everyone really did know about it? Even Fuligni himself, who in addition had hooked up with a young Romanian. Just a little meaningless affair, not something to shed blood over? "Thanks for the information," he said, still coughing from the effort of the jog.

"Just don't tell anyone you heard it from me."

"You would be under witness protection."

"That makes me feel better already. I'm going to let my wild horse here gallop on a bit," Paulette called back. "The mistral makes the animals nervous." She spurred on the animal, waving good-bye as she rode off. Blanc finished his route, more confused than ever, and for more than one reason.

Later Blanc found himself crawling through Gadet in his car. He was wearing a light jacket over a white T-shirt because the gusting wind had made it noticeably cool. The mistral caused a flurry of leaves and little white disposable plastic bags to dance along the sidewalks. The cars along the main street were parked at such oblique angles it looked like an earthquake had shaken them; men and women crossed the street with shopping baskets and trolleys without taking any notice of cars or motorbikes. He spotted Tonon and wound down the window.

"What are you doing out and about so early?"

"Friday is market day in Gadet." The fat lieutenant held up an empty wicker basket. "Park your car at the gendarmerie and come back here. We're going shopping."

"Won't the food have spoiled by evening?"

"We have a fridge in our office, in case you hadn't noticed. I haven't lived here just since yesterday."

Blanc sighed, but he thought it was best to go along with his colleague. He wasn't going to do any work over the next hour or two anyway. So ten minutes later he and Tonon were strolling through the packed little square behind the restaurant. The blue-and-white sun canopy of a fish stall billowed in the wind. Mountains of vegetables. Jars of honey. He was impressed and even a little intimidated by the gourmet produce and the energetic housewives and laughing pensioners pushing past, heading for specific stalls where they were kissed on both cheeks. He wondered if Tonon had been whispering in the ear of Paulette Aybalen.

"This is not how you do it," his colleague, who had already filled his basket, said. He got a plastic bag from one of the stalls and said, "Now I'm shopping for you."

Marius held a cheese wrapped in dried green leaves under Blanc's nose. "Banon," he explained, "ripened in oak leaves." Then came black olives, tomatoes, a melon from Carpentras, a bag of cherries. Blanc was expecting the plastic bag to burst at any moment. "Right, now we get ourselves a couple of baguettes and then it's home to Daddy Nkoulou."

Blanc didn't want to imagine what would happen when their boss found them in the gendarmerie station laden down with all the shopping. Or the look on his face if he heard himself referred to as "Daddy." But he said nothing, just hurried into the office and piled all the stuff into a little camping fridge purring away under Tonon's desk.

Just at that very moment the door was thrown wide open and Corporal Baressi forced his massive form into the room. "I thought this might interest you," he said, tapping on a piece of paper in his left hand. "This is just in from Saint-César. Pascal Fuligni is dead."

A Fatal Boating Accident

Blanc turned on the blue flashing lights and pulled out of the parking place with screeching tires. "Are you trying to catch up with Fuligni in the next world?" Tonon cursed at him as he tried in vain to put on his safety belt in the swerving Renault. "No matter how fast you go, you're not going to bring him back! And in any case the report said it was an accident. A fisherman saw Fuligni's yacht drifting across the Étang de Berre with no one at the helm, and in the water next to it the drowned owner was floating with a huge bump on the back of his head."

"How do you end up with a bump on your head on a sailing boat? Somebody must have hit him on the skull."

"There was no one on the *Amzeri* when the fisherman got there. Not a soul. No other boat anywhere near. Nobody swimming nearby," Tonon said.

Blanc raced through Gadet and turned onto the *route départementale* 16. He passed a few cars and a single truck, which on a Friday around here was the height of business traffic. "Do you sail, Marius?" he asked between clamped lips, not taking his eyes off the narrow road.

Tonon shrugged his shoulders. "Now and again a friend takes me out to the Calanques. But that's in a motorboat. I've never really worked out how all that stuff with sails, rudders, and the wind works. How about you?"

Up north everybody went out to sea, the stormier and colder, the better. Blanc, who hated his origins, had for that reason alone never set foot on a sailing ship. He shook his head.

Tonon scratched his chin in amazement. "Still, now that I think about it, it occurs to me that sailors normally stay in port during the mistral. The wind is far too strong and far too cold."

"Maybe Fuligni was on a little trip and left yesterday?" The captain reflected on how mild the weather had been on his walk to the Bernard vineyard. "Then this morning the mistral caught him by surprise."

The road headed downhill toward Saint-César. They had a view over the houses to the Étang de Berre. Small steep waves rushed across its surface, sending up spray from the crests; it was as if the lake was coming to a boil. In the yacht harbor the gusting wind was rocking the vessels from side to side in their moorings, creating a cacophony of plastic and steel sterns knocking against the wooden piers. Blanc screeched to a halt at the parking lot, immediately recognizing Fuligni's silver Mercedes coupe. Then he flinched. Not far away stood a white Audi Q7. Lafont? The mayor of Caillouteaux was nowhere to be seen. At this early hour there wasn't much going on down at the harbor, except for the policemen and forensic experts in their white protective garb, two photographers who the captain assumed to be photojournalists. Two police corporals held up a tarpaulin screen, but it was fluttering so violently in the wind that it didn't conceal anything. Behind it, a woman was kneeling down on the wood, bent over something that looked like a bundle of wet towels. Dr. Fontaine Thezan had pushed her big sunglasses back onto her hair and was examining the body with an apparatus of some sort that Blanc couldn't make out. He hurried down the pier, waved through by the corporals—and found himself standing next to the corpse of the building contractor.

Fuligni was wearing a T-shirt and light summer trousers, both dark and heavy from the water. He was barefoot, and had brownish seaweed wrapped around his lower arm. His eyes were closed, his mouth unnaturally wide open. Blanc watched as Dr. Thezan carefully examined the body. The air smelt of marijuana and brackish water, but something else too: decomposition. He took a step back.

"A fisherman reported it to us at nine thirty-one A.M.," one of the corporals who had taken out a notebook and was reading from it told him. "He was still out on the Étang de Berre, called in from his cell phone. He had already pulled Fuligni on board his boat. Then he came here as fast as he could, and we just unloaded the body onto the pier."

"Any witnesses see what time Fuligni set out on his yacht? Whether he was alone or not?"

The corporal shook his head. "We asked the harbormaster and the few other people who were already on their boats. Nobody saw anything. The harbormaster was on duty from around eight A.M., and would have noticed Fuligni if he had left Saint-César after that time. So it must have been earlier."

Blanc glanced at Tonon and nodded in the direction of the corpse. "T-shirt, summer pants, no jacket, no shoes. Very underdressed for somebody intending to go sailing in the mistral." He waited until the pathologist called him over.

"First fire, now water," she said by way of greeting. "You seem to be a master of the elements."

"Sounds as if you think I killed them."

"It would be a new twist." She gave him a brief smile, then turned serious, carefully touched the corpse's head and turned it so that Blanc could see the back of the skull. She had combed Fuligni's thinning hair to one side, and indicated a serious swelling on the skin. "Hematoma," she explained. "Must have been a pretty hefty blow."

"Fatal?"

"Probably not that bad. We'll only know at the autopsy, but I suspect the skull wasn't damaged. He probably drowned. It's a fairly common sailing accident, I've had a few amateur sailors with similar wounds on the dissecting table. *Morbus nauticus* in Latin."

Blanc looked at her in surprise. "With blows to the head?"

"Usually to the rear, but sometimes to the forehead or temples." Fontaine Thezan got up and pushed her sunglasses back down to cover her eyes. "Particularly in a heavy wind the boom swings round." The captain looked at her blankly so she pointed at one of the moored vessels nearby. "That's the long beam that sticks out at an angle behind the mast. The mainsail is fastened to it. If the wind is strong, and particularly if you're not perfectly on course, it often happens that the wind fills the sail and swings the boom round from one side to the opposite right across the boat. If you're not incredibly careful or don't get out of the way fast enough, it will hit you on the head, hard—with two potentially fatal outcomes: The blow knocks you out, and at the same time the swinging boom knocks you overboard. You fall into the water unconscious and drown straightaway if you aren't wearing a life jacket. Unless of course you were lucky enough for someone to see you fall and haul you out straightaway, which is very unlikely if you're out sailing alone."

"Are you trying to tell me Fuligni's death was an accident?"

She shrugged. "I'm sorry if I'm spoiling your fun, *mon Capitaine*. But that's what it looks like, from a purely medical point of view. You'll get my report, of course." Dr. Thezan packed up her things and strolled off down the pier, ignoring the questions of the two reporters, and climbed into her battered Jeep.

"Merde," Blanc swore under his breath.

"Putain," Tonon corrected him. He seemed to be in a good mood, waving to the forensics team who were all over the *Amzeri*. "Strange coincidence, isn't it."

"Damn strange." He told the lieutenant that he had found out about the relationship between Miette Fuligni and Lucien Le Bruchec. He didn't mention who had told him.

Tonon shrugged indifferently. "You hear things now and then. Miette is hardly a woman who'd appreciate being left on her own."

Blanc thought of his own marriage. "That's a lesson I've learned."

"Do you think Le Bruchec hit Fuligni on the head and then pushed him overboard?" Tonon asked. "On his own boat?"

"It wouldn't be the first time a lover disposed of the troublesome husband."

"And before that Le Bruchec had executed and immolated

Moréas? After sixty peaceful, respectable years our architect suddenly turns into a serial killer?"

"Maybe the two cases are unconnected."

"Maybe this isn't a 'case' at all, just an accident. Dr. Thezan didn't exactly give you grounds for hope."

Blanc interviewed the fisherman who had found Fuligni's body, and the harbormaster. Neither told him anything he didn't already know. Then Marius came up to him and pointed to a little white motorboat battling through the waves to the tiny lighthouse at the end of the last pier, in order to turn into the quieter waters of the harbor. Over the howling of the mistral they could make out the dull groan of a powerful outboard motor. At the stern, on either side of the outboard, were two tall deep-sea fishing rods. At the wheel in the middle of the open-topped boat, dressed in blue and white oilskins, was Marcel Lafont.

"The mayor's going to have a heart attack when he learns that his old friend, who's supposed to be building his beloved *médiathèque*, is dead." Tonon said it as if he were indifferent but Blanc could hear a note of tension in his voice.

Lafont had noticed the police and journalists on the pier, accelerated, and hurtled toward them, leaving a wide wake behind him. "What's happened," he called out, even before he had tied up.

"I suggest you get on to dry land first, *Monsieur le maire*," Blanc replied calmly.

Two minutes later Lafont was staring down at the soaked corpse of his friend. He said nothing, but the color had drained from his face, and his lower lip was trembling. The gendarmes discreetly pulled back to give him some space. "What happened?" he managed to ask at last, clearly shocked.

"We don't quite know yet," the captain said cautiously. "Monsieur Fuligni may have been the victim of an accident." He told him what the pathologist had said. "One way or the other, he wasn't exactly dressed for going out on a boat during the mistral. You look better kitted out."

Lafont absentmindedly ran a hand over his oilskins. "I went out at three in the morning, to go fishing, over by Istres. It's something I like to do before starting work. I don't sleep much these days." He nodded toward the hilly, wooded shore opposite Saint-César. "I was in the little bay behind the hill over there. You can't see it from here. It's very quiet and the fish bite. It was still calm when I went out but Météo-France warned the wind was rising. It started to get rough about five A.M. and I put on my oilskins."

"Did you see Monsieur Fuligni when you arrived at the harbor during the night?"

The mayor shook his head. "I saw his Mercedes. Pascal often drives down here in the evening and spends the night on his boat. He treats it a bit like a holiday home, but it was all dark on his yacht and so I didn't think about waking him."

"So at three A.M., when you got here, the *Amzeri* was still at the pier?"

"Yes, as normal. Who on earth would take a boat out at night, the day before the mistral?"

"Monsieur Fuligni never went sailing during the mistral?"

Lafont was about to answer, then hesitated and made a vague gesture. "Well, not to go any distance. Whenever he had repaired something or had a new toy—a new large foresail, a sonar, depth finder, whatever—then he would always go out for a few minutes to try it out just beyond the harbor. Even if it was raining cats and dogs. I suppose it's possible he went out this morning, to test something."

"That might explain why he was so unsuitably dressed, and so careless," said Tonon, not without a hint of irony in his voice.

Lafont stood up straight. "A stupid, meaningless death, you're right there. But death is death. Don't make things too difficult for his family."

"A tragic accident, but hardly a scandal," Blanc reassured him. He assumed that the mayor didn't want too thorough an investigation, which might only make things worse for his relatives. Or was it possible he had seen more than he was saying, out there in his fishing boat? Or might it be that he just didn't want Miette and Pascal's marital problems to be exposed by the searchlight of a gendarmerie investigation?

"What's going to happen to your *médiathèque* now, *Monsieur le maire*?" he asked incidentally.

The politician scratched his head, cast a final glance at the body of his friend, and muttered, "It'll get built. Now more than ever."

"It's not a crime," Nkoulou insisted, when they were standing in his office a little later, presenting their report.

"That's not been proved yet," Blanc protested. "It might even have something to do with the Moréas murder. It's a bit of a coincidence that—"

"Do not make the situation unnecessarily complicated. You're trying to dive headlong into a second murder investigation before you've even cleared up the first. Or maybe because you can't?"

Blanc stared at his chief. The muscles of his jaw were so tense that he was getting a pain in the temples. Nkoulou was bound to notice. Relax, he told himself. "Should we at least wait until we get the reports from the forensics team and the pathologist?"

"But of course. That's normal procedure." The chief nodded and dismissed them.

"Do you think Lafont might have been on the phone to him again?" Tonon whispered, when they were back in the sanctuary of their own office.

Blanc shrugged. "Maybe. Maybe Nkoulou really does consider us such a pair of losers that he won't trust us with more than one case at a time. I'll have a chat with *Madame le juge*."

"Over the commandant's head?"

"I promised Madame Vialaron-Allègre to keep her up to date on all developments. I intend to do that. If she sees Fuligni's death in the same way Nkoulou does, then I'm out of luck. But if she thinks otherwise, then she may choose to have a word with our dear commandant."

"Sounds like you're just desperate to make friends. In any case, *Madame le juge* is working from home today."

"Are you coming with me this time, Marius?"

"I'm leaving the lady to you."

Blanc already had his hand on the door handle when he turned around. "Don't you find it a bit strange that Monsieur Lafont went out at three in the morning with two fishing rods to an area where the fish are famed for biting, but came back to the harbor with not a single fish?"

Tonon gave him a sympathetic look. "Just do me a favor and don't tell the *juge d'instruction* that you now consider the mayor of her town to be a suspect because the fish weren't biting."

Blanc's phone rang en route. He pulled to the side of the road in the shadow of a pine tree and answered. It was one of the forensics team. The gusts of wind were breaking dry twigs and scattering them along the asphalt, the wind in the trees making so much noise he could hardly understand what his colleague was saying. "Lots of fingerprints on board the *Amzeri*. Fuligni's, but also those of lots of other people, maybe just visitors, fellow sailors, the harbormaster, his wife, whoever. It won't be easy to find out."

"Any sign of a struggle?"

"No, and no traces of blood either."

"Not even on that piece of wood with the sail?"

"You mean the boom? No. Mind you, on this boat it's made of aluminum."

The captain nodded. It would have been too easy. Fuligni's injury was a blow, not a blood wound. He thought back to what Lafont had said about his friend. "Was there anything on board that looked new? Anything Fuligni might have been trying out?"

The forensics man was quiet for a second. Blanc could hear the howling wind coming through the phone. The man was probably still on board. "No, but I'll have a look around. The front sail is still packed away, complete. The mainsail was flying above the boom, but it's old. The compass, radio, GPS all look pretty well used. All the indications are that Fuligni had breakfast belowdecks, came up briefly, and, whack, the boom swung round and took him out."

"He had breakfast?"

"There are croissant crumbs on the table belowdecks, and in the galley an old coffeepot with grounds in it. Still moist. *Putain!*" Suddenly the man's voice vanished.

"What happened?" Blanc shouted.

The voice came back. "There are two coffee cups in the sink."

"Two?"

"I'm an idiot. I should have spotted it straightaway. We'll check them out."

"I'll look forward to your next call." Blanc turned off his Nokia. Two cups. Now the business was beginning to get interesting.

Just as he was about to pull back out onto the road, a dark blue Citroën C5 came speeding down the hill. The driver didn't notice the patrol car parked in the shadow of the trees, but the captain recognized her: *Madame le juge.* He cursed and put his foot down. But Aveline Vialaron-Allègre knew the winding, narrow *route départementale* better than he did, and was driving like a lunatic. After just three bends he had lost sight of her. Still at the wheel, he pulled out his cell phone and tapped in a number, the blue Mégane swaying from side to side across the road, the tires screeching.

"Marius?" he shouted into the Nokia.

"Corporal Baressi on Lieutenant Tonon's phone."

"*Merde.* Sorry. Where is Tonon?"

"Not at his desk."

"I thought as much." *Connard*. "Are you expecting Madame Vialaron-Allègre?"

"*Madame le juge* has been informed of the tragic accident of Monsieur Fuligni."

"It wasn't an accident. Who informed her?"

"No idea. In any case she wanted to get a full picture of the situation."

"Tell her that I'll be in her office in a few minutes and I'll fill her in."

"*Madame le juge* is not coming in to the office. She wanted to see the boat. And the body of the unlucky Monsieur Fuligni."

Blanc put his foot on the brake quickly enough to still be able to turn onto *route départementale* 70D, leading to Saint-César. Somebody had told Aveline Vialaron-Allègre. She wanted to see the crime scene and the victim herself. Why? Because she didn't trust Blanc to do the job properly? Or did she have an altogether different reason?

A few minutes later he parked the patrol car next to the C5 down by the harbor. On the pier the forensics team were clearing up their last bits of equipment. They had taken off their white protective clothing and were standing around smoking. Stretcher bearers had lifted the body, covered with a sheet, and the *juge d'instruction* was standing a little to one side, by the edge of the pier, staring into the water. Blanc hurried past the yachts, stopping briefly with the forensics team next to the *Amzeri* to ask, "Anything new with the coffee cups?"

"Nothing." Young Hurault, already nearly bald, the one who had searched Moréas's house, shook his head. The captain recognized that it had been his voice on the phone. "We'll send them to the lab, but they look to me as clean as if somebody had scalded them."

"On board a sailing boat?"

The forensics man nodded toward the galley. "There's a two-hob gas cooker in there, more than enough to bring a few liters of water to boiling point in a few minutes."

"Anything to suggest that's what happened?"

"Can't be sure. All I can tell you is that there is a normal, relatively full propane gas canister attached. That makes it at least technically possible."

"Do you normally scald your coffee cups in the morning, Monsieur Hurault?"

The young man looked at him in surprise, then shook his head. "Just a dash of washing-up liquid, a rinse with warm water, and then leave them to dry. That's what everybody does."

"So if we think someone was trying to get rid of any clues," Blanc muttered to himself, "then you might think just rinsing the cups was hardly enough."

"And why leave two cups in the drainer? If you want to get rid of any evidence, surely you'd put them back in a cupboard."

"Maybe our Monsieur X didn't have the time. After all, boiling the water and pouring it over them will have taken a few minutes. Or perhaps he didn't want to touch the cups he had just poured the boiling water over for fear of leaving new traces."

"Well, that's your problem," Hurault replied, and peeled his thin frame out of his overalls. "I'll send you the report from the lab if we find anything of interest."

Blanc walked down to the end of the pier. He hesitated before taking the last few steps, preferring to wait until the *juge d'instruction* noticed his presence and turned around. She'd been crying, he realized with some surprise. "I was on my way to you," he said, trying not to show he had noticed the state she was in.

"Monsieur Fuligni was a friend of my late father. He was practically part of the family," she said, clearly having noticed his surprise at her grief. She stretched and gave him a questioning look: "You're here because you don't believe it was an accident?"

"I have doubts, primarily because of two clean coffee cups," he said, telling her what he had discovered.

"And now you think that Monsieur Fuligni wouldn't have gone out in this weather." Aveline Vialaron-Allègre followed his line of thought. "He was sitting belowdecks, having breakfast, with a guest."

"A guest who afterwards took care to remove the evidence."

"After he had hit Pascal on the head, untied the boat, and then pushed him overboard outside the harbor?"

"It's a possibility."

"But when the fisherman came across the *Amzeri*, there was no one on board."

"Maybe the culprit jumped into the water and made his way back to land."

"But you have no witnesses."

"Unfortunately not." Reluctantly, Blanc acknowledged that he was enjoying her putting him to the test.

"And what motive might this hypothetical murderer have had?"

Blanc hesitated, wondering if it might be such a good idea to tell the *juge d'instruction* that her much-valued family friend's wife was cuckolding him. *Merde alors*. He briefly summarized the rumors about Miette Fuligni's affair with the architect Le Bruchec. Aveline Vialaron-Allègre didn't look too shocked, as if it were the first time she had heard the story.

"You named Lucien Le Bruchec as a suspect in the Moréas murder case, and now, a few days later, you're naming him again, this time as the killer of Pascal Fuligni. It's not hard to tell you're not from around here. Nobody who knows Lucien would take that seriously, even for a second. It's absurd that a man like him would shoot a suspected burglar and then just days later kill a rival in a love affair."

"I'm not accusing anybody. I have no intention of arresting anybody." He could feel his heart rate rising. "You asked me for a possible motive. I gave you a possible motive. The oldest in the world: passion."

"The oldest motive in the world is greed," the *juge d'instruction* replied.

"I'm not ruling that out either."

"If there's anything in what you've just said, it implies that both murders were carried out by the same person. But we have neither a suspect nor a motive." Blanc was about to interrupt her, but she gestured at him to be silent. "Please explain to me then the difference in the killer's approach: In the one case a man is mowed down with a Kalashnikov, then set on fire, in the other he's hit on the head and dumped in the water off his yacht in the Étang de Berre. Coffee cups rinsed in boiling water. That's the act of someone doing everything possible to conceal the evidence. The exact opposite of what happened at the garbage dump. The first looked like an execution, the second was supposed to look like an accident."

"That doesn't mean there aren't parallels: cold-bloodedness for a start. Efficiency. A killer adapting the method to the circumstances. On a garbage dump, where it's noisy and dirty and there are moments when there's nobody about, a salvo from a machine gun could be considered efficient, fast, and unlikely to be noticed. At the same time the killer doesn't have to get close to a violent man like Moréas, who could be dangerous at close quarters. He kills him without warning from a distance. In the harbor here at Saint-César a single shot would have everybody sleeping on their boats jumping out of their beds. A blow to the head, possibly belowdecks, wouldn't be noticed by anyone. Once again the murderer would be taking the least possible risk, attacking from behind. And in both cases the killer eliminates all the evidence: first by fire, then by making it look like an accident."

"And rinsing the coffee cups with boiling water?"

"An eye for detail."

Vialaron-Allègre lit up a Gauloise. "What does your boss think about all this?"

"Commandant Nkoulou thinks it was an accident."

"I'll talk to him," she said, nodding to dismiss him.

"So is this an investigation or not?" Blanc called after her, confused.

"Of course," she replied. And for a brief moment they smiled at one another, almost as if they were friends.

Blanc got his phone out. He had to talk to Miette Fuligni, firstly to break the terrible news to her, but also, as discreetly as possible, to ask her a few questions. But he wanted to talk to the architect, Le Bruchec, first, before news of the death got around.

For that reason he rang the gendarmerie first, but Tonon still didn't answer. Instead he got through to Fabienne Souillard, who wasn't exactly thrilled but agreed to drive out to see the widow. It took him a while to get through to Le Bruchec. The architect was at home. "I'd like to come and ask you a couple more questions," Blanc said, as vaguely as he could.

"Well, hurry up about it, I've got an appointment to play tennis."

With Miette Fuligni perhaps? Blanc wondered. On the other hand Le Bruchec didn't exactly sound as if he knew his lover's husband had been fished out of the Étang de Berre dead.

"Tell me, Monsieur Le Bruchec, are you a sailor?" he asked when he was sitting in the inner courtyard of the architect's house fifteen minutes later.

"I was when I was young. A 470."

"Sounds like a weapon."

The architect laughed. "Feels like one too. A 470 is an Olympic racing dinghy. Very sporty. Spend an hour in a good wind in one of those beasts and you'll feel like you've got on a bucking bronco."

"So you don't sail anymore?"

He shook his head. "I sometimes go out fishing in a friend's motorboat. But I'm too old for the little dinghies, and I don't have the time to indulge myself with a big yacht. For every hour you spend out sailing, you spend two hours in port. There's always something to fix or fiddle with or clean. Dreadful. I prefer tennis." Le Bruchec was already dressed in a white Lacoste tennis shirt with matching pants, though he was still in flip-flops. "What's the point of these questions?"

"This morning Monsieur Fuligni was pulled out of the water near his yacht, outside Saint-César harbor. Drowned."

Le Bruchec stared at him vacantly a moment. Then he flinched, his left eyelid flickering. *"Mon Dieu,"* he mumbled. "What happened?"

"He was hit on the back of the head and fell overboard. It may have been a tragic accident."

"Does Miette know yet?"

"My colleague is with her now."

"The boom," the architect said, more to himself than anyone else. "A loose cord and the thing swings across. It's happened to every sailor."

"On the other hand, the mistral is blowing and Monsieur Fuligni might not have gone sailing. It is possible that someone delivered the fatal blow. Someone on board with him," Blanc explained flatly.

The architect looked at him, irritated. "Why do you say that? And why do you suddenly turn up here and ask me questions like that?"

"Because you're in a relationship with Madame Fuligni."

Le Bruchec opened his mouth as if he was going to launch into a tirade, then closed it again, got up, and began striding up and down the inner courtyard, like a tiger in a cage. "Are you accusing me of murdering him?"

"Do you deny having an affair with Madame Fuligni?"

"That doesn't exactly make me a killer."

"Where were you last night? And where were you this morning?"

"That's absurd." Le Bruchec wiped his right hand across his bald head, which had begun to sweat.

"Please just answer the question," Blanc said calmly.

"I was here. In my house. I have been since yesterday after-noon."

"Have you any witnesses to that?"

The architect glared at him. "No. It was my cleaning lady's day off yesterday. And I had no visitors." He sat down. "Listen to me, *mon Capitaine*. I've known Miette forever. I've always liked her. But we were friends, nothing more. But then when my wife died six months ago . . ." His voice failed him and he was silent for a minute. "Well, whatever, I was lonely. It was the same with Miette. Pascal neglected her, had done for ages. Then there was that Romanian girl, his secretary. It was both a scandal and ridiculous at the same time. Miette and I met regularly at the tennis club—and at some stage things happened. But it's only an affair, nothing more. We were consoling each other, you could say. It was always clear to both of us that Miette wasn't going to leave her husband for me. And I didn't want things to go any further than occasional . . ." He looked for the right phrase. ". . . togetherness."

Blanc looked hard at the architect. He had no alibi—and he did have a motive, whatever story he came up with. He was still young enough to want a new partner after the death of his wife. But he was well known round and about. He needed to keep a good reputation if he was to keep getting commissions. In the long term an affair might harm him, though most people already seemed to know of it. But if Miette suddenly became a widow through a tragic accident, then he could make their relationship more or less public. After a suitably decent length of time, they might even get married. And someone who regularly played tennis would have a strong arm, strong enough to knock a man out with a stick or other blunt object in a single blow. "Can you please give me the make, license plate, and color of all your cars?" he asked. Perhaps one of his cars might have been seen in the harbor at Saint-César.

A few minutes later he said good-bye, still without more than a vague suspicion. Nothing he was going to get a search warrant with, let alone an arrest warrant. He said, *"Au revoir,"* hoping it sounded like a threat. Le Bruchec shook his hand absently, staring at his tennis equipment lying in the hallway. He didn't look like he was about to play his match.

Back at the gendarmerie he went to see Fabienne in her office. His young colleague was pale. "That was the first time I've ever had to inform someone of the death of a family member," she whispered.

Blanc was grateful she didn't hold it against him that he'd made her do it. "How did Madame Fuligni take it?"

"Silently, horribly silently. I think I would have found it easier if she cried or collapsed. I would have been able to offer her consolation or called the medics or something. But she just stood there looking at me for what seemed like ages. I didn't know how to react."

"Were you able to ask her any questions?"

"Yes. Later. Madame Fuligni rang an old friend, and when she arrived, she seemed to come round a bit. She told me her husband had gone down to the boat last night, with the intention of sleeping on board, something he did often. She thought nothing about it, watched television for a while, and then went to bed."

"Witnesses?"

"She said she was alone the whole time."

"Yes, too much to ask for."

"You don't think Madame Fuligni herself dumped her husband in the Étang de Berre?"

"I was hoping for a good, solid witness statement to rule out that possibility. But she had a motive. Also she knows the harbor and the boat, and her presence wouldn't seem out of the ordinary. She's fit too, fit enough to knock someone out with a blow to the back of the head."

"Statistics are against you. Nine out of ten murders are committed by men."

"Women don't get caught so often."

"What about the coffee cups with boiling water poured over them? Miette Fuligni would only have needed to put them back in the cupboard. If her prints had been found on them or anywhere else on board, it would have been totally normal. She'd been on the *Amzeri*, so what? She's his wife. She must have been there a hundred times."

"Maybe she's an obsessive cleaner."

Fabienne just laughed and pointed to a few sheets of computer printout. "This came in from the forensics lab while you were down at the harbor. It's the report on the bullets used to kill Moréas."

Blanc read the first few lines, then whistled through his teeth. "So, not the weapon we found under Moréas's bed. But a 'hot' gun," he whispered. "Seven-point-six-two-millimeter ammunition was used in a Zastava M70, a Yugoslav Kalashnikov copy. The cartridge cases had characteristic marks from the ejector system. Some of the cases showed two ejector marks, implying they had been reloaded and ejected, then fired this

time. Cartridge cases with similar marks had been found last
year in one of the suburbs north of Marseille, in the stairwell of
a dilapidated apartment block where someone had shot dead
a North African drug dealer." A murder that still hadn't been
cleared up. "I wonder if our killer is the same man," he said.

His colleague shook her head. "I'd bet a month's wages the
gun was bought cheap in Marseille. After every murder the killers buy a new weapon—Kalashnikovs are cheap. That way a
murder can never be laid at their door even if we find them with
a weapon. Our colleagues in Marseille in any case haven't been
able to find any link between the dead dealer and Moréas. The
dealer had only arrived from Algiers three months before his
death. He didn't know his way around, did some business on the
turf of one of the Corsican clans. That alone would have been
enough to send an assassin after him."

"Who buys hot guns like those from known killers?"

"Pros from the Balkans who couldn't care less whether or
not the French police are looking for a particular weapon. Or
kids looking for the cheapest they can get. Opportunists who
don't realize they're being sold a 'hot' weapon."

"Well, that reduces our number of suspects."

"You're joking, I assume."

"On the contrary. At least now we can be fairly certain that
Marseille drug dealers aren't mixed up in this, even if our perpetrator copied their technique. Maybe that was a deliberate
attempt to divert our attention." All of a sudden Blanc's mind
switched to the death of Fuligni. That too had been arranged
to suggest one specific solution, even though there were lots of
possibilities. "Our killer is fastidious," he mumbled to himself.
He read the rest of the report. The Kalashnikov they had found

in Moréas's house hadn't been fired for years. It had never come to the attention of the police either in Marseille or anywhere else in France. As far as instruments of murder go, it was still a virgin.

The door opened and Corporal Baressi stuck his head round it. "We've sent a couple of people down to the harbor at Saint-César with the details of Le Bruchec's cars." The chubby gendarme glanced down at the list in his sweaty hand. "Nice wheels. I wouldn't mind a couple of these. But neither the harbormaster nor anyone else spotted any of them. The architect wasn't down at the harbor."

Fabienne Souillard gave him a scowl. "Le Bruchec doesn't keep a boat down at the harbor," she said icily, "and therefore he wouldn't have had the code for the parking lot. If he had been down at Saint-César he would have had to park in one of the side streets. Did you ask around there too?"

Baressi disappeared without answering.

"I have something else for you," Souillard said. "It's about the German painter. Almost certainly meaningless."

At that moment Tonon came in with a half-eaten croissant in one hand and a cardboard coffee cup in the other. "So this is where you've been hiding," he said to Blanc, kissing Fabienne on the cheek. "Well, it's prettier than in our old boys' office." Hanging from his gun belt was an ancient silver mobile CD player with a thin headset cable leading up to his hairy ears.

"Is that a brain pacemaker?" Fabienne asked sarcastically.

Tonon pulled out his earbuds and tinny music drowned out the whirring of the computer's fan. Blanc thought he could just make out the voice of Serge Gainsbourg. "Used to belong to one of my kids. Can't remember which. I found it while cleaning up."

"You're so nineties."

"My best years."

"What were you about to tell me, Fabienne?" Blanc interrupted the pair of them. He wasn't exactly thrilled at his partner only just showing up and acting as if he was on vacation.

"Gérard Paulmier called, the former *La Provence* journalist. He said he had been speaking to his old colleagues again about Monsieur Rheinbach's visit. He said he thought it would floor you, and that it was something you might want to know."

"He knows his people."

"You men are so transparent. Anyway, it would appear Rheinbach asked not just about Moréas, but more specifically about his involvement in the attacks on tourists."

Tonon, already slurping at his coffee, took a gulp and coughed, sending a fine brown spray across the desk. Souillard turned her eyes away, and used a Kleenex to wipe her computer and iPad.

"What precisely did Monsieur Rheinbach want to know?"

"It seems first of all he just wanted to read the original articles about the attacks and the arrests after the tourist was killed. There were quite a lot of reports at the time, including about the arrest of Moréas, although his name was never mentioned, just 'a suspect from Caillouteaux.' But if you know the story then it's pretty obvious they're referring to Moréas. It soon became clear, however, that Rheinbach had already read the stories. He just wanted more information and kept pressing them, as to who wrote the story, for example. It was as if he was after information that didn't make it into the published piece at the time. But the journalists turned him away."

Blanc looked at his colleague. Tonon had gone pale, the paper cup in his hand shaking. "That old story," he mumbled, "that same damn old story."

. Blanc had been intending to ask Tonon to look into it, but he began to realize Marius obviously wouldn't exactly relish going back over the old case. Instead he said to Fabienne, "Would you look into it? Find out why a jigsaw puzzle painter should be so interested in this grubby old story. Why this Rheinbach was so obsessed with Moréas. Was he intending to blackmail him? Had he found out something that had been missed all these years?"

Tonon snorted indignantly.

"Or maybe Rheinbach was just after something he could use as a defense because he felt threatened by Moréas?" Blanc continued, unperturbed. "Or was he trying to threaten Moréas himself? Maybe there are some documents relating to their properties? Or maybe one of the two women who had a brief relationship with Rheinbach had also hung around with Moréas?"

"Moréas had annoyed this timid painter when he was out in the forest with his canvas and brushes," Tonon grumbled. "He just wanted to know who he was dealing with. That's all."

"I've never gone down to a newspaper to try to find out details about a neighbor's involvement in some ancient incident," Blanc said. "I think that in itself is something worthy of investigation."

"Discreetly," advised Tonon, "very discreetly."

Blanc and Souillard both nodded, though neither of them

had any idea what their colleague felt they needed to be so discreet about.

"Come over for dinner tonight," Blanc said to Marius a bit later when they were back in their own office, bent over their ancient computers. Tonon seemed to be particularly worked up about their digging into the old highway robbery case again. Probably, Blanc thought, because he saw it as a lasting accusation against himself, that he had made a mess of the case and never brought Moréas to justice. Now here was some cop from Paris and a young lesbian who were going to open it all up again. What if they were to find something he had missed all these years?

"I'll bring a few things along so we don't have to eat out of cans," he replied, attempting a smile.

Nkoulou appeared. "You two are to continue investigating the Fuligni death. The *juge d'instruction* insists on it," he told them. "I'll give you time, until the autopsy report is done. If you don't have anything by then, I shall tell Madame Vialaron-Allègre that somebody has called a false alarm." And with that the commandant slammed the door behind him.

"He's going to explode with anger if you keep on like this," Tonon whispered.

Blanc grabbed the phone: "Have you got the pathologist's number?"

"It's on speed dial. Hit '8.' You're not going to put pressure on Dr. Thezan?"

"On the contrary. I'm going to tell her to take her time with the autopsy."

If Fontaine Thezan was surprised by his call, she didn't show it. "I'm going to cut open the body today," she replied. "I assume we won't find anything new, but I can order blood and tissue samples to be taken and test them for drugs and such. That can take a while."

"I owe you a coffee," said Blanc.

"I drink green tea," the pathologist answered, and hung up.

Blanc spent the rest of the day writing up a report for the files. At some stage Tonon disappeared. "Buying ingredients," he announced. "See you this evening. Shall we say around eight?"

The captain shut down his computer early and got to his feet. There was nothing more to be done for the day. It was an unusual feeling. He decided to go home, sort out the house a bit, and relax. There was no mobile reception in the old mill, although if he took a few steps out from the plane trees he could just about get a weak connection. He spent a little time surfing the Internet hoping maybe to get mail or other news from his children. On Facebook he found he had a friend request from Fabienne Souillard. He confirmed it. Three more of his former Paris colleagues had disappeared from his fast-shrinking list of FB friends. But his daughter had posted something: two party photos with a few people he hadn't seen before. But nothing from his son. His daughter had wished her mother a good vacation in Martinique. What was Geneviève doing in the Caribbean? Had she already gone or was she about to leave? Was she with her new guy? He turned the damn Nokia off. Across the river Serge Douchy was rattling along on his asthmatic tractor and nodded to him. Blanc thought the goatherd was being ironic, but he realized he was probably imagining it. He raised a hand and waved. Don't feel sorry for yourself, he told himself.

A dented old Fiat Marea turned into the olive oil mill's

drive. Tonon honked his horn and dragged his huge frame out the door. He was wearing pale linen pants and a blue and yellow Hawaiian shirt, his eyes concealed behind an ultramodern pair of sunglasses with jagged lenses.

"You could be in the next Dany Boon film," Blanc said by way of welcome.

"That would be a good career move," Marius grunted. "Give me a hand." He opened the trunk.

"Have you got a cannon in there?"

"It's a barbecue grill."

"It looks like a heap of junk."

"Well, now it's yours." Tonon set up the huge, rusty piece of apparatus outside the mill, and then produced a bag of charcoal, a plastic bag dripping fat, a string bag full of eggplants, and a small bag of potatoes.

"What is this? I invite you over for dinner and you bring everything with you?" Blanc said, only halfheartedly. His stomach was rumbling.

"Pure egoism. I just don't trust your cooking skills." From his plastic bag from Géant Casino supermarket he also pulled out a bottle of Ricard. "Pastis is better than yoga for relaxing."

Blanc dragged a table and two chairs into the open air, while his colleague set up the grill, piled charcoal in, and put a fire lighter in the middle. They poured a finger of pastis into two glasses and added ice and water. Tonon raised his glass and toasted him. Blanc sniffed the aroma of almonds, took a sip, and let the pastis rinse his mouth with alcohol and the taste of licorice. It also quenched his thirst. Tonon downed his glass in one, and refilled it.

Over the next hour Tonon grilled a dozen merguez he had

produced from the plastic bag, piercing the spicy lamb sausages with a fork so that fat dripped onto the steaming charcoal, while the merguez themselves shrank to dark hard sticks. Marius wrapped the eggplants and potatoes in foil along with rosemary and thyme and threw them onto the grill. Blanc learned that his colleague had two grown-up children. "The boys are so left-wing they are embarrassed to have a cop as father," he said, laughing. It wasn't quite clear whether or not he was still in contact with them. Blanc thought of his own kids and the fact that Facebook was really his only link to them, and decided not to ask his colleague for too much detail. He took another sip from the glass of pastis, the scent of cooking meat and vegetables sending him into a mild state of euphoria. Before long the bottle of Ricard was empty. He opened a bottle of Bernard rosé, wondering how his colleague intended to get home later.

They enjoyed the spicy merguez, eggplant, potatoes, a baguette with cheese, and wine. "Not exactly Michelin star, but tell me when you ever ate better in Paris?" Tonon challenged.

"You are an artist," Blanc admitted. He decided he would fix up an improvised guest bed for Marius. They would finish off another bottle of rosé, and neither of them would go anywhere for the rest of the evening.

Then the Nokia he had left outside rang. Souillard. "Fabienne, don't tell me you're still at work?" Blanc said, with more than a touch of guilt.

"Not really. My girlfriend is away and I was just surfing the Internet in the office," she said dismissively. "But this woman appeared."

"On the Internet?"

"No. Waiting in the office next door. A cleaning lady, who'd been working in her boss's house this morning. Over the years he's usually left her money in an envelope on the kitchen table—but not this time. Also the fridge had been left to thaw, and a few suitcases were missing. Nothing like it had ever happened all the time she's worked for him. She was puzzled, but did her job. Later on she tried to get hold of her boss—calling him at home, in the office, on his cell phone. But every time it went straight to voice mail. This evening she talked to her husband about it and he advised her to go to the police and file a missing person report."

Blanc already had an inkling of what was coming. "So who is this missing boss of hers?" he asked, trying to get rid of the alcoholic fug clouding his brain.

"The architect, Lucien Le Bruchec."

The Last Text Message

"We need to get down to the gendarmerie," Blanc called to his colleague. "I'll drive."

Tonon took his time emptying his wineglass. "I hope we're not going to have to see anything that will bring my sausages back up."

They climbed into the Espace, but it only spluttered when Blanc turned the key in the ignition.

"Did you forget to fill up?" Tonon asked.

"I filled up with more than enough this evening," Blanc grumbled. "We'd better take your car."

His colleague threw him the keys, but they missed him by several yards, leaving the two of them fumbling around on the ground in the dark until they found them. Blanc readjusted the seat and rearview mirror to fit his height. "Where are the lights?" But Marius had already put his head back on the passenger seat and was snoring away. *Merde.* Blanc felt his way around the controls until he found the light switch. By the time they finally got on the road, he felt as if it had been half an hour since Fabienne's call. He drove down the middle of the *route départe-*

mentale for fear of ending up in a ditch on either side. Only then did it occur to him that Tonon hadn't even asked why they suddenly had to be on duty at this late hour of the evening. "Le Bruchec has disappeared," he shouted into the lieutenant's ear. "Open your eyes and turn your brain back on."

At the gendarmerie he greeted the corporal who was on night shift, and hurried to Souillard's office, the bleary-eyed Tonon dragging behind him. "I sent the cleaning lady home. It's late," she said on seeing them. Then, *"Mon Dieu*, what happened to you, Marius?"

"We had a barbecue," Blanc explained.

"So what do we do? Issue an arrest warrant for Le Bruchec?"

"No, we don't have evidence enough against him for that. We'll send out an alert giving his description to every police station and the border posts in Italy, Spain, and Switzerland, as well as the Marseille airport and all the main stations. Do we have any photos of him?"

"There are dozens on the Internet. I've already downloaded one and prepared an alert. But are you sure it's legal?"

"We'll reformat the cleaning lady's statement as a missing person report, and then it will look official," Blanc said. "Consider it a shortcut."

"I asked the cleaning lady to leave us her keys."

"I'm going to recommend you for a promotion."

"As far as Nkoulou is concerned, a recommendation from you is the kiss of death for my career. Do you intend on taking Marius with you?" she asked, indicating Tonon, who had already nodded off in his seat.

"Is it going to annoy you if I leave him here?"

"Not as long as he doesn't start to snore."

Blanc nodded thankfully. "It won't take me long. Then I'll come back and will take Marius home."

As he left the office she was staring at her screen again.

The mistral was still rustling the tree branches. Blanc could see little more than shadows. It sounded as if he was in the midst of a waterfall. The woods were full of demons. But as he got close to Le Bruchec's house halogen lights concealed in the ground and triggered by invisible motion sensors enveloped the house in bright white light. It reminded Blanc of the spaceship in *Close Encounters of the Third Kind.* He opened the door, flipped on the lights, and went from room to room. The house was clean and tidy. Too tidy. He found the main bedroom. A vast built-in wardrobe along one wall, a monument in mirrors and aluminum. The door slid back silently at the touch of a finger. Shelves of neatly folded polo shirts, pants, underwear. Some of the piles were higher than others. Below was a row of suitcases, with one empty space. The bedside table had been cleared. At first glance there didn't appear to be a cell phone in the house, not a notebook, or paper, or cash, a checkbook or glasses. In the kitchen the doors of a huge American-style refrigerator stood open, the interior thawed out.

Blanc went out to the garage and opened the doors. A Range Rover, a Porsche, a BMW. One space was empty. The captain took out his phone and called Fabienne: "Give me a list of all Le Bruchec's cars."

Within a few moments he knew that Le Bruchec had taken the smallest, least conspicuous of his cars, his late wife's VW

Polo. Blanc remembered what the farmer who had been at the garbage dump the day of Moréas's death had said: There had been a little red car parked there. And then he remembered that the farmer had admitted seeing Le Bruchec—but roaring past him in his Range Rover. I've had too much wine, he said to himself. An hour later he had finished with both house and garage and was driving back, slowly, to make sure he didn't end up in a ditch.

In the gendarmerie, Fabienne—still frighteningly fresh and lively—smiled at him. "Half of France is on the lookout for Le Bruchec now."

"And the other half is out for the count," Blanc muttered, nodding toward his colleague, who hadn't moved from his chair. He got the corporal to help him drag the massive Tonon, reeking of pastis, rosé, and sweat, out into the passenger seat of the Fiat. "Drive on ahead to Lieutenant Tonon's house," he ordered him. He followed the patrol car to Saint-César, where they parked by one of the giant pillars that soared above the rooftops supporting the viaduct far above their heads. Tonon's house was narrow and looked as if it had been squeezed in as an afterthought between two much larger buildings: two stories, an old door, wooden shutters, pale plasterwork of an indistinguishable color. "This place could do with a bit of a makeover," the corporal coughed, as they dragged the lieutenant toward the door. Blanc fumbled in Tonon's pants pocket until he found the key, and managed to open the door, all without letting go of one of his arms. A few minutes of cursing and swearing later and they had managed to lay Tonon, in uniform but without his shoes, on the bed.

"Now I'll show you a house that really, really needs a makeover," Blanc said to the corporal. "Drive me to Sainte-Françoise-la-Vallée."

By the time he got back to the old mill and watched the taillights of the patrol car disappear, all he wanted to do was sleep. A few of his neighbor's goats were bleating in the dark; one of them kicked at the wooden gate with its hoof. Then Blanc flinched as a rough voice yelled at him from across the river: "Next time, watch your damn barbecue grill. There are still embers. The mistral is here, *putain*! One spark and the whole valley would have gone up in flames."

"At least then we'd have had grilled goat," Blanc called back. Goddamn Douchy. He swayed into the house.

Next morning Douchy's cockerel woke him up. The mistral was still rattling the shutters. A Saturday morning in July: He should be sleeping it off in a big soft bed, breathing in Geneviève's perfume, feeling her soft skin beneath his fingers. Instead, he struggled to his feet from an old camping mattress on an iron frame and about as comfortable a bed as in an interrogation cell. A cold shower. Strong coffee. Only then did his brain cells struggle to come to life.

Then he dragged himself into the Espace, which at least started straightaway. But Blanc was too tired even to wonder what had caused this sudden change of heart in the old car. A couple of curves down the road and his phone rang. Blanc braked, pulled to the roadside, fumbled in his pocket for his Nokia, then dropped it between the pedals. He cursed, fished the phone up with his feet, and didn't even glance at the display to see who he had just missed a call from. Later. He drove to the gendarmerie, where Fabienne greeted him with a smile, looking as fresh as if she'd had ten hours of sleep. Tonon was nowhere to be seen.

"I tried calling you," she said.

"My phone decided to develop a life of its own in the car."

"They've caught Le Bruchec."

Blanc was suddenly wide awake.

"Who? Where?"

"At the toll booth on the A7, outside Lyon, just before three A.M. A motorbike patrol of the *Sécurité routière* just happened to be there. The officer spotted the red VW Polo. Le Bruchec didn't seem too surprised when he was waved over. He's on his way here and should be with us in half an hour. I just wanted to make sure you'd be in the office."

"I couldn't be better," Blanc lied. "Does Nkoulou know yet?"

"The commandant can't wait for the result of your interrogation."

Blanc wondered if he ought to call Madame Vialaron-Allègre. He decided against it. Better to hear what the architect had to say first. "Half an hour should be just long enough to have a coffee," he said, and went into one of the Gadet bars for his second wake-up shot of the day.

Exactly thirty-six minutes later, he was sitting opposite Le Bruchec. The architect was pale, unshaven, and looked ten years older than the last time they met. Blanc had brought three cups of coffee from the bar, and pushed one across the table to him. The second was for Fabienne, who was going to take notes. He had brought the other for Marius, but he hadn't turned up yet. So he knocked back the bitter brew himself.

"You've done cleverer things in your life than choosing now as the time to disappear," Blanc began.

"Well deduced. You should apply to join the police," Le Bruchec replied. The coffee seemed to have done its work.

"Where were you heading? Abroad?"

"Nonsense. I was going to Paris. I have friends there from my student days. I just wanted . . ." He searched for the right word. "A chance to breathe. To clear my head. It's not against the law."

"Absolutely not. But you must have realized that disappearing like that was bound to cause alarm. You vanished without even a word to your cleaning lady."

"I needed peace and quiet."

"Monsieur Le Bruchec, can we go back to the Sunday when you met Charles Moréas at the garbage dump?"

The architect sighed. "It's like having teeth pulled."

"A dentist can't arrest you," Blanc replied softly. "So, you say you bumped into Moréas there about three P.M. and exchanged no more than a few words with him. A quarter of an hour later you left the dump, and Moréas was still there."

"I can prove that," Le Bruchec said, though he sounded more resigned than self-confident.

"Last time we spoke you said you had no witnesses."

"Last time we spoke you knew less about my private life. Madame Fuligni was with me. She called me when I was down at the dump and told me her husband had gone down to his yacht. We arranged to meet at three thirty."

Blanc scribbled a note on a sheet of paper and gave it to Souillard. *Get the cell phone data for LeB and M.F. Check if they spoke on Sunday about 3:15 P.M.* She nodded and turned to her computer screen.

"How long was Madame Fuligni with you?"

"Until just before eight P.M. She wanted to get back in time for the evening news in case her husband turned up."

The captain closed his eyes. He had a pain behind his eyes, his stomach was chafing from too much coffee, and he still felt tired.

"It's the mistral," Le Bruchec said, with just a touch of schadenfreude in his voice. "It's like wine: Some people can take it, while others get headaches."

Blanc pulled himself together. He would check out the architect's story. If it was true, then the man had an alibi until eight o'clock on Sunday evening. Maybe they would be able to strike him off the list of suspects altogether. It would certainly be enough to let him go. No judge would issue a warrant, and Madame Vialaron-Allègre in particular would scratch his eyes out if he even suggested anything of the sort. And on the second death, they had got no further at all: no progress on Pascal Fuligni.

"You can go," he said wearily. "Apologies for the inconvenience. But we would appreciate it if you would let us know the next time you intend to go away, until this case is declared over. We may need another statement from you, as a witness. You would appear to be the last person to see Charles Moréas alive. Apart from his killer."

For a moment the captain wondered if he should ask one of the ranks to drive him to Fuligni's house, then decided he was up to driving himself. He took the Espace rather than turn up in a blue gendarmerie patrol car outside the house of a woman who'd been recently widowed. It was going to be hard enough.

As he pulled up to the house, he noticed a taxi outside. The driver was putting a huge suitcase and a full blue Ikea plastic bag into the trunk. Nastasia Constantinescu was standing next to it in a thin top and short black leather skirt. Her large sunglasses only partially concealed the fact she had been crying.

"Are you leaving, Mademoiselle?"

She attempted a smile. "Now that Pascal . . . Monsieur Fuligni has been taken from us, nobody knows how to carry on the business. Madame no longer needs me either, so I'm going to my sister in Toulon."

Blanc took down her sister's name and address. He didn't think the young Romanian had anything to do with either murder, but you could never be sure. *"Au revoir,"* he said, and waved good-bye.

The door was open. He knocked and went in. Miette Fuligni was sitting at an oak table in a large open-plan kitchen/living room. She had two bowls in front of her, one of *café au lait*, and yogurt mixed with cherries in the other. The cherries had left red streaks in the yogurt, like bloodstains. Madame Fuligni was wearing pale blue linen pants and leather sandals; her toenails were painted red. The top two buttons of her short white blouse were open, offering him a clear view of the cleavage between her perfectly formed breasts. Good cosmetic surgery, Blanc thought, and looked out the window.

He greeted her with a nod. "I'm afraid I have to ask you a few awkward questions," he said.

"You have a wonderfully old-fashioned way of expressing yourself, *mon Inspecteur*. Lucien warned me though." She nodded toward the iPhone lying on the table. "He just called. I believe he's been a guest of yours."

Blanc cleared his throat. "At least that spares me a few explanations," he muttered, angry at himself at the same time. The two would have had time to coordinate their stories. "Were you at Monsieur Le Bruchec's house last Sunday?"

"I do hope your moral standards aren't quite as old-fashioned as your means of expression."

"Around what time?"

She shrugged her shoulders. "Afternoon." She thought for a moment. "Lucien says he was back home about three thirty P.M., so it must have been about then. I was back home before the evening news. We took turns in going to each other's house." She didn't seem embarrassed in the slightest.

"Were you also with Monsieur Le Bruchec on Thursday evening? And Friday morning?"

"You want to know whether I was with my lover when my husband died?"

"That would make a few things easier."

"No, I was alone. I had called Lucien around noon on Thursday. But he wasn't free. He said he had a commission he needed to work on. So I went to play tennis at the club and then spent the evening in front of the television."

Blanc forced himself to ignore his headache. If Lucien Le Bruchec and Miette Fuligni had planned together to get rid of Pascal Fuligni, this would have been their ideal opportunity to create an alibi. Madame Fuligni, who already knew the cop was aware of her affair, only needed to say she had spent the hours in question with her lover. That way they would both have given each other an alibi. See what you can do about that! But as it was, neither had an alibi for either Thursday evening or Friday morning. Paradoxically that might indicate that neither had anything to hide. So maybe it really was an accident? Or was there a third party involved? He felt faint.

"Would you like a *café au lait, mon Inspecteur*? Or maybe a pastis?" Miette was giving him a look that was half sympathetic, half ironic. Even at that moment she was a tempting woman.

"One would give me a heart attack, the other finish my brain off."

"*Inspecteur*," she called after him at the door. "When will the pathologist release my husband's body?"

"Why do you want to know?"

"To prepare his funeral."

"*Pardon*," he stammered, suddenly embarrassed. "I'll ask, and request that they finish the investigation as quickly as possible." Amazing how easy it was to lie when his brain was on fire and all he could think of was fresh air. At that moment his Nokia rang.

"*C'est moi.*" It was Fabienne Souillard's voice. "It didn't take long to check out the phones. Madame Fuligni's phone called Le Bruchec's number about three eleven P.M. on Sunday. The call lasted about a minute and a half. That ups his credibility."

"I'm afraid so."

"Then this won't please you either. Nobody saw any of the architect's cars in Saint-César on Friday. The big parking lot near the yachting harbor, the one anybody can use, is just in front of the Office du Tourisme, a converted old church. They have a surveillance camera, and on the footage from Thursday evening to Friday morning, none of the cars of interest to us show up."

"Footage from a single camera is hardly proof. He could have parked somewhere else without anybody noticing the car. And an architect more than anyone else would notice details like a surveillance camera on a building. He would never have parked there."

"Even so, we don't have anything to contradict Le Bruchec's statement."

"You can't always be lucky."

"It would appear you don't believe my husband was the victim of an accident?" Miette Fuligni asked as Blanc terminated the call. She was standing in the door. Just two steps outside the captain could feel the mistral tugging at his jacket.

"I'm not ruling anything out, Madame," he replied cautiously.

"My husband had no enemies. Even I loved him, despite the fact that our marriage was . . . difficult." She looked exhausted all of a sudden, like an actress who's been onstage too long.

Blanc took a step closer. "Your husband never felt threatened?"

"Not remotely. He got angry about this Moréas. And he broke into a tirade about you when you more or less accused him of murdering the guy at the garbage dump." She waved away the contradiction. "That was just Pascal: always shouting and complaining. But he quickly got it out of his system."

"Did you notice anything out of the ordinary in the days before his death?"

"Depends on what you mean by ordinary. That he flirted with his little Romanian hooker in our house and I had to watch the pretty little performance? That had been going on for weeks."

"Was your husband nervous? Anxious? Was he, for example, spending more time down at the boat than normal?"

"His daily routine was the same as always. Very predictable."

Blanc considered the fact that Miette Fuligni had left Le Bruchec in time to be home for the evening news. A very predictable family life, up to a point. "Did your husband have any unusual guests recently?"

She shook her head. "The usual friends. Lafont, a few fellow sailors. Building workers."

"Anything unusual in the post? A parcel? A letter?"

"Who still writes letters these days? No, not as far as I know."

The captain went over the scene down at the harbor again, the first time he had met Fuligni. The builder had been using his phone. But on Friday the forensics team hadn't found a cell phone. Maybe it had fallen overboard along with him and was lying somewhere on the murky bottom of the Étang de Berre. "Is your husband's cell phone here?" he asked, just for the sake of it.

"Maybe," Miette Fuligni answered dismissively. "Pascal was always forgetting it. I keep telling him he would . . ." She gulped, suddenly realizing she would never talk to her husband again. "I'll just go and look on the bedside table," she whispered, and disappeared into the house. A few seconds later she came back with an iPhone in her hand. "This is his," she said.

Blanc took it out of her hand. It was locked.

"You don't by any chance know the code."

"It's zero-three-zero-eight," she replied. "Our wedding day." She swayed on her feet.

Blanc could see the tears welling up. "You've been extraordinarily helpful, Madame," he said quickly. He suddenly felt himself surprised by a wave of empathy toward this woman, so stubbornly and bravely fighting the depredations of age, lack of confidence, loneliness, and now grief. "We will sort everything out," he told her, meaning not just the death of her husband but also the unspoken accusations against her lover.

"The sooner the better," she said, attempting a smile and waving to him as she closed the door.

Blanc drove off without looking in the rearview mirror. But he was too impatient to drive straight back to the gendarmerie station. Instead he pulled to the side of the road and took out Fuligni's iPhone. The code was correct. He looked through the list of incoming calls, but none of the numbers meant anything to him. He would let Marius deal with them. Or Fabienne. That would be quicker. He checked the text messages: a meeting, apparently with his bank manager. An address, for the delivery of a wheelbarrow to a certain Luca. An order for a ten-foot-by-five-foot cast-iron fence. A few fairly obscene messages to a woman designated only as *ma chatte*, which Blanc was fairly certain did not refer to Madame Fuligni. The last text, sent on Thursday evening about 4:25 P.M., was a few lines to Marcel Lafont: *It's all going to come out. There'll be enough blood spilt to fill the harbor.*

Blanc sat there a while gazing out of the windshield. The mayor of Caillouteaux. The wind was still blowing just as strongly through the branches of the pine trees, making the treetops spin in an absurd ballet. Fuligni's old friend. The air was so clear it seemed as if every color—the gray of the asphalt, the brown of the ditches, the red of the poppies—all seemed to have been painted over with lacquer. Lafont, the man who at the time of Fuligni's death was also out on the Étang de Berre, out of sight on the opposite side of the lake, or so he said. A crow emerged from a battered oak tree, fluttered its wings in vain against the mistral, then retreated back into the branches.

Blanc turned the key in the ignition and set off slowly. He needed time to think about what to do next.

Back at the station he nodded to Fabienne Souillard. Weekends in Paris almost everybody was at their desks as normal. Down here he was on his own except for his young colleague and a solitary sleepy gendarme at the front desk. "I need to make a couple of calls," he said with a brief apologetic smile, "then I have a bit of a story to tell you."

He closed the door of his office and sat there staring at the landline. Who should he call first? The *juge d'instruction*, and then his boss. Ought he to mention Fuligni's last text message? He couldn't make up his mind. It was a lead. But he had had so much grief whenever he made accusations, the last thing he wanted now was to involve the mayor. He needed to find out more first. Discreetly.

He called the *juge d'instruction*'s number first. A man's voice answered. *Merde*, it was the weekend. He had the minister on the line. He gave his name and asked if he could speak to Madame Vialaron-Allègre.

"You're calling my wife at midday on a Saturday?" The nasal tone was indignant and sarcastic all at once.

"It's about a case we're investigating."

"You can tell me."

Blanc's mind whirred. The matter was confidential. Then

again, if he refused he would find himself posted to Lorraine. He gave the briefest possible summary of the two deaths and the architect who had disappeared and been picked up at a highway tollbooth.

"Sounds very confusing. Are you coping?" Vialaron-Allègre sounded as if he knew the answer but just didn't want to hear it.

Blanc could feel his pulse racing. Don't let him wind you up. "I need to discuss the next steps with *Madame le juge.* We put out a search warrant for Le Bruchec, brought him in for questioning, and let him go again. It wouldn't be a good idea if the first she heard of it was on Monday morning, possibly in the newspaper."

Silence on the other end of the line. "You're right," the minister finally admitted, although it was fairly obvious he would have preferred to say nothing of the sort. "My wife will be with you in a minute."

Blanc felt himself relax when the judge came on the line. Ridiculous. But he forced himself to keep calm and repeated the story of what had happened over the previous few hours.

"We don't have enough to arrest Monsieur le Bruchec," she said calmly.

"No."

"You were right to put out a search alert for him. But you were also right to let Lucien go again so quickly."

"I have other leads that I'm following."

"On the weekend?"

"I'm afraid so."

"Call me if you have anything new." A slight pause. "And thank you for keeping me up to date, even on a Saturday."

Blanc put the phone down and stared out of the window. Could have been worse, he thought. Much worse.

He was in a mild state of euphoria and therefore less cautious than he might have been as he dialed the second number. Nkoulou. Blanc had intended to give a brief military-style report and took a deep breath when the receiver was picked up, but then stopped without saying a word when he heard a woman's voice: "*Allo?*" It was a young woman's voice, with an accent Blanc didn't immediately recognize. The word was slurred slightly, as if whoever was speaking was drunk, on drugs, or had a disability. "Who is this?" the voice said, and then, "*Putain.* It's Saturday."

"Captain Blanc speaking. Is this the number for Commandant Nkoulou?" He sounded to himself like a complete idiot.

There was a noise on the line as if someone had tossed the receiver to one side. "Hey, Nicolas," in the distance. Crude. Blanc thought back to what his colleagues had said about Nkoulou's nonexistent private life and the bet he had been automatically included in since his first day in Gadet. Seems I might be on to a winner, he thought. But even so he found it hard to imagine any correlation between his punctilious boss and this impolite woman.

"Nkoulou." The voice was slightly breathless and shaky, as if there was a touch of anger or even fear in it.

For the third time that day Blanc related the story of Le Bruchec's disappearance and reappearance.

"You're calling me up to tell me this shit?!" Blanc held the receiver away from his ear. He had never imagined the boss capable of yelling like that. "The man defrosts his fridge and you send out a nationwide arrest warrant for him?"

"It wasn't an arrest warrant, it was—"

"Whatever the hell it was, it's of about as much interest to me as the contents of my small intestine! You had a respectable citizen stopped on the highway as if he were a bank robber on the run! You have him brought nearly two hundred miles in a patrol car at night and put him in an interrogation room, only to let him go five minutes later. *Pardon*, all a bit of a misunderstanding."

"Should I have not done anything when I discovered he had disappeared?"

"You didn't need to organize a military-style alert. There are other ways of doing things. What if Monsieur Le Bruchec lodges an official complaint against us?"

With Minister Vialaron-Allègre perhaps, Blanc thought. He was never going to understand the Midi. "I'll deal with it," he said, a sentence that meant everything and nothing. He was not keen on the idea of apologizing to Le Bruchec. He wasn't letting him off the hook quite yet.

"Don't spoil my weekend again, *mon Capitaine*, or I'll spoil every one of your weekends for the next twenty years." A clunk. Nkoulou had hung up. Blanc waited until the dial tone came back, then put down the receiver as if it were nitroglycerine. He wondered whether his boss's fit of rage was really to do with the steps he had taken in the investigation, or whether it was because he had accidentally spoken with a woman whose voice he should never have heard.

"You look like you've got a bad stomach," Fabienne said when he walked into her office.

"Are you on weekend shift?"

"Voluntary overtime, but I'm heading off on my Ducati in a moment."

"Leave your thunderbird where it is for five minutes." Blanc pulled out Fuligni's phone and showed his colleague the dead builder's last text message.

"Hmm, he was a better builder than writer: 'There'll be enough blood spilt to fill the harbor.' Think that's got anything to do with his row with Moréas about the mooring?"

"What is there that could come out regarding that? And why would he text Lafont about it?"

"We don't really know what he's talking about here. Or whether it has anything at all to do with his death. It might be irrelevant. Forget it."

"Have you ever received a text about the harbor flowing with blood? You don't think it's a bit of a coincidence that the man who sent it should be found dead a few hours later, in the harbor?"

"Does Nkoulou know about it?"

"The boss didn't want to be disturbed. He was with someone."

She gave him a dirty look. He raised his hands and in as few words as possible told her that the boss had given him the cold shoulder. "We'll add Fuligni's phone to the list of potential evidence, and list the text message in the files, but we don't need to tell anyone else for now."

"So when Nkoulou takes fire at you, I'll be in his sights too?"

"It's something of a consolation to know I won't be going to Lorraine on my own."

Souillard laughed. "Bet I can get to Metz faster on my Ducati than you can in that old mom van of yours," she said, grabbing her helmet. "See you Monday. Have fun with your secret files."

When he was finished in the office Blanc drove around the local countryside aimlessly for a bit in the Espace. Next to one of the minor roads stood the ruins of what must at one point have been a very grand farmhouse. Its yellow stone walls were covered with vines gone wild while the branches of an oak tree had grown around the blackened broken beam that had once held up the roof like the fingers of a man in a cell. Radio Nostalgie switched from an old Bee Gees hit to *"Joe le Taxi"* by Vanessa Paradis. Blanc reached for the switch and silenced her little girly voice. He wound down the window but the mistral was blowing so icy cold it made his ears hurt. He parked in the dark shadow of a cypress tree and stared up at the bright blue sky above him. Light. Wind. It was real painter's country. Van Gogh had gone out of his mind down here. But a cop? Blanc realized he couldn't stand facing an empty weekend.

He wouldn't sit down this evening with his kids making plans for a Sunday excursion. He wouldn't go out to eat with friends. He wouldn't pile into bed alongside his wife. *Merde.* He couldn't even settle down and watch some stupid movie, because he hadn't a television in his wreck of a house, and in any case reception here would be awful. House? Shack. It would fall down before long if he didn't do more than he had done up to now. A lot more. In any case that would be better than sitting in a battered minivan staring out of the window.

Blanc drove on until he came to a roundabout with a sign

to Salon. Within ten minutes he reached a suburb that was cut through by a major highway. A giant supermarket. Car dealerships on either side. And down a grimy dead-end street next to the highway: *Bernard Philibert—Matériaux et Bricolage*, a green and white building with pallets, stones, tiles, and bags of concrete next to its parking lot.

"*Voilà!*" he mumbled. "My weekend is saved."

Blanc parked outside the DIY store, grabbed a trolley, and pushed it down the aisles, piling stuff into it almost at random. An electric drill that looked as evil as a machine gun. A hammer you could kill a bull with. A saw the length of his arm. Wood varnish, or wood lacquer? He took a two-gallon can of each. Paint brushes of every size. Plastic sheeting. A dusty sack of mortar. Trowels. Blanc had never done up even a room in his entire life. The fat woman at the checkout, past her best years, chatting away knowledgeably to paint-covered workmen and wiry pensioner types as if she had built a dozen houses single-handedly (which she probably had) looked at his overflowing trolley the way a winner of the Tour de France might look at the superlight bike of a weekend cyclist. "You're sure you haven't forgotten anything, Monsieur?"

Just for the hell of it he lifted down a measuring rod from a shelf next to the cashier and put it on top. He paid with a check from his Paris bank. He would need to change branches. But he would have to do that during the week. *Merde.*

When he got back to Sainte-Françoise-la-Vallée, he piled up all his booty in the kitchen. Should he deal with the floor first? Or clean and paint the walls? The ceiling? What did you do with a wooden ceiling? Or should he tackle the window frames? Take a look at the electricity wiring? He felt exhausted already, worn out, discouraged. He was going to end up facing an empty weekend all the same.

Then he heard a car engine. He went out of the house and blinked. Bruno Micheletti's old blue Peugeot 504 rolled up to the house. He rolled down the window and called out, "Hey, neighbor, do you fancy having dinner with us the day after tomorrow?"

Blanc felt like it was his birthday. "What would you like me to bring?"

"Anything but wine," Micheletti said with a laugh, and roared off.

Later that evening Blanc lay in bed thinking. Mayor Lafont. Fuligni's old friend. Not far away the morning he died. What could that text message have meant? Was it a warning? A threat? That reference to the harbor overflowing with blood. Was it just some unfortunate metaphor? Or had he really been talking about the harbor at Saint-César? But it wasn't part of Lafont's *commune*. And was any of that in any way helpful in the Moréas murder? No. And that was the more important investigation. Nkoulou had him in his sights. If he messed up the Michelettis wouldn't have the chance to invite their new neighbor over again.

The next morning he was woken out of a deep sleep by his cell phone. It was Sunday but he had forgotten to turn off the alarm app. He tapped around on the touch screen until he turned it off. But in so doing he noticed he'd received a text yesterday, while he was running around like a maniac in the DIY shop. It was from Fabienne: *Sorry to disturb you. Was fidgety yesterday and went through the old files. Found the name of the tourist who was killed. We need to speak. Talk tomorrow?*

A Dead Tourist, and a Red Car

The Espace wouldn't start. Blanc lifted the hood and stared at the maze of metal, cables, and wires. He had bought enough tools to build a city the previous day, but nothing of any use in this morass, not that he had the slightest clue where to start. Then he heard a loud engine on the main road and thanked God for it. He ran out onto the *route départementale* swinging his grotesque hammer and gesticulating wildly at the old blue Alpine, which screeched to a halt just inches from his shins.

"Have you gone over to the dark side?" Jean-François Riou spluttered. "From cop to hammer murderer? Or are you trying to kill yourself? In which case you'd do better throwing yourself under a train than this vintage motor."

Blanc smelled the hot oil and gas fumes coming from the old sports car. "I was just trying to imitate your miracle from the other day."

"You're trying to fix a Renault Espace?" Riou laughed, as if it were the best joke he'd ever heard.

While his neighbor fiddled around in the entrails of the

minivan, Blanc found himself gazing enviously at the Alpine, with a certain embarrassment. "You have an extravagant hobby," he said.

Riou looked up, nodded, and smiled, also embarrassed. "Every Sunday morning I take the old girl out for a spin. At least that way I'm out of my wife's hair while she's cooking."

"An hour driving around, another hour tinkering."

"Not at all!" His neighbor was horrified at the idea. "These old motors are a lot more reliable than the modern computers on wheels. And cheap too. Or at least cheaper than most of what you see around here."

Blanc was about to respond with some meaningless pleasantry, when he thought of Le Bruchec's Range Rover and Lafont's Audi Q7. "You mean this Alpine is cheaper than all these giant SUVs?"

"*Bien sûr.* Throw in a few extras and those four-by-fours cost easily a hundred thousand euros. And then you need a small car too. One of those monsters would never get into one of the multistory car parks in Marseille or Aix-en-Provence. You need to have a boss who pays you a packet to buy one of those. Or a hand in the Marseille cocaine business."

Blanc didn't reply, just concentrated on staring over Riou's shoulder to try to see which screws he was turning. "Right, done. Until the next time." Riou wiped his hands and banged the hood down. Thirty seconds later he was gone, leaving just tracks on the gravel and a hint of gas in the air.

"He frightens my poor horses every time he does that." Paulette Aybalen was reining in her nervously snorting steed, before having it trot up to Blanc's house. Behind her, by the edge of the road, her daughters sat on two other dancing animals. Like a troop of amazons come into the twenty-first century through some gate in time from antiquity, Blanc thought.

"Going jogging in the woods again today?"

"I'm going to work, actually."

"You're not wearing a uniform."

"I have to put in a few unforeseen hours of overtime." He was still thinking over Riou's comments about expensive 4×4s. Paulette knew all the gossip in town; after all she had been the first to tell him about the relationship between Miette Fuligni and Lucien Le Bruchec. "May I ask you a question?"

"Professional or personal?"

"Professional."

For a second a shadow of disappointment flitted across her face, then she shook her head as if surprised at herself and turned to her daughters. "Ride on, I'll catch you up."

The elder girl laughed, "You're too slow for us, *maman*."

"Then wait for me at the top of the hill next to the burnt pine tree." The girls galloped off.

Paulette Aybalen jumped down from her saddle and gave Blanc a questioning look. "You're a hunter," she said. "A bloodhound. There's something bugging you. That's why you're working even on a Sunday. Were you sent down here from Paris to deal with some particularly serious case?"

"I was sent down here from Paris because I had already dealt with a particularly serious case there. They didn't want it to happen again."

She said nothing for a minute, then smiled. "So what is your question, *mon Capitaine*?"

"How does Monsieur Lafont earn his money?"

Paulette Aybalen stared at him blankly for several seconds, maybe because she was taken aback or even shocked, he couldn't say. "You're not out to slaughter the biggest bull in the meadow, are you? No wonder they moved you away from the capital."

"I'm not out to slaughter anybody. I simply asked a question."

"People around here either talk quietly and respectfully about Marcel Lafont, or else not at all. Not at all is usually best."

"Sounds as if he's some godfather figure."

"He's been mayor as long as I can remember. He's made something of Caillouteaux. The place could have gone to seed. Just look at Berre. That used to be a wonderful town on the lake. Nowadays nobody would have named the lake after a town like that. It would be too embarrassing. Berre today is dominated by oil tankers and the refinery, with flames leaping from the chimney all through the night, and the air stinks of petroleum fumes so much it would make you sick. It could have been the same here. Lafont found a better solution."

"So everybody is pleased with him?"

"He keeps getting reelected."

"Maybe not forever."

Paulette Aybalen took a step closer to him. He could smell her perfume. She lowered her voice. "Compared with Lafont, this FN cow is the conductor of a children's choir. Our beloved mayor had a pretty wild youth, if you believe the rumors."

"In Corsica? Marseille?"

"Nobody knows exactly. But they're not mutually exclusive. He may still have old friends in both Corsica and Marseille."

"Friends who would not be at all happy if I started treading on Monsieur Lafont's toes?"

"I've got used to having you about. It would be a pity if you were to suddenly vanish one day," Paulette Aybalen replied. She said it without a smile, and shook his hand in farewell, very coolly. Then she leapt back into the saddle of her Camargue horse. "Don't put in too many overtime hours, *mon Capitaine*. That's not how we do things down here in the Midi." She dug her heels into the horse's flanks, and rode off.

Blanc watched her go, trying to concentrate on her words. But what he was really concentrating on was Paulette Aybalen's agile body springing back up onto her horse. He wouldn't have got to know a woman like that in Paris.

On the short journey into town, Blanc called Marius. Only to get the beep of his answering machine. He left a message, apologizing and asking his colleague to come into the office. He could only hope that at some stage over the course of the day Tonon would check his messages. When he got to the gendarmerie the officer on duty avoided looking him in the eye. There was a palpable silence in the building, almost a physical tension in the air—like a haunted crypt. All the office doors on the second floor were closed, except for that of the office Madame Vialaron-Allègre had taken over. He found himself pleased to see that the *juge d'instruction* had unexpectedly turned up at the office on a weekend, and stuck his head in her door.

"You're more curious than is good for you, *mon Capitaine*." It was her husband, the minister.

Blanc could have kicked himself.

"I was expecting to see *Madame le juge* sitting here," he replied lamely.

"My wife is pruning the roses in our garden. She likes cutting the heads off pretty flowers."

Not quite certain how to interpret that, Blanc just looked at him silently.

"Sit down, won't you, now that you're here." Blanc sat down, feeling as if he were in an interrogation room, on the wrong side of the table. "You paid a visit to our friend Marcel the other night. He was not exactly overjoyed to see you."

"Mayor Lafont?" Blanc was alarmed. This was going in the wrong direction.

"He's more or less part of our family. And we're in the same political party." Vialaron-Allègre watched to see what effects his words had: He looked less than happy. "There are elections coming up soon. Marcel is a bit worried. For no good reason, if you ask me, but then Marcel is a cautious man, always fears the worst. I do my best to stop the worst happening. That's the least one can do for a friend—in a situation like this."

"Monsieur Lafont should consider himself lucky to have such a good friend."

The minister blinked for a second then gave him a cool smile. "You must know that construction of a *médiathèque* would greatly help Marcel's election chances."

"The mayor left me in no doubt."

"*Bon*. Now, through a tragic accident, the very man who was supposed to build this *médiathèque* is no longer available. Marcel is going to have to find somebody else as soon as possible. In the middle of the summer, and at the beginning of an election campaign. On top of all his other day-to-day duties."

"*Monsieur le maire* does not take any vacation time?"

"In a situation like this? You're not a politician, *mon Capitaine*." The minister cleared his throat. "Whatever. In a delicate situation like this I just don't want to see Marcel having to waste time and energy on unnecessary police investigations."

"Our investigations are never unnecessary."

"To be more precise, I don't want Marcel troubled. Do we have an understanding, *mon Capitaine*?"

"Absolutely, Monsieur Vialaron-Allègre." Blanc was glad to be able to get up and go. He wondered if *Madame le juge* was aware that her own husband was hindering police investigations.

He had only been at the desk in his own office for five minutes when the door opened and Tonon came in. He was wearing an Olympique de Marseille soccer shirt, its bright blue colors reduced to a sort of turquoise shade by too much sunshine and too many washes, khaki-colored three-quarter-length pants with baggy pockets, and a pair of fraying boating shoes. He looked as if he'd been sleeping in the outfit. "I hope you've got a good reason to call me in like this on a Sunday," he grumbled. In his right hand he held a bag of freshly baked croissants, the paper dark with leaked butter. He didn't offer Blanc one.

"We'll have to see if it was a good enough reason," the captain admitted. He closed the office door, which Tonon had left open. "We've got a visitor, the minister."

"*Putain.* That's a reason not to be here."

"Vialaron-Allègre would like us to leave Lafont in peace. I'd rather haul the mayor in."

"I should never have listened to the fucking answering machine."

"Lafont stinks of dirty money."

"That's how all the politicians down here smell. You're not

leading a corruption investigation. It's a murder case. Or maybe double murder, if somebody hit Fuligni over the head."

"That's just the point. His last text message was to Lafont: 'It's all going to come out. There'll be enough blood spilt to fill the harbor.'"

Marius thought for a moment. "A message from a man who's better with a trowel than words."

"The threat of a man under pressure. Or at the very least a drastic warning. Something had to make Fuligni nervous enough to send Lafont a text like that. What was going to come out? Was Fuligni threatening to expose something? Or was he afraid of something being exposed? A few hours after sending this message to the mayor he's found dead in the lake. And our mayor's out in his motorboat not far away."

"Okay, call Lafont in, if you want, best of all today, while the minister's still here. That'll be the biggest storm ever to hit Gadet, and at the end of it you and I will be clouds of ash drifting over the Touloubre."

"That's why I disturbed your Sunday. The way we did it in Paris was, as soon as you've found a big spider lurking at the heart of the web, you have to immediately talk it over with your colleagues. You need to be careful."

"That's how you became such a big success?"

Blanc ignored the sarcasm. "We need to keep on Lafont's tail," he said conspiratorially. "But he mustn't know. Nobody must know. At least not yet. We dig quietly in the dark until we come across the pot of gold."

"In Lafont's case you're more likely to come across a crock of shit."

"What is it that links Lafont and Fuligni? What's their secret?"

"The *médiathèque*. The pair have between them built half of Caillouteaux. The new project is the biggest contract Lafont could ever have handed to his friend."

"Agreed, but it's a public contract. Anyone who's interested can have access to all the details of the deal: an eight-million-euro deal for Fuligni. For Lafont a prestige project sure to get him reelected. Maybe the budget is a bit too high, maybe the timing a bit too convenient, but it's all legal. Nothing to cause one of them to send a sinister text to the other."

"Eh bien?"

"So there has to be something else going on between them. Maybe it really is something that concerns the harbor. After all, both of them had boats down there. Or maybe it's some other building project? Maybe it was the town hall renovation, when Lafont got his hands on all the antiques? Or maybe an affair? Fuligni wasn't one to miss out on a good thing. And his wife isn't exactly a prude. Maybe it wasn't just a Romanian secretary and a widowed architect in this little love circle. Maybe the mayor too? Or the mayor's wife?"

Tonon gave him a sympathetic look. He bashed a few keys on his keyboard with his big paws and said, *"Voilà.* Carole Lafont."

Blanc looked at the screen and saw an old story from the Internet edition of *La Provence.* A photo of the mayor's wife with some smiling children and two nervous-looking female teachers. Madame Lafont was a matronly woman in her midfifties with gray hair piled on top of her head, heavy jowls, and a huge bosom.

"Not exactly Fuligni's type, to put it mildly," Tonon muttered.

"Certainly not a lady you'd want to quarrel with," Blanc replied, trying to keep his end of the story up. "Maybe Fuligni's Romanian secretary was servicing the mayor as well. Fuligni wouldn't have objected, for fear of losing his contracts. But eventually he decides he's had enough. He threatens to tell Madame Lafont, at which point, in order to avoid a scandal, the mayor nips down to his yacht at the harbor and—"

"Maybe you should start writing TV soaps. Fuligni was far too proud to share his young chicken with anybody else. And Lafont might have made a lot of mistakes, but not even his most bitter political rivals over the last thirty years have suggested he's run around after other women."

But Blanc was still looking at the photo. There was something alarming about it, but he couldn't work out what it was. Carole Lafont? An opulent lady in a gray suit with a light red scarf and a friendly smile. The children and the two intimidated teachers. He took a close look at each and every face. Never seen any of them before. What was there of note about the school building itself? The wall was plastered yellow with a bronze plaque on it, which he couldn't make out in the photo. An open wrought-iron door, and in the background a parking lot with a battered Peugeot 106, a red Mini, and a white delivery van. The leafy branch of a tree, almost certainly a plane tree, protruding into the frame from the right. A patch of bright blue sky. Blanc zoomed in on the photo until nothing but pixels could be seen. He still couldn't read the bronze plaque. He looked at all the faces, the hands, even their shoes. Harmless, normal, completely inconspicuous. He shook his shoulders resignedly and closed the photo.

"Does the boss know what you're up to?" Tonon asked. He'd been observing Blanc all the time, while finishing off his second croissant.

"I spoke to Nkoulou on the phone. He seemed preoccupied. Probably best not to bother him."

"At least we agree on that point."

They heard the roar of an engine outside, someone cranking up the revs. Then it stopped dead. Blanc went over to the window. A motorbike had just pulled up before the gendarmerie: a fire red gas tank, tiny handlebars, vintage wheels. Two figures in black leather suits with integrated helmets, dark visors; they looked like storm troopers. The driver took the protective headwear off and shook her long brown hair in the wind. Fabienne. A tall, slender woman who had been sitting behind her on the pillion also took off her helmet, to reveal short-cropped blond hair. "That's how I imagine a lesbian," said Marius, who had joined his colleague to look out.

Fabienne joined them a few minutes later. "Roxane Chelle," she introduced her girlfriend. She had eyes the color of a swimming pool and a jaw like Rodin's *The Thinker*. Instead of greeting the two men with a kiss on the cheeks like Fabienne did, she shook their hands with a grip that made Blanc think Marius might have known what he was talking about.

"Let's go to the computer in my room," said Fabienne. "It's a lot quicker than those old tin boxes you have." She told Tonon, who was following them along the hallway in a state of some puzzlement, that she had been looking through all the material online relating to the car robberies that Moréas had been involved in.

Marius went white. "What do you think you're doing? You

think you can get any further with this damn thing just by doing a bit of surfing on the Internet before heading out to a nightclub?"

"You did everything you could," Blanc interrupted to calm him down. "But sometimes a fresh look from an outsider can spot new connections."

"That sounds more like psychiatry than detective work."

"Deflate your egos, boys," Fabienne said in a conciliatory tone of voice. Her girlfriend gave a sarcastic smile that seemed to shut Tonon up.

"Take a look at this," their colleague said, nodding toward her screen. "The tourist who was run over and killed was German; Claudia Meier. That was in the old newspaper clippings too. I was rather naïve at first and tried Googling her, but it would seem half the women on the other bank of the Rhine have that name."

"Not that it matters," Tonon grumbled. "She died back when the Internet hardly existed."

"Yes, but the Net has sucked up the past. When I realized I had a million women with the name Claudia Meier, I took a long shot and tried adding 'Lukas Rheinbach' in the search field. They're both German, right? And the painter was asking questions about the accident, wasn't he? *Voilà.* All of a sudden a lot fewer hits, and most of them rubbish. But you also end up here: on a site where you can look up old school friends. They host old school class photos. Like this one." She zoomed in on one photo. "This is the final-year photo taken at a school outside Cologne."

Blanc found himself looking at around a hundred men and women dressed in a fashion he dimly remembered lined up outside a grim-looking concrete building. It only took him a few minutes to recognize the German painter, aged about twenty. Below the photo was a list of names, among them "Claudia Meier," eighth from left. Blanc counted along the row: a pretty girl with long, dark blond hair, beaming into the camera. Next to her stood Lukas Rheinbach, his arm around her shoulder.

"Putain," Tonon swore.

"We need to go through the files from the investigation into the highway robberies thoroughly again," Blanc mumbled, all of a sudden feeling uneasy.

"They're over here," his colleague said, pointing to a filing cabinet in the corner. "I always keep them within easy reach."

Within seconds they were leafing through yellowed pages of old reports, from police and pathologists, from the days when they were all done on typewriters; black-and-white photos; fingerprint cards; sketches of the crime scenes; pictures of the victim; a copy of her passport; photographs of the crime scene; documentation from the autopsy in the Salon hospital. A series of documents that in nightmare fashion detailed the transformation of a beautiful woman into a heap of flesh and bones. Blanc took the copy of the passport and held it up next to the computer screen, not that it was really necessary: The victim was identical to the girl with Lukas Rheinbach's arm around her shoulder.

The captain worked his way further through the files. Lukas Rheinbach had also been in the car when it was attacked, an old Citroën 2CV with a German number plate. The files contained a copy of his passport too, as well as details of his address and occupation ("art student"), their last address in France: a hotel in Bonnieux where he and Claudia Meier had taken a room together. Rheinbach had been named as a witness, after which his name no longer featured in the files.

"You owe me an explanation, Marius," Blanc said when he had finished. "You've allegedly been after Charles Moréas for murder for some twenty years. But when we find ourselves talking to the boyfriend of the victim, you don't mention it. To be honest, you gave me the impression you had never even seen Monsieur Rheinbach before, never even heard the name."

"I wasn't present when they took witness statements. It didn't seem to matter; he was just a foreign tourist. I knew who the guilty party was. I just wanted to nail Moréas. *Mon Dieu.* I'd seen the dead girl's body lying on the road!" Tonon didn't look him in the eye, just glanced around the room.

"Your name doesn't even appear in the files. You weren't involved in the investigation," Blanc stated. His tone was friendly enough but nobody in the room, not even Souillard's girlfriend, who wasn't even in the police, could mistake the change in attitude: This had become an interrogation.

Tonon covered his eyes with his big paw. *"Putain,"* he swore softly. "Is this thing never going to let me go?" He took a deep breath and finally turned to look at Blanc. "I'd been suspended from duty by then," he admitted wearily. "On that very night I was sent to the crime scene. Somebody had called the police from a farmhouse. I think it was a long-distance truck driver passing by. I raced down there with a couple of men and came across the body first, then the robber's wrecked car. Most of them had already run off, but a couple were still there. They were in shock but they fought back. It was dark. Nobody knew exactly what had happened. Had it been an accident? An attack? My men and I approached the car. Suddenly somebody

fired a gun. Well"—he hesitated, searching for the right words—
"we returned fire. Or I should say, *I* returned fire. I'd already
had a couple of glasses of rosé. I nearly shot one of my colleagues. No, I actually did shoot one of my colleagues. It was
only a grazing shot, luckily. By then the others had overpowered
the guys and secured the crime scene. The usual stuff. I was
taken away and, overnight, suspended from duty. It was a few
weeks before I was allowed back into the gendarmerie, by which
time people had glossed over it all. There was no official investigation into my behavior. But it was made clear that for the rest
of my life I would remain a lieutenant in this station and only
be given cases where I could do the minimum damage. But as
none of my colleagues were still bothering with the robbers
and nobody was getting anywhere with the case, I grabbed hold
of the files, if only to stop them moldering away. I didn't really
read through them, because I knew it had been Moréas, and I
just went after him. Everybody else just let me get on with it,
happy not to have anything to do with me. *Voilà.* Now at least I
had a hobby to keep me busy."

"And for all these years you never bothered with Monsieur
Rheinbach?"

"It didn't seem important." Tonon scratched his head.
"Moréas was the perpetrator, right? But the original investigation had failed to nail him, right? So I looked for a different way
to go about it. I wanted to get him for another crime. Any crime.
Putain. The guy must have been guilty of a dozen things. Sooner
or later, I hoped, I would be able to pin something on him, no
matter what it was. Then, when I had got my hands on him, I
would have been able to bring the old case up in front of the
judge as well. I had been watching the guy for years, paying

attention to every detail I could find about him: his shit tattoo, the medallion with the cobra, the shack in the woods, his threats against harmless walkers, even the ridiculous charge of speeding on his motorbike. I just wanted to get the asshole for something."

"But . . ."

"Leave it, Roger," Fabienne interrupted him gently. "It doesn't do any of us any good crying over spilt milk. What matters is we now have a lead in the case we're dealing with. That is all that matters. Don't torture Marius."

For several long moments Blanc stared at the black-and-white photos of Claudia Meier, then nodded. "Okay, so, Monsieur Rheinbach."

"So, do we just bring him in?" asked Fabienne. He could hear the disappointment in her voice at the prospect of interrogating the painter—the ideal culprit, the foreigner nobody cared about.

"You and your friend here can take to the road again," Blanc replied. "We won't bring anybody in this weekend." He nodded toward the door. "Not while we still have a guest from Paris with us."

"Vialaron-Allègre won't be interested in who we're interviewing," she replied.

"There's nothing he's not interested in. The gendarmerie is so quiet he'd be bound to notice if we bring in Monsieur Rheinbach. He'd get involved, want to know who we're interviewing and why. The minister wants to do his friend and fellow party member a favor. If we bring in a German painter as a suspect, he'll insist we arrest and charge him. As far as the mayor is concerned that would be the Kalashnikov murder solved and his

FN rival would have one less string to her bow. And we would no longer be breathing down his neck. As long as the minister was happy, Nkoulou would be happy. That would be the case done and dusted. Except that it wouldn't be."

"If that slimy bastard gets involved in the Moréas murder then he'd also be likely to find out how I botched up," Tonon added glumly. "My career's been gathering cobwebs for long enough but at least they still leave me here in the Midi. Let the minister root around in that old *connerie* and he'd probably post me somewhere else, if only to do Nkoulou a favor."

"So let's all go home and wait until the minister has gone back to Paris. We'll talk again on Monday," Blanc concluded.

Blanc spent the rest of Sunday dragging the remaining furniture out of the ground floor of his house, and then tackling the walls. He scratched and scraped patches of old wallpaper and oil paint from the walls until they were stripped bare, down to rough, crumbly stone: yellow, white, gray, the cracks between them filled with ochre mortar. Half of his expensive new tools were either too large or too small, the other half unusable, and he hadn't bought most of the materials he actually needed. But eventually he was finished, dripping with sweat and his shoulders aching. It's looking good, he told himself. It was the first actual thought he had formulated in hours: He had been running on automatic, totally engrossed in the work—a fusion of hard graft and Zen.

It was only when he had showered, pulled on a pair of shorts, and squatted down behind a wall to protect him from the mistral to watch the swallows, with a glass of rosé in his hand, that he finally allowed himself to think over the events of the morning. Monsieur Rheinbach. He found himself somehow annoyed by the idea of arresting the German painter. Yet so much of it fitted: Rheinbach was unlucky with women, this Claudia Meier might not have been just a youthful fling but the love of his life. The character with her death on his conscience lived just around the corner, scot-free and acting like a bully. Could Rheinbach have known all along that Moréas was a suspect in her death? His name had never been mentioned in the paper, but Rheinbach had been there at the time, had been a witness, might even have seen something incriminating on that fateful evening. Had he been looking for something on the attack when he was at *La Provence*'s editorial offices? And why had he spent so much time in the Caillouteaux records office? He had to have known who Moréas was.

Then he remembered the words of the farmer who had been down at the garbage dump at noon on the day of the murder—he had mentioned that there had been a little red car parked nearby. Rheinbach drove a wine-colored Clio.

"You are going to have some explaining to do, Monsieur Artist," Blanc mumbled to himself. "Or you're going to be painting jigsaw puzzles from memory for the next few years."

And still . . .

Le Bruchec. Lafont. Fuligni's text message. Fuligni's unexplained death. Did all that really have nothing to do with the case? It wasn't just the mistral that was disturbing his train of thought. Blanc felt sure he had overlooked some decisive factor. He wished there was someone he could discuss it with. In the past he would occasionally have talked over his investigation with Geneviève if he got stuck on a case. He wasn't supposed to but what did it matter really? She never said much. To tell the truth he now suspected that all those years she had never really listened to a word he said. But it had been good to talk about it. It helped him to get his thoughts in order, made him feel as if he had dealt with it on an intellectual level, and more often than not he would stumble across a new lead.

But now? Should he call Fabienne? He liked her and she was bright. But she was very young, and had a thirst for life. At the weekend she had the right to enjoy herself and not have to sit listening to the musings of a colleague who'd been transferred here against his will. Marius? He had his own demons to battle, problems enough without Blanc's doubts and questions. And apart from anything else Blanc couldn't quite bring himself to ignore the nasty little voice whispering away in his head: What if it was Tonon himself? A cop who, after twenty years of frustrating investigation in vain, had just grabbed a Kalashnikov and taken out the guy who had ruined his career? A cop whose fuse had simply blown? Tonon's car was white, not red. Nobody had spotted him down by the dump. There were no other leads pointing to him, and there was certainly nothing to link him to Fuligni's death. But even so . . .

Blanc despised himself for even thinking of his colleague as a possible suspect, but there was no way he could bring himself to say he could trust Marius one hundred percent.

He didn't go to bed until the wine bottle was empty. He didn't feel drunk, just tired and defeated. Then all of a sudden he thought of someone he would be happy to discuss the case with: the *juge d'instruction*. Madame Vialaron-Allègre would have heard him out, would have understood him; with her sharp intellect she would have helped him get his thoughts in order. He could hear her voice, see her face. As a result Blanc fell asleep thinking about the very woman he wasn't sure was going to help him or end up being a threat to him.

An Artist Without an Alibi

The mistral was still rattling his shutters on Monday morning. Blanc had been so exhausted the night before that he had only brought in the essential pieces of furniture. In the meantime the wind had blown over two chairs, and an old tablecloth now hung like a ragged sail in a plane tree on the other side of the Touloubre. He shrugged. He would buy a new one at the market. Eventually.

After three days of the mistral, almost everybody at the station was exhausted from lack of sleep and as bad-humored as if Olympique de Marseille had lost a home game against Paris. But at least the minister had vanished. His wife was at work in her office. Blanc would have liked to tell her what he had found out on Sunday, but she had the phone to her ear when he knocked on her door and went in. She scribbled something on a piece of paper and passed it across her desk to him, while still on the phone. *Urgent meeting in Aix. Will have time this afternoon.* Her handwriting was large and extravagant, with large curving loops like some Renaissance letter. Blanc was disappointed but nodded and closed the door carefully behind him, taking the piece of paper with him.

Nkoulou was working next door, as cool and correct as ever. The commandant raised a hand to his forehead as Blanc passed, but said nothing. It was as if the phone call on the weekend, with his furious outburst and the woman with the vulgar voice, had never taken place. Blanc was relieved but remained on his guard. A few minutes later Fabienne Souillard arrived. She was wearing a freshly starched uniform that made her look ten years older and six inches taller. Blanc glanced briefly at the gun in her holster then looked away. I hope she doesn't lose her nerve, he thought. They had to wait another half hour before Tonon turned up. When he eventually arrived, he looked dreadful. The veins in his eyeballs had burst into a red net on the whites. He was unshaven and his uniform was as crumpled as his face. As ever, his holster was empty.

"Let's go visit the painter," Blanc said, reaching for the car keys.

Nkoulou glanced at them through the open door, but still didn't say a word.

"I thought you might be back," Rheinbach said wearily, opening the door to them.

Blanc was relieved that the man wasn't being difficult. He produced the copy Fabienne had made of the old school photo. "I'd like you to tell us something about your younger days," he said.

"It's not exactly a story with a happy ending." The artist led them into the house and asked them to sit down. He looked anxious and relieved simultaneously at being asked to tell the story. "My parents used to take us camping down to Saintes-Maries-de-la-Mer every summer. That's something that stays with you for life. I have always loved the South of France, even before I knew I was going to be a painter. And long before I met Claudia. It was a high school romance. After graduation, we went on to university together. That summer we took my old 2CV down to Provence to go painting. I think you know how that vacation ended." He turned and looked out the window.

"Did you know who was responsible?" Fabienne asked him.

Rheinbach shook his head. "The men were wearing masks. I gave a witness statement. Then my parents came to collect me and we dealt with the rest of the formalities."

"Formalities?"

"For bringing the body back to Germany."

They all sat in silence for a few minutes. Then Blanc cleared his throat and said, "I'm amazed you came back to Provence after something like that."

The painter gave them a weary smile. "My friends said that too at the time. I didn't come back here for years. I finished my studies, got married, began to work as a freelance painter, and tried to forget the whole episode. But my marriage fell apart, and my career followed suit. So at some stage I came back here, where I could at least make a living as a second-rate contract painter. Better than driving a taxi around Cologne."

"And you want us to believe that it was purely by chance you ended up living next door to Charles Moréas?"

Rheinbach held up his hands. "I don't want to make you believe anything. I bought this old place because it was the only thing cheap enough for me to afford. After a while I realized that my neighbor wasn't exactly the kind of person you'd invite round for supper, but his name meant nothing to me. It remained like that for years, until my other neighbor dropped by. The architect."

"Le Bruchec came to see you?"

"We'd bumped into each other from time to time and said hello. But we moved in different circles, if you know what I mean. He earns in one hour as much as I make in a month. That's why I was so surprised when he dropped by just a few weeks ago."

"After the death of his wife?"

"Yes. He was worried that our mutual neighbor could break into his house. He said he'd seen him hanging around the house and asked me if I could keep an eye on it for him. He suggested we might both complain about him to the gendarmerie. I didn't want to get involved in anything and made an excuse. But then Le Bruchec said he wanted to see 'this highway robber Moréas locked up.' The juxtaposition of 'highway robber' and 'Moréas' suddenly rang a bell with me, although I couldn't think why. It was possible I had heard the name 'Moréas' when I was giving my statement twenty years ago and had since forgotten. Then the architect began to tell me all the old stories about Moréas, the rumors that he had been involved in robbing cars. I suddenly felt sick with fear and had to ask Le Bruchec, as politely as possible, to leave the house. After that he never mentioned Moréas to me again. But I began to make my own inquiries."

"In the town hall archives. And at the editorial offices of *La Provence*."

"I can hardly say any of them were particularly chatty. But I picked up a few things. Enough to put two and two together."

"You found the missing pieces of the jigsaw."

Rheinbach made a face. "At some stage I found myself sitting here, in this chair, realizing that by some horrible turn of fate I was living just a few hundred yards away from Claudia's killer, who was free as a bird. He didn't even bother to keep a low profile, didn't even have a bad conscience. He ran around the place getting in people's hair and acting the tough guy. Maybe he had even completely forgotten Claudia's death. Whereas I certainly hadn't forgotten."

"And so you killed him."

The painter inhaled sharply as if he had been punched in the stomach. "There were moments when I would have loved to. But it wasn't me."

"Where were you on Sunday, the thirtieth of June?"

Rheinbach shook his head resignedly. "I think you might be able to work that out. I wanted to confront Moréas once and for all. I wanted to confront him with what he had done. I wanted him to confess to my face that he had killed Claudia." He gave a bitter laugh. "How naïve was that? It just so happened that as I was driving along, I spotted him roaring down the road between our two properties on his motorbike. I did a U-turn and followed him, just like in the movies. Except that Moréas was on a rusty, battered motorbike and I was in an aging Clio. Not exactly Steve McQueen stuff. It ended by the garbage dump next to the main highway. I parked in the main lot near the entrance. Moréas had driven straight over to one of the Dumpsters. He had no idea I had followed him. I sat there behind the steering wheel for an hour wondering what to do. It was absurd, me and that guy hanging around in a garbage dump in the heat of the day. What was I going to do? I was just about to give up and drive home when along came Le Bruchec in his big four-by-four with a trailer full of trash. He and Moréas started talking to each other. I couldn't make out what they were saying but it certainly wasn't very amicable. It was like watching some bizarre play."

"Did they argue long?"

"Maybe a few minutes. I can't be certain. Then Le Bruchec emptied his trash and drove off."

"Did either of them notice you?"

"I don't think so."

"And then?"

"Then I finally picked up my courage, got out, and walked straight over to Moréas." Rheinbach closed his eyes. Blanc realized he was too ashamed to look any of them in the eye. "The guy gave me a dirty look," he continued at a whisper. "He knew who I was. Had known all these years that I had been the one he and his gang had dragged out of the car along with Claudia. And he could tell by looking at me that I knew it too now. And he just laughed." He took a deep breath. "I wanted to talk to him, to look him in the eye, to appeal to his conscience. To shatter him morally, can you understand that? I thought he would cringe, be ashamed, deny everything. I was an idiot. He had no sense of shame at all. He just laughed at me."

"Moréas was sick in the head," Tonon said sympathetically. "He would have enjoyed that."

The painter gave an agonized smile. "I couldn't get a word out. I just stood there in front of this guy, staring at him. And he stared back, until eventually I blinked first and looked away. I turned around to head back to my car. I felt more miserable than I ever had before, even on that night twenty years ago. And then I was overcome by a wave of anger. I didn't think twice." He paused.

At that moment Blanc was certain that Monsieur Rheinbach wasn't his murderer. The sad man sitting in front of him was telling the truth. There was no way he would have lifted an automatic weapon and emptied the entire magazine, let alone set fire to the body afterward. "What happened next?" he asked wearily.

"I was insane with rage," Rheinbach admitted. "I bent to the ground, picked up the first stone I found, and hurled it at Moréas."

"Did you hit him?"

"Yes. I don't think he had believed I would do anything."

"On the head? Did it knock him out?"

"No, no. It only hit him on the hip, I think. He cried out and swore, but he must have been in pain, since he didn't charge at me. He swayed and then fell over."

Blanc remembered what Dr. Thezan had said: the old motorbike accident, that Moréas had an artificial hip joint. The stone must have hurt him really badly. "You couldn't have hit him in a better spot," he murmured.

"I suspect him stumbling saved my life. Moréas was absolutely furious and threatened me all the time he lay there on the ground. But he was too badly hurt to come after me. I ran to the car and drove off. All night long I hid in the house waiting for Moréas to burst in at any minute like some raving monster. The next day I decided there was no point in hanging around until he got me. I packed up my easel and a few paints, with the intention of heading off for a few days, somewhere he wouldn't find me. And then you turned up . . ."

Blanc stared out of the window at the perfect blue sky. They would take the painter with them down to the gendarmerie station and get him to make a statement. Nkoulou would read it and then have the man detained in custody. What the German had just told them could easily be taken as a partial confession. All that remained to be done was to drag the rest of the story out of him. The boss wouldn't permit them to allow Rheinbach to return home. Not as long as there were politicians putting pressure on him. If the commandant held him as a suspect, neither the mayor nor the minister would have anything to complain about. "Monsieur Rheinbach," he said, with resignation in his voice, "we must ask you to come with us."

A few hours later, after all the formalities had been completed, they had a foreign jigsaw puzzle painter in the sole cell in the Gadet gendarmerie station, normally used for drunks to sleep off their hangovers or to hold a thief caught in the act until he could be sent to Aix-en-Provence or Marseille. If Rheinbach was to be caught up in the wheels of justice, then soon he would be gone. Blanc might well never see him again, but he would have solved his first case in the Midi, and Monsieur Vialaron-Allègre would have no excuse for any more plots against him. But instead of closing the files and heading off to have lunch with Fabienne and Marius in the shade of the plane trees, he busied himself in his office until nearly everybody else was out at the restaurant. Then he went to the office next door, to see *Madame le juge.*

She was smoking and gave him an inquisitive look from behind a cloud of cigarette smoke. *"Mon Capitaine,"* she said.

"Every cop in Gadet is jealous of your success. But you don't exactly look like a hunter who's just bagged a trophy."

"I think I might have had the wrong buck in my sights."

"Commandant Nkoulou considers the case as good as open and shut. He seems very relieved. He was even singing your praises."

"He might be somewhat premature."

"You want to ask me not to prepare the case for the prosecution yet?"

She used her cigarette to point to a chair. "Now I understand why certain people in Paris were pleased to see the back of you." She smiled and Blanc realized Madame Vialaron-Allègre meant it as a compliment. At that moment he finally decided to trust her.

"Let's reconstruct the day of the murder," he began. "Sunday, June thirtieth. Nobody knows how Moréas spent the morning. Maybe he was on his own, at home or on one of his bits of land. The pathologist found traces of alcohol in his blood. Maybe he had been drinking the day before and was sleeping it off. But things begin to get interesting just before noon: Moréas turns up in Saint-César harbor and spends some time on his boat. The building firm owner Pascal Fuligni confronts him at his mooring and offers him five thousand euros for it. Moréas just laughs in his face. The pair get into a loud argument. Shortly after, Moréas drives off. Fuligni remains in the harbor—at least according to him. We have no witnesses to the fact.

"Apparently, Moréas goes directly to the garbage dump. Around midday or shortly after he's seen at the scrap metal Dumpster. Probably looking for stuff that other people have thrown away but he can reuse. Lucien Le Bruchec turns up, the neighbor who suspects him of trying to break into his house and is planning to make a formal complaint, though he has not yet done so. They have a brief, argumentative exchange of words, and then the architect takes off again. He admits as much himself. And that is also what Monsieur Rheinbach says, who turns up around the same time. He is crouching down in his red car, unnoticed by everyone else, taking in the whole scene. The farmer who was dumping trash also noticed the red car, but apparently not anyone inside it. We've asked him again, and he can't remember seeing anyone.

"*Bon.* Next, early in the afternoon, we have the confrontation between Rheinbach and Moréas, which apparently ends with Moréas lying in pain on the ground, swearing, while our stone-throwing artist makes a run for it. Our colleagues from forensics have already turned his house upside down and found paints and paintings, but not the slightest trace of any Kalashnikov from Marseille. How do we suppose Monsieur Rheinbach could have got his hands on such a weapon? Just to be sure, I asked our colleagues down in Marseille if the German had ever turned up on their radar. Not a thing. Except for his witness statement all those years ago, his name has never turned up in a single French police file. I also asked the same question of our German colleagues. Nothing there either. The painter is as clean as a nun."

"You wouldn't have taken him into custody?"

"Commandant Nkoulou insisted. And in one respect he's right: Following the row with Rheinbach, nobody we know of saw Moréas alive. No witnesses, not that that is particularly remarkable: Who's going to be hanging about in a garbage dump on a hot Sunday afternoon? It's only first thing on the Monday morning that an employee comes across the still-smoking body. So, who was there at the garbage dump after Rheinbach? Only the murderer."

"That's unless the painter himself is the murderer."

Blanc pulled out his notebook and leafed through it. "On Friday, five days after the murder, the builder Pascal Fuligni is found dead in the Étang de Berre. No link between him and Rheinbach."

"There is also no link between the two deaths. At least not officially," Aveline Vialaron-Allègre reminded him. "You're not going to save Rheinbach by claiming there's no way he could have been involved in another unsolved death."

Blanc hesitated for a moment. Trust this woman, he told himself. Who else do you have? "There's one more thing . . ." He extended across the table to her the piece of paper on which he had noted Fuligni's last text message—*It's all going to come out. There'll be enough blood spilt to fill the harbor*—and explained to her what it was.

The *juge d'instruction* stared long and hard at the piece of paper. "Did you ask Marcel about this?" she asked eventually, lighting up another cigarette.

"I haven't been to see your friend."

"Marcel is my husband's friend, a political friend."

Blanc leant back in his seat. He felt like celebrating, but forced himself not to show any emotion. She's watching my back, he thought, she really is watching my back. "I don't know what those few lines mean," he said. "But I refuse to believe they are unimportant—that it is all coincidence, that Fuligni's death was a tragic accident, that two deaths within five days just happens to be 'one of those things.'"

"You want a couple of days' breathing space, so that with my permission you can investigate an allegation of murder against Marcel Lafont? Against the man who has for the past thirty years been mayor of Caillouteaux? Against the trusted friend of my husband, a government minister?"

"I will be extremely discreet."

"But you still want my protection. And that I don't mention a word of this to my husband."

"I couldn't have put it better myself."

"And if I don't offer my protection, will you carry on with the investigation regardless?"

"I think you already know me well enough to answer that question for yourself, *Madame le juge*."

Aveline Vialaron-Allègre had forgotten all about her cigarette. "You want to make me your accomplice in a secret, indeed possibly illegal investigation," she murmured. "Have you ever done anything like this before? In Paris?"

"Cops sometimes set up small, secret teams. But sometimes I went out on a limb on my own. However, I have never compromised a *juge d'instruction*."

"So this will be a first for both of us."

And with that, Blanc finally realized that he would at least have a couple of days to investigate Mayor Lafont in peace.

For the rest of the day Blanc shut himself away in his office, working at his ancient computer. The police had never carried out a single investigation of the mayor although he had on numerous occasions been called as a witness. Nonetheless, an Internet search on his name came up with countless hits: Monsieur Lafont opening a bridge, Monsieur Lafont at a meeting of Midi Provence, Monsieur Lafont at the party congress that elected the last presidential candidate. Now and again he popped up in statements by the opposition. The usual political rhetoric in general; only if you read them closely, and knew what Blanc now knew, you could decipher some of them as allegations of corruption. It obviously hadn't been of any use. Three years ago Marcel Lafont had been awarded the Cross of the Legion of Honor, France's highest honor. And just over a month ago, a columnist in *La Provence* had speculated that Lafont could end up in the senate before long. Or might be named chairman of Midi Provence. Or both. The column had been published the day after the press conference at which Lafont had first publicly announced his plans for a *médiathèque*. There was also a photo of the event, with Fuligni standing next to him.

"*Merde,*" Blanc muttered. This damn *médiathèque* was more than just Lafont's ticket to reelection as mayor, as he had suggested himself—it could also be his ticket to ride a whole series of gravy trains. He had the feeling that over the course of Lafont's long political career there had to be more than a few dark closets to which the doors had never been opened. But he also knew that even an experienced team of cops with regular permission to carry out an investigation would need more than a few days, a lot more. A lone wolf working in secret didn't have a chance.

"Have you got a construction permit for that?" Douchy yelled at him from his tractor when Blanc parked outside his house early that evening. His neighbor was pointing at the mountain of stripped wallpaper and other rubbish that he had piled stones around to stop the wind blowing them all over the place.

"I'm stripping wallpaper. Since when does that require a permit?" Blanc shouted back at him.

"You need a permit to build an extension," Douchy replied, unperturbed. "Otherwise I'll lodge a complaint at the town hall."

"Then please give my best to Monsieur Lafont. I have business to discuss with the mayor every now and then."

As soon as he mentioned the mayor's name the surly farmer immediately seemed to lose any enthusiasm for a fight. Instead he just drove off on his tractor without saying good-bye. Life in the Midi can sometimes be easy, it would seem, Blanc thought.

He had not forgotten that the Michelettis had invited him over for dinner. Bernard. Bring anything but wine. In the old days he had left it to Geneviève to decide what to take when they were invited somewhere. It was time he got used to his new way of life. The first house on the right when you came into Sainte-Françoise-la-Vallée from Gadet, behind a thick hedge that separated it from a field of olive trees, was a little garden store. He had driven past it on several occasions. This time he had stopped and bought a large hibiscus plant and, remembering Paulette Aybalen's words, a little thyme plant in a bright red terra-cotta pot. He realized to his own surprise that he was rather excited. He dressed a bit more presentably and climbed into the car.

The approach to Domaine de Bernard was on the road to Saint-César, but it was a long and winding route to reach the winery, which in fact was hidden away behind oaks and pine trees but actually only a few hundred yards away from his old olive oil mill. Amidst the trees a few brave cicadas were still clicking away against the rushing mistral. The few other drivers he encountered on the *route départementale* were driving like lunatics. Blanc was beginning to feel nostalgic for the gray days of Paris in the fall, when at least there was no wind. He turned off the road onto a gravel and brownish red sand track. It was quieter amidst the oak trees. When he trundled down into the depression where the vines were planted it was all of a sudden hot and warm. He immediately relaxed.

Bruno Micheletti was sitting on an ancient blue tractor with tall, thin wheels on which he was carefully navigating his way among the rows of vines. Behind him an apparatus attached to a plastic tank was spraying a brightly colored liquid in a fine rain over the leaves. That won't be water, Blanc thought to himself, and tried not to breathe in too deeply.

"Just drive on up to the house," Micheletti called out over the stuttering noise of the tractor's diesel engine. "It's at the end of the track."

Blanc drove on, along a winding track that dipped and rose again, peacocks wandering amid the vines, or perching on low stone walls that had conserved the sun's warmth, or even half hidden amidst the lower branches of the pine trees. The estate was much larger than he had imagined. Blanc was no expert at guessing these things but it had to be dozens of acres at the very least. On his walk in the wood he had only come across one tiny corner of it. Eventually the gravel and old asphalt track led him up a hill that could have been the seat of a little castle overlooking a sea of vines. There was a little dovecote that sat some fifteen feet above a barn with a closed wooden door that reeked of wine and wood and vinegar. Next to it was a little garden with a freshly watered lawn in front of a nineteenth-century house made of brownstone. On a terrace sheltered from the wind by the house itself, beneath a yellow umbrella, was a long wooden table where glasses and cutlery shone in the oblique rays of the sun.

Blanc parked carefully behind a peacock that was strutting along the gravel and didn't seem to be remotely stirred by a huge car coming threateningly close. One of its long tail feathers suddenly rose up and was taken by a gust of wind that whipped it out and sent it dancing, a flash of silver and violet against the sky.

"It's that time of year," said Sylvie Micheletti with a laugh. She had been standing on the stone steps of the terrace, and now came toward him. "In summer the males lose their tail feathers. We tie them into little bundles and give them to our customers. At least to those who don't already have enough three-foot-long bird feathers." She kissed him on each cheek. Blanc felt truly honored at such a friendly greeting. He opened the tailgate of his car and took out the presents he had brought. Sylvie looked so slight that the mistral might blow her away. He hesitated to put the two pots in her little hands. But she just laughed and took the plants from him. "These are a boon for both body and soul," she exclaimed.

Bruno drove up the track, leapt down from the tractor, and disappeared into the house through a side door. Blanc followed Sylvie onto the terrace. There were four place settings. But before he could say anything Paulette Aybalen came out of the patio door carrying a huge bowl of salad. Now there's a coincidence, Blanc thought to himself, amused rather than alarmed.

Quite clearly the Michelettis, out of the friendliest of motives, had determined to use a good meal to turn their near neighbors into a couple. Blanc smiled, agreed with Paulette on the familiar "*tu*" rather than the more formal "*vous*," but was equally determined to behave impeccably. After twenty years of marriage without cheating, he believed that it was wise to be cautious when shopping again on the love and lust market.

They ate melon from Carpentras with raw ham and drank glasses of glittering white wine. Then Bruno brought out a ceramic platter with dark meat straight from the oven. "Wild boar. Shot it myself," he declared proudly. "We have a herd of them around here who spend every night plowing up half the forest."

"Marinated in red wine?" Blanc asked, vaguely remembering a recipe he had once read.

"Red wine is for drinking, not for making sauce!" his host exclaimed. "A little olive oil, some thyme, and a hot oven, and . . . *voilà*!"

Sylvie served couscous and cold ratatouille. They were now on the rosé. The sun had long disappeared behind the treetops by the time they tore apart a baguette and passed around a wooden board with ten different types of cheese, accompanied by a red wine. Blanc began to wonder if it would be wise to drive back home later. He noticed that Sylvie was the only one of them who had not drunk any wine, and had not been offered any by her husband. Before the cheese course she had popped into the kitchen and unobtrusively brought out a wooden box from which she took four or five pills of varying colors. Bruno and Paulette had paid no attention, so he had made a point of lifting his glass so as to conceal the fact he had noticed.

By midnight, when he finally got up from the table, full of food and just a little under the influence of the wine, he realized he was happier than he had been for ages. I've arrived, he told himself, finally arrived. He had also realized that Paulette Aybalen had come on foot, and said that of course he would give her a lift home. A good move, he thought. They spent the few minutes in his car in silence but without embarrassment. He parked outside his own house and accompanied her the few dozen yards to her door on foot. He leant down toward her, her long hair smelling of pine, hesitated the tiniest of seconds, his face close to hers, then kissed her on both cheeks.

It was so dark he couldn't tell if she was disappointed or pleased that he hadn't tried to take things any further. "Good night, neighbor, and thank you," she whispered. At least she didn't sound upset.

Blanc strolled back home, feeling as if he were floating. I have arrived, he thought again. The wind rushing through the plane trees outside the house was so loud he almost didn't hear the ringtone on his phone. The number on the display meant nothing to him, though he noticed that whoever it was had been trying to call him all evening. He never turned his phone off, but it appeared that out in the woods there was no signal. He took the call.

"Have you been spelunking? It's as if you've been underground for hours."

Blanc took a few seconds to recognize the voice. *"Madame le juge!"* he exclaimed.

"I've been unable to rest easy since we last spoke," she said, ignoring his apparent surprise. "I dug up a few documents."

"Me too," he replied. "Lafont is a hard nut to crack."

"This is not about Lafont," Aveline Vialaron-Allègre replied impatiently. "It's Moréas. He's the guy all this fuss is about, right?"

Blanc stood there, scarcely daring to breathe. "You've found something?"

"A copy of a document in the town hall files. One Marcel neglected to mention to you when you first went to talk to him in Caillouteaux. One you were unable to find the second time you were there, possibly because someone had cleverly hidden it. I came across it in my husband's poison cabinet, a fact that he is definitely not to be made aware of."

"His poison cabinet?"

"Where he keeps documents that might be useful. That's how you make a career in politics, *mon Capitaine.* My husband collects copies of documents relating to his party colleagues. All of them, young and old, big beasts and little. All public documents, perfectly legal to file away. But who does things like that? *Eh bien:* In the documents relating to his fellow party member Marcel Lafont, I found the planning permission for the *médiathèque.*"

"The eight-million-euro job."

"Forget the eight million. That was building money. But first you need somewhere to build. The *médiathèque* is supposed to be built on the edge of the plateau, because in this ancient town there is no room anywhere else. Nearly all the common areas belong to the *commune.* But there is one important strip of land in private ownership."

Blanc leant back against the trunk of a plane and suddenly felt the world closing in on him. "What an idiot I am," he whispered.

"I'll make a note of that admission," the *juge d'instruction* responded coolly.

"Moréas inherited five parcels of land from his parents,"

Blanc said wearily. "Land he did nothing with. Four of them in the woods, where he would chase off hikers, and one . . ."

". . . in the town, on the edge of the plateau. An excellent site on which to build, for example, a *médiathèque*."

"But an antisocial character like Moréas would never sell. Fuligni can whistle for his eight million and Monsieur Lafont can watch his pet project melt away, along with his chances of reelection and a seat in the senate. And there's nobody who can force the guy to sell."

"Marcel was under so much pressure that he revealed plans for his *médiathèque* to the press before he had even solved the problem of acquiring the land. Maybe he hoped that putting public pressure on Moréas would have persuaded him to sell. Or maybe he just underestimated the stubborn recluse because he came into town so rarely and Lafont didn't really know him."

"Or Monsieur Lafont knew that Moréas would conveniently die just when it mattered?"

"Get to the gendarmerie early in the morning. We are going to have to take two or three others into our confidence. I'll leave it to you to do that. I have a meeting in court tomorrow morning that I don't want to miss because it would only cause attention. Come and see me at midday at our house in Caillouteaux. Then we can go over the steps we should take next."

"That will be a pleasure."

"Don't come in the patrol car. I don't want anyone to know you've come to see me."

"I picked up a few things like that in Paris."

"*Mon Capitaine?* Next time do me a favor and check your cell phone more regularly."

An Inappropriate Affair

Tuesday marked the fifth day of the mistral. But it wasn't just because of the wind that Blanc couldn't sleep. He was fixated by the call of the hunt. Fabienne was at the gendarmerie early and for once, luckily, they didn't have to wait too long for Marius. Blanc closed the door to the office and told both his colleagues about the strip of land that was needed for the *médiathèque*.

"Where did you get that from?" Tonon asked.

Blanc hesitated for a moment. He didn't want to compromise Aveline Vialaron-Allègre unnecessarily. "From a reliable source."

"Clearly a good-looking woman," Fabienne teased him, not knowing how close she was to the truth.

"We're going to tread on Monsieur Lafont's toes," Blanc said.

"You'd better tell the boss first," Tonon warned him.

"You really think Lafont shot Moréas and set fire to his corpse, just to get his hands on a strip of building land?" Fabienne asked skeptically.

"In order to save his own career. Either he did it himself or he got some of his friends from Corsica or Marseille to do the dirty work for him. But, yes, I actually do think it was him. And he didn't want anyone else making inconvenient allegations."

"But there was someone else: Fuligni."

"He might not have known for sure, but almost certainly would have had suspicions."

"But why would he send Lafont that text about blood in the harbor?"

Blanc raised his hands. "Pass. Maybe he was intending to blackmail him."

"After his pal Lafont had handed him an eight-million-euro contract?" Blanc's young colleague was still looking skeptical.

"Sometimes even eight million isn't enough. Maybe Fuligni's building business was in trouble. Maybe his affairs with women were costing him a lot of money."

"Romanians are cheap," Marius muttered indignantly.

"Nonetheless I believe Lafont decided to silence his friend down at the harbor. Lafont knew Fuligni liked sleeping on board his yacht on his own, he admitted as much. On the night of Fuligni's death he was out on the Étang de Berre on his own in his fishing boat. He decides to pay a visit to Fuligni on board his yacht, they have a drink, and then he hits him on the skull. A blunt instrument needn't make a noise. Nobody would have heard anything. Lafont unties Fuligni's yacht, takes it out of the harbor, throws his unconscious body into the water, and lets him drown. Then he gets back into his own boat, disappears into a bay, and only comes back the next morning, posing as the deceased's shocked best friend. *Voilà.*"

"It's all too dangerous. Lafont is too powerful," Tonon insisted. "The mayor has already complained to Paris. He's put pressure on the commandant. He thinks he'll be left in peace now. When he finds out we're coming after him again, he'll go ballistic. It's better we tell Nkoulou. He'll have to know sooner or later anyhow."

"And what if he forbids us from investigating further?"

"Then you go to your friend, the *juge d'instruction*. If she says no, then we go for lunch and sort out the troubles of the world on our own. I'll pay." It sounded as if Marius was already counting on them being happily dismissed and sitting in the shade of the plane trees in just a few hours' time.

"Madame Vialaron-Allègre has already given us her blessing."

Fabienne gave him an oblique look: "*Eh bien*, in that case we may as well knock on the chief's door."

Nkoulou looked up, shocked to see three of his subordinates come into his room at the same time. "Close the door," he ordered them, even before any of them had said a word.

Blanc took a deep breath. The next few minutes would decide whether or not his career was down the drain. As concisely as possible he told his boss where the investigation had gone over the past few days.

Nkoulou listened to him in silence—starched, ironed, immaculate as ever, save for the little ring of sweat that sat on his forehead like a diadem. "Do you know what you're about to do?" he asked when the captain had finished. His voice was calm, considered.

"Monsieur Lafont is a powerful man."

"He is not just one man. Lafont has been cultivating friendships for decades, doing favors, handing out presents of all sorts. Dozens, hundreds of respectable people have profited from his friendship: farmers, shopkeepers, doctors, teachers . . ."

"Building contractors," Tonon added.

"They will all be shocked if we bring Lafont in, especially if it's in connection with a murder case," Nkoulou continued determinedly. "Your neighbors, *mon Capitaine, mes Lieutenants*, the bakers you buy your baguettes from, the doctors who prescribe your painkillers, your children's teachers, the electricians who repair your worn-out fuses." He gave a small sarcastic smile. "I just hope that is clear to you. As clear as glass."

Blanc thought of Paulette Aybalen's advice that it was wise to speak softly about Lafont, and better still not to speak of him at all. "Perhaps one or two of them might not be all that unhappy," he said.

The commandant gave him a long, searching look. "Over the past few days Monsieur Lafont has been on the phone to me a lot more often than I told you. He has been very polite, very respectful. But also, how should I put it, very firm. It would make my life easier if I threw you all out of my office here and now and forgot all about this business of yours." He was silent for what seemed like an eternity, the expression on his face rigid, the beads of sweat glistening. Blanc had an absurd urge to take out his handkerchief and wipe them away, before they ran down the side of his face. "But I hate it when amateurs get involved in my business," Nkoulou said at last. "Society has rules, regulations, laws. They can be tedious but they contain the wisdom of generations. I took an oath to enforce those laws, not to dismiss them because the phone keeps ringing. So get on with it."

They got to their feet and hurried to the door.

"*Madame, Messieurs,*" Nkoulou called after them. "Not a word of this to any of your other colleagues. I don't want news of a potentially incendiary investigation like this to get out. Least of all to Monsieur Lafont."

"I don't want that either, *mon Commandant,*" Blanc replied.

"Sometimes, it can be an advantage that Nkoulou insists on everything being done by the book," Tonon whispered, clearly relieved and somewhat amazed when they found themselves back in the hallway, having first made sure that they'd closed the chief's door behind them.

"It would appear that the first time we went to see Lafont to ask about Moréas, he concealed the existence of the documentation on the land issue from us," Blanc said, back in their own office. "But the planning permission documents for the *médiathèque* can't have completely vanished. Not when it's such a grand and pressing project."

"But you searched the archive," Marius reminded him, unnecessarily.

"Yes, but I was only looking for documents in which Moréas was mentioned. Lafont could easily have removed those. He had more than enough time. But if we searched under '*médiathèque*' then we'd be bound to find documents—not even the mayor can hide everything relating to an important public project on that scale. Then at least we'll have tangible documentation of our own, rather than secondhand material, which is what we've had to deal with up to now."

"So you're going to go back and have another go?" Fabienne asked.

Blanc gave an apologetic smile. "This time it's your turn.

They know me down there and it would only alert Lafont if I went back digging around again. None of them know you. Go home, change out of your uniform, and try not to wake up all the dozy bureaucrats with your Ducati. Leave it on the edge of town and go the rest of the way on foot. Give your own name, but don't tell them you're a cop. Think of some excuse for wanting to go through the archives." His own renovation work suddenly sprang to mind. "Tell them you're thinking of buying a house locally and that you've heard about the *médiathèque* that's supposedly going to be built nearby. You want to see the plans in case a year after buying the property you find yourself looking out the window onto a parking lot. Sound naïve, but hard-nosed."

Fabienne raised her left eyebrow. "At least you said naïve rather than stupid," she said.

"Do it however you want, but just make sure we ascertain that the strip of land owned by Moréas is exactly where Lafont wants to build his fairy palace."

Blanc and Tonon sat around twiddling their thumbs for two hours until their young colleague came back. Fabienne had put on a nondescript pale yellow dress, flat shoes, and a pearl necklace—she looked serious, dull, and not in the least threatening. Then she had donned her helmet and driven like a lunatic up the hill to Caillouteaux, putting on her most disarming smile as she went into the town hall. It had been no trouble at all to get the bored clerk to produce all the documents and to make copies of them. Then she had repeated her journey in the opposite direction back to Gadet where, breathless but triumphant, she presented them with a pile of photocopies.

"An extract from the land registry showing the precise area

of land owned by our charred friend," she announced. "An official request from the *commune* of Caillouteaux to purchase said piece of land. But no record of any response from Moréas."

"He'll have given his response orally," Tonon muttered. "I can imagine his very words."

"And obviously there's no deed of purchase. The land would still belong to Moréas today if he hadn't already departed this world for the happy hunting ground."

"You're a star," Blanc told her.

She gave him a sarcastic smile. "Well, at least that sounds better than naïve. As it happens, I'm more of a star than you realize, *mon Capitaine*." She laid out the photocopies on the desk. "The woman at the archive was having difficulty keeping her eyelids open. As I was already there, I thought I'd make the most of her sleepiness, and took it upon myself to examine one shelf on which the dust had not yet settled. If you have no living relations at time of death, your estate goes to the government. Normally that can take a while—the lawyers seek out the fabled nephew in America until they are absolutely sure none exists. That can take months, even years. In the case of Moréas, the search for an heir began on Monday, the first of July."

"As soon as his death was reported!" Tonon exclaimed.

"When we got to Caillouteaux that day, it was already gone five P.M. The town hall was dead. There was nobody there but Lafont."

"You'll find that, surprisingly enough, the search for an heir was not listed under Moréas's own name, but instituted on behalf of the *commune*. Which, of course, could appear to be purely routine. There's more to come: Simultaneously the *commune* put in an official request to purchase the land as necessary for an important urban development. Equally apparently routine. And perfectly legal."

"From a purely legal point of view the land does not yet belong to the *commune*," Blanc interjected. "But in practice it already controls it as if it did. It's been taken out of the public domain, as if there never had been a strip of land owned by Moréas there. And if cops like us come snooping around we wouldn't find anything relating to the sale, because there never was one. All very clever, very inconspicuous. The sort of trick that you'd need quite a lot of experience to pull off."

"Who initiated the search for an heir and who made the land purchase request?" Marius asked.

"Both were signed by *Monsieur le maire* personally. Lafont. We've got him! *Mon Capitaine*, I invite you to kiss me on both cheeks and take me to lunch."

Blanc did as he was told, regretting for a moment that his young colleague was only interested in other women. "We've got the noose," he said, "but we still have to get Lafont's head in it. The only breach of the rules we can prove is that he instituted the search for an heir somewhat prematurely. But who would bother to search the globe for relatives of a guy like Moréas? And even if someone did lodge a complaint, the process would only be delayed. A trifle. As far as Lafont is concerned, it would be no more annoying than getting a parking fine. None of this is enough to put him in the frame for actually killing Moréas, and certainly not Fuligni."

"You think the *juge d'instruction* will hold us up, even despite these documents?" Fabienne asked, suddenly brought down to earth.

"I hope not. On the contrary, these documents may be

enough for her to let us bring Lafont in for questioning, to turn his world upside down and do something that will take us a step further."

"It's a miracle that this Vialaron-Allègre woman even considered letting us poke our noses into the bigwigs' toilet," Marius said skeptically. "Are you really going to tell her you believe a respected town mayor is a cynical double murderer? That you want to launch a murder investigation against him in the middle of an election campaign? All because of a premature auctioning off of the pile of garbage that Moréas managed to accumulate throughout his miserable life? Or because the *commune* bought up a strip of land that nearly everybody thought it already owned? The judge will shoot us down in flames. And if she doesn't, then her slimy husband in Paris certainly will."

"We'll see," said Blanc, getting to his feet.

He parked the Espace next to two public tennis courts that had been cut into the slope of the Caillouteaux hill just below the summit. Very new tennis courts, very well maintained. That must have cost a bundle too, Blanc thought. He pulled his baseball cap down low on his forehead and put on his large sunglasses. But even that would not exactly make him inconspicuous: He was a tall, pale-skinned foreigner in a land of small, olive-skinned natives. He took an alleyway that brought him out onto a knoll opposite the church. All of a sudden it was quiet— the terraced houses sheltered the square from the mistral. Their stone glowed in the sunlight, and there was a smell of tar. His own footsteps seemed improbably loud. There was nobody around. The shutters were closed. Lunchtime. Even so he felt as if he were being watched by a thousand eyes.

Blanc came round the side of the hill where the wind blew fiercely, carrying pine needles up from the valley below that struck him like tiny bullets. Still nobody to be seen. Somewhere a wooden door was banging to and fro in its frame. He came across a dusty, weed-strewn piece of land with a sign posted in the middle: CHANTIER—INTERDIT AU PUBLIC. And beneath it an architectural plan of the *médiathèque*, that looked like a UFO landed in the middle of a Romanesque monastery. Just a few square yards of thistle-covered land, but worth more than a human life.

He approached the home of the *juge d'instruction* in rue du Passe Temps not from the church but from the opposite side, turned to look around him one more time, then rang the bell. He took off his sunglasses and baseball cap to look into the little security camera. A few seconds later Aveline Vialaron-Allègre opened the door.

"Nobody followed me," he said.

"You hardly need to whisper," the *juge d'instruction* told him calmly. She was barefoot and wearing a cream, knee-length dress, her toenails painted red. Blanc inhaled the scent of Chanel No. 5 and Gauloises as he followed her into the house. She had carefully bolted the door behind him, turned off the electric doorbell, and muted both the house telephone and her cell phone. Instead of leading him into her office, she took him into a little room upstairs, looking out onto the internal courtyard. "It's our guest room," she told him. "Nobody can see in from the street, and nor can any of the neighbors. Relax, *mon Capitaine*." She offered him a seat on a sofa bed, while she took the solitary chair in the room.

Blanc got the impression it was not the first time his hostess had entertained guests in confidence. Instead of making him feel relaxed it only boosted his adrenaline.

"I have taken two colleagues into my confidence," Blanc told her, "and Nkoulou as well. We are in possession of documents that confirm Charles Moréas's land holdings. And rather more than that." It did not take him long to bring her up to speed with the progress of the investigation. The room was pleasantly cool and shady. The noise of the mistral was distant. The shutter slats filtered the midday sun into bright stripes to flicker minimally on Aveline Vialaron-Allègre's skirt. Blanc had to concentrate in order not to stare at them. And her bare calves. And her painted toenails. A secret visitor in a hidden place. He was all alone with a beautiful woman. And beginning to fantasize.

"So, you have a motive," the *juge d'instruction* said, looking him in the eye. For a moment Blanc thought she was talking about his fantasy rather than the case.

"For the murder of Moréas," he said, just a little too hastily. "The *médiathèque* is not just important for Lafont's reelection but could also be a ticket to the senate and to ensure the finance of Midi Provence. But it was a ticket that couldn't be used as long as an antisocial character like Moréas held on to a patch of dusty weed-infested land that just happened to belong to him. You were right: Greed is the oldest motive of all. Greed for power and money turned Lafont into a killer."

"He gets rid of the man who stood in the way of his *médiathèque, d'accord.* But then why would he also kill the man who was going to build his *médiathèque?*" She had got to her feet and was walking up and down. Blanc couldn't avoid watching her.

"Fuligni might have been his favorite builder, but he was

hardly the only option," he said. "He might well have been the only available builder in a hamlet like Caillouteaux, but there are dozens round and about. Who else is building all the new houses Le Bruchec keeps designing? Fuligni might have been dependent on Lafont to keep him in business, but there's no way Lafont was dependent on Fuligni. Even on the day Fuligni was found dead, he told me, down at the harbor in Saint-César, he would just have to find someone else. 'Now more than ever,' was how he put it."

"Yes, but that's hardly a motive. If I were to kill all the people I'm not dependent on, then I'd be the last person alive in France."

Blanc declined to comment. "I was thinking about that last night," he said, "and this morning, while I was waiting for my colleague to come back from the town hall with the documents. And I was still thinking about it on my way here. Could Fuligni also have been involved in killing Moréas? I doubt it. If he had intended to get rid of him, he would hardly have offered him five thousand euros for his mooring place. Nor would he have had a public altercation with him with dozens of people listening. But Fuligni had known his pal Lafont for years, would have known more about his past in Corsica and Marseille than we do. As a builder he would have known that the owner of a strip of land was blocking his pet project. Then suddenly the man in question is shot dead. With a Kalashnikov, the weapon of choice for murders in Marseille. Within hours there's nothing to stop the diggers moving onto the land. That might well have given Fuligni cause for thought. He doesn't know what his friend Lafont might have done. But he has an idea. He says nothing, because he doesn't know for sure. There may well have been instances before when he didn't ask too many questions about how Lafont got hold of the land and the money to finance other building contracts he'd been given. But this time there's another factor he didn't have to reckon with in the past—"

"A cop like you turning up," Aveline Vialaron-Allègre interrupted him. "None of us expected that. Apart from my husband, of course." She sat down on the sofa bed next to him. A ray of sunlight fell on her face. Blanc looked at her elegantly curved upper lip, her straight nose, her long eyelashes.

"I questioned him down at the harbor because his row with Moréas over the mooring had made me suspicious," he continued. "I was on the wrong track, I now realize. But it had never occurred to Fuligni that the investigation spotlight might turn on him. All of a sudden he would have felt under threat— the one man who really had an idea who the killer was, felt under threat of being accused of the crime himself."

"So how does he protect himself? He turns to the actual killer."

"He doesn't say anything directly to his face. Instead, after I interrogate him, he sends Lafont a cryptic text message, part plea, part threat. Lafont will have understood: Get me out of the line of fire or else it'll all come out. And who knows exactly what he might have meant by 'all'? Who knows what secrets Fuligni might have been privy to, what he might have revealed?"

"Easy enough to get himself killed on board his own yacht, even if he had been useful. All you have to do now is get me the slightest shred of proof for me to consider believing this crazy story of yours."

"I'll bring you more than a shred. I'll bring you the Kalashnikov. But you'll have to give me a search warrant for Lafont's house. Tomorrow lunchtime. I've done my research. Monsieur

Lafont always takes lunch at home. He'll be there, but nobody else will. It'll be as discreet a house search as any can be. No press."

She laughed in amused surprise. "The front page of *La Provence* the next day will still carry the story that a gendarmerie captain believed our mayor has a Kalashnikov hidden under his bed. Do you really think you'll find a Kalashnikov in Marcel's house?"

"Even cold-blooded murderers have problems afterward with the weapon used. Weapons carry evidence, sometimes related to the victim, always related to the perpetrator. Every idiot knows from television that DNA traces are hard to eliminate, there are almost invisible traces of blood, microscopic fibers, and a thousand other indicators. No matter how well a killer cleans the weapon he used, he can never be certain that he has eliminated every trace of the evidence pointing at him. So what does he do with it? Throw it away? He would be afraid to the end of his days that somebody might stumble on it and he would end up being caught. In any case it's not that easy to get rid of a large weapon like a Kalashnikov, least of all when you're the mayor, known to everybody for miles around."

"What's to stop him simply dropping the gun over the side of his fishing boat?"

"Fear. His car is about as inconspicuous as a tank. The minute he opens the door down at Saint-César harbor, there'll be somebody there to say hello. You really think he can then take a Kalashnikov wrapped in a blanket out of the trunk, or a box or wherever he's hidden it, and calmly walk across the parking lot, down the pier, past dozens of other boats with his friends and acquaintances sitting on them, watching him? Take the weapon on board his little boat, which doesn't even have a cabin? Then throw it overboard on the lake, with dozens of other boats out there? Or go out onto the lake at night, the sole boat out there, with an outboard motor loud enough to be heard in the middle of the town? And even if he did, the weapon would only be a few dozen feet under the surface of the water, in a lake where there are fishermen out every day with lines and nets? 'Oh, what's this I've caught? Better call the cops . . .'" Blanc shook his head. "Or maybe Lafont goes out into the wood, spade in one hand, automatic weapon in the other? And then somebody on a horse comes by, or a hunter? Or some wild boar unearths it some night rutting up the soil? Or some farmer's wild goats? Nope. Not likely."

"He could bury the gun among the foundations for his *médiathèque*. That would do the trick. It would be safe there. Rather fitting, don't you think?" Aveline Vialaron-Allègre moved closer to him.

"Not until the building work has started. As long as the foundation stone hasn't been laid, Lafont will have the Kalashnikov hidden somewhere."

"If you go in and search the mayor's house just before the elections, there'll be a scandal whether you find the weapon or not. It's the sort of situation my husband refers to as Ancien Régime: No matter what you do, you end up with your head under the guillotine. He's got a lot of experience in avoiding situations like that. There's absolutely no way he'd allow you to carry out the search."

"Even a minister of state has no power to prevent a search if it's been ordered by a *juge d'instruction*. That would be against the law."

"There are laws that are upheld, and laws that aren't upheld." She gave him a long, searching look. "Why, *mon Capitaine*, are you rushing headlong into an adventure in which you have nothing to win? Do you do it for the thrill of the risk?" She was sitting right next to him now, her perfume overwhelming him.

"My job is to uphold the law, no matter what. And I simply don't like seeing a criminal get away with it." He hesitated. "And yes, if you must know, I do enjoy the thrill of the risk."

Aveline Vialaron-Allègre gave him a bewitching smile, spontaneously closed the last few inches between them, and kissed him on the lips. Blanc felt her hair on his cheek and his hands on her skin and for a moment he was deliriously happy.

She slipped casually out of her expensive dress, nonchalantly letting it fall to the floor as she lay back on the sofa bed, naked. "We don't have a lot of time," she whispered. "I have to be back in court."

Ancien Régime, thought Blanc.

Search Warrant

The next morning Blanc was tempted to believe his hour with Aveline Vialaron-Allègre had been a hallucination of a brain disturbed by the mistral. For a brief, confusing, passionate moment he had held in his arms a beautiful, experienced lover. But after they had both exhausted their lust she had got up without a word and disappeared through a door. He heard the sound of rushing water from the shower and then embarrassingly found himself still lying there naked on the sofa when Madame Aveline Vialaron-Allègre reappeared in a Chanel suit and smart shoes, makeup and hair perfect. "I think you should go now, *mon Capitaine*," she said, lighting up another Gauloise.

While he was hastily getting dressed she went downstairs and was using her laptop to control the security camera by the door, turning the lens to left and right to scan the length of the rue du Passe-Temps. "There are advantages to living in an out-of-the-way place," she murmured. "Nobody will see you leave."

Thirty seconds later he was back on the edge of the Caillouteaux plateau, her house behind him, as silent and empty looking as all the others. The wind blew the last vestige of her scent from his hair. Aveline still says "*vous*" rather than "*tu*" to me, it occurred to him absurdly. He wasn't sure he would ever again be as intimate with her as he had just been. Or indeed, whether he wanted to.

He drove back to Gadet and told his colleagues that the *juge d'instruction* was prepared to issue a search warrant for Lafont's house at midday the following day. Fabienne had given him an odd look as if she didn't quite trust him. Nkoulou was remarkably relaxed and made the necessary arrangements for a couple of cars and a few gendarmes to be ready, without telling any of them what they were to be ready for. Tonon was in a state of shock. It had simply never occurred to him that one day he might be about to turn over Lafont's house.

Blanc returned to Sainte-Françoise-la-Vallée early, but it wasn't just the mistral that kept him awake lying there on his hard bed, turning to and fro, but thoughts of death and love.

He thought about the action they were about to take against Lafont. In twenty-four hours' time the mayor would be finished. Or else he would be. France might be a country in which the boss of a billion-dollar company couldn't even fire a doorman without the trade union setting tires alight outside the gates, but Lafont and Vialaron-Allègre would find one way or another to hound him out of the gendarmerie. They would fire him. Or, what did he know, maybe Captain Roger Blanc would also end up lying like a peppered, grilled chicken in some godforsaken corner of the Midi.

And then there was the hour he had spent with Aveline. Happiness and passion, but along with them the worry about even the idea of starting an affair with this woman of all people and at this time of all times. That was if it even was the start of an affair . . . As the gray dawn approached, he had persuaded himself to forget the hour they had spent together. What he had done had not just been unprofessional, it had been idiotic. *D'accord*, it had been Aveline who had seduced him. But lust had consumed him, even though it was precisely the woman who had described it as the second oldest motive in the world who had inflamed it. But their hour together was hardly love. It was revenge. Revenge on Geneviève. Revenge on the minister. The action of a beaten man, already on the floor but still trying to get in one last kick. Not exactly something to be proud of. And certainly not love. He would never make the slightest mention or insinuation of it to anyone, least of all Madame Vialaron-Allègre. It would be as if he had never even gone to see her.

It was only when he set off in the Espace that he realized his baseball cap with NOVA SCOTIA on it was nowhere to be found. The only explanation could be that he had left it in a house in Caillouteaux.

He did manage to locate his phone, however. He wanted to make the most of the few hours before midday and called Miette Fuligni. "I'd like to take a look at some of your husband's papers," he told her when she answered. "Do you know where he kept the documentation relating to the planned *médiathèque*?"

"In his office. I used to keep things in order for him, filed his documents away and things like that. But then that Romanian tart arrived and took charge. Or rather didn't take charge. It looks like a whorehouse in there. Good luck trying to find it. Marcel also came by looking for something and left in a bad mood."

Blanc gasped. "Monsieur Lafont? When was this?"

"The same day my husband's body turned up. He came to pay his condolences. What did you think?"

"Is it okay if I come by?"

"If you want, but come now; I've arranged to play tennis with Lucien later."

Quite the grieving widow, Blanc thought to himself, wondering how anyone could manage to play tennis in the mistral. But at the same time he was more angry with himself for not preventing Lafont from going through the dead man's papers. He had the feeling he would be wasting his time.

A few minutes later he was standing next to Madame Fuligni, who was wearing a thin red tracksuit, in the dead building contractor's office. There was still a heady smell of perfume in the air. Miette wrinkled her nose and opened the window wide. "Just like a whorehouse," she muttered.

Blanc went over the dozen or so boxed files on the shelves on the wall. Someone had used a felt-tip pen to mark each with a date and a note—either a surname or a street name or a place.

"Those are all Pascal's projects over the last ten years," she explained. "From the initial estimate to the finishing details. One file per house."

Up at the top was a box file marked "*médiathèque*" in different handwriting to all the others. The letter "H" had been inserted as an afterthought. "His girl didn't even know proper French," Miette Fuligni added.

The box file was empty. "Was your husband in the habit of opening a file with nothing to put in it?" Blanc asked.

"Don't talk nonsense. Pascal always had masses of paperwork: estimates, contracts, drawings, plans, anything you can imagine. It was only when the pile on his desk got out of control that he called me for help. Or rather his Romanian more recently—she probably lost them all."

No, Blanc thought to himself. The girl might have made a few mistakes, but she wasn't that useless. Lafont hadn't come to pay his condolences, he'd come to clean up. "Did the mayor stay long, when he turned up on the Thursday?"

"He might have been here for a couple of hours. I don't look at my watch much and on that day I probably didn't bother at all."

Time enough to go through not just that file but all of them. Blanc was disappointed. Maybe there would still be something, some tiny grubby little story from Lafont and Fuligni's relationship. But it would take a team of cops days to find something like that. Forget it, he told himself. He went over to the desk, looked through what was lying on it, what was in the drawers. It was impossible to tell if everything was how Fuligni had left it or if someone else had already been through it. Routinely he looked through the papers, flicked through the calendars and notebooks: measurements, orders for building sand, telephone numbers, a drawing of a curved staircase, roughly scribbled with a ball pen, but surprisingly elegant in design. When Blanc lifted the two issues of *Paris Match* that lay spread open on the desk, Miette Fuligni snorted in anger. The magazines smelt particularly strongly of the cheap perfume. He flicked through them—and pulled out a letter that had obviously been used as a bookmark in the most recent issue. It was a letter from the *commune* of Caillouteaux.

The letter was unsigned, just a routine note to all those involved in the *médiathèque* building project, informing them that all the water pipes were to be laid on the land belonging to

Monsieur Charles Moréas. Somebody had ringed the name in yellow felt tip. I doubt very much that was the Romanian, Blanc said to himself. The date on the letter was the previous Wednesday. Fuligni must have got it on the Thursday. He could imagine the scene as if it were a movie: The building contractor reads the letter. Just a routine matter. Then he sees the name Moréas. Maybe that's when it all finally becomes clear to him, seeing it in black and white: the name of the victim and his niggling suspicion coming together. Fuligni himself has already had the police question him. Now the victim's name crops up in a document addressed to him. What if the cops turn up and find all the documents with the name Moréas on them in his office? Panic. He scrawls a ring around the name and sends his pal Lafont a text asking him to do something to get him out of the firing line. Then he dashes out of the office. The young Romanian, who hasn't a clue about anything, picks up the letter and uses it as a bookmark in her magazine. Lafont does indeed react to the text message, but not in the way Fuligni had been expecting. He kills his old friend, goes to visit his widow to pay his condolences, and searches the office. But how could he know that the last letter from the *commune* would be in a copy of *Paris Match*? He misses this one tiny piece of evidence . . . It made a great story, all too credible, as Aveline Vialaron-Allègre might say if one had the slightest bit of proof. Don't let yourself get led astray, Blanc told himself. "Did your husband have any contact with Monsieur Lafont that Thursday prior to his death?"

Miette Fuligni shook her head. "Not as far as I know."

"Really?" Blanc was disappointed.

"As far as I know. Marcel wanted to speak to him, I remember. He called at some stage in the afternoon, got me on my cell phone because he couldn't get hold of Pascal. His Romanian girl didn't bother to pick up the office phone, I imagine. And Pascal had left his iPhone on the bedside table, as you know."

"Did Monsieur Lafont say what he wanted to talk to Pascal about? Did he leave a message?"

"He just wanted to know where he could get hold of him. I told him Pascal had gone down to his yacht and was going to spend the rest of the day there and the night as well. That wasn't the wrong thing to do, was it?"

"No," Blanc lied, "not the wrong thing at all."

Leaving the Fuligni driveway, the captain was about to turn onto the *route départementale* heading for Gadet when to his left he spotted a car rushing toward him at high speed. He halted to let it pass, distracted by his thoughts. Then he noticed that it was a little red car. A Mini, with an elderly lady at the wheel whom he vaguely recognized. A matronly figure with gray hair and a large bosom. Where do I know you from, Blanc asked himself. Then he realized.

The online edition of *La Provence*. The photo taken outside the school: Carole Lafont, the mayor's wife.

Carole Lafont. A red Mini. The red Mini that had also been in the photo, in the parking lot in the background. A parking lot, like the parking lot down by the garbage dump. The statement by the farmer that he had seen a small red car down by the dump on Sunday morning. No, he hadn't just seen it, he had had to drive around it. Rheinbach in his Clio had been there too, but he had parked outside the gate, not in anybody's way. Then he remembered Lafont's words the first time they had met: *"But I grew up in Marseille, politically too. I still have lots of friends there. I was down seeing them just last weekend. They had a good laugh at my expense. My Audi was in for service and I had to take my wife's car. A red Mini, a woman's car. You wouldn't believe the ribbing they gave me."*

He had only ever connected the mayor to his huge monster of a car. But he had taken the Mini. To go to Marseille. To get a Kalashnikov from a friend down there, possibly? But would Lafont, who never got his hands dirty, let someone pass off a hot weapon on him? Or might he deliberately have bought a gun that had previously been used in a murder, to divert attention in the direction of Marseille? Whatever the case, on the day of the murder he hadn't been driving around in his big, conspicuous Audi Q7, but in his wife's little red car. He parked in the entrance road to the dump in order to take out Moréas. On a Sunday, so that the next morning he could make his claim to his strip of land. But he had had to wait. The farmer Gaston Julien was getting rid of his roofing felt and got annoyed at the red car he had to drive round. And then a scrawny red-haired man turned up, Moréas laughed in his face, the man threw a stone at him, and Moréas fell over. The ideal opportunity for Lafont. As soon as Rheinbach raced off there was nobody else left at the dump— except for Moréas, who could hardly stand up, and was certainly in no situation to run away. He was an easy target . . .

It was another good, plausible story, but still one he had no proof of. Don't make a fool of yourself. Don't go falling in love. Unless he found the Kalashnikov, Blanc knew he was finished.

At the gendarmerie station they were waiting impatiently for him. Everybody knew there was something in the air, but not what. Nobody could have rung Lafont secretly to warn him.

Aveline Vialaron-Allègre wasn't there, which was good. He would be able to concentrate better, even though he was a tiny bit disappointed not to see her. Blanc took Fabienne and Marius into his office, closed the door behind them, and told them about the files in Fuligni's office, Lafont turning up supposedly to offer his condolences, and the mayor's wife with her red Mini.

"Sounds a convincing tale," Fabienne said.

"As convincing as an old-fashioned novel," the old lieutenant interjected. "You don't really think you could win a case in court with a story like that, do you?" Tonon was freshly showered and wearing a clean uniform with skewed creases, evidence that he had obviously ironed it himself. He didn't reek of rosé, but his hands were shaking ever so slightly. His gun was in his holster. Blanc wondered if it might not be better to avoid taking him to search the mayor's house, but he couldn't think of a suitable excuse to leave his colleague behind.

"Where is *Madame le juge*?" Fabienne asked.

"She's going to be there with us," Blanc assured her, realizing that he didn't sound one hundred percent certain of that.

"We're diving headlong into a heap of shit," Marius said gloomily. "I've almost completed my thirty-second year of service. Finish it and I can retire and wander around Saint-César market watching the girls' asses. Instead Lafont and his pals will have our guts for garters. The *juge d'instruction* has vanished in a puff of smoke. Nkoulou has shut himself away in his office. We're left out here in the cold. They'll hang us out to dry by our balls."

"They might have a problem with that in my case," Fabienne said, giving him an encouraging smile. But Blanc saw it wasn't easy for her either.

"Stay here, both of you," he suggested. "I'm in the firing line anyway. I'll go on my own with the lower ranks, you can hold down the fort here."

Marius looked as if he was about to agree, but his younger colleague spoke up first. "So that you get all the glory and a medal for finding the Kalashnikov? Out of the question." Tonon murmured something that sounded more like a curse.

On the ground floor a dozen gendarmes were waiting along with four plainclothes members of the forensics team with their kit. Their faces suggested they already knew they would find nothing. Outside a couple of Méganes were parked, as well as a white delivery van. Most of the doors to the downstairs offices were closed. Blanc went to see Nkoulou. "We're good to go," he said.

"I've given the men their instructions. You're in charge now."

"You aren't coming with us?" Blanc had Tonon's grim prediction in his ears.

"I can't drop everything else on my plate for one operation. You're perfectly competent enough to carry this out without me. I wish you success, *mon Capitaine.*" Nkoulou turned his eyes down to examine in detail a file that lay open on his polished wooden desk.

As Blanc was leaving, the door to the office of the female chain-smoker whose name he could never remember opened. She waved to him, and then suddenly her waving hand drew a line across her throat.

Corporal Baressi on the reception desk muttered, "*Au revoir, mon Capitaine,*" though it sounded sad rather than sarcastic, then called after him, "*Bonne chance.*"

"See you later," Blanc replied, forcing a smile. Where is Aveline? he wondered worriedly.

He could feel a dozen pairs of eyes on him as he walked out of the building. "We are going to search the house of Monsieur Marcel Lafont, who is a suspect in the murder of Charles Moréas," he told them. "The main item we are searching for is the weapon used in the murder, a Kalashnikov." He gave them a few more details, handed around photographs, issued a few specific orders. But he had the impression no one was really paying attention.

Eventually one of the younger men said, "You really do mean Mayor Lafont?"

"Don't be intimidated by his office."

"I'm just glad I'll be wearing a mask," one of the forensics team said. There was a burst of nervous laughter.

Blanc paid no attention and walked over to the patrol car with Marius and Fabienne. They would lead the little column. The others piled into the remaining cars. Blanc tried to ignore the whispering but couldn't fail to overhear a few words: "Paris . . . posted here . . . Vialaron-Allègre . . . *Putain!*"

Marius directed them to an unmarked route that ran through the woods down the slope from Caillouteaux. The Mégane rattled over a few potholes, then braked before a new, green-painted gate in a yellow wall some six feet high. "Looks a bit like a jail," Fabienne muttered.

"In that case Monsieur Lafont won't have anything new to get used to," Blanc replied, leaning out of the window to press the bell. "Gendarmerie," he said into the speaker.

They heard the sound of an electric motor, then the gate

swung open and they drove through. Beyond the gate the rickety track became a gravel roadway, leading to a pink-plastered villa. Very new and very big. The curved white bow windows looked as if they had been taken from a château, though they turned out to be modern and made of PVC. To the side of the house was a swimming pool as blue as the cooling tank in a nuclear power station.

"It'll take us a week to search this palace," Tonon muttered disconsolately.

"We're not looking for some misplaced strand of hair, we're looking for a Kalashnikov," Blanc replied, noting at the same time how sharp and nervous his own voice sounded. He opened the car door.

Lafont came out to meet him, a sly smile on his face. He would have seen us drive up on surveillance cameras, the captain reckoned. He saw the cars and knows what's coming. He didn't even bother to pretend to be surprised. Maybe somebody did warn him after all.

Blanc shook hands very formally with the mayor, told him why they were there, and handed him a copy of the search warrant. The other gendarmes got out of their cars, timidly. Not one of them made any attempt to go into the house. The forensics team piled out of their van. They really all were wearing their masks.

"I'm aware that a lot of cops are naturally right-wingers, but I wasn't expecting you in particular to be in the pay of the Front National," Lafont said, handing back the search warrant as if it were a dirty photo. He spoke loud enough for all of them to hear him.

"I am in the pay of the French Republic," Blanc replied.

"For now at least, *mon Capitaine*," Lafont said, and nodded toward the house. "I do hope you have adequate insurance. To cover any breakages."

Marble floor, white walls, wooden ceilings with LED lighting, casting soft light even at midday on old oil paintings of landscapes in gilded frames. Tonon took a look around and inconspicuously nodded toward the living room: Louis XVI chairs, a cabinet from the same period, an ancient table sparkling from multiple coats of oil. It all must have looked good when it was still in the town hall, Blanc thought to himself.

The gendarmes followed him, as shy as schoolchildren visiting a museum. The forensics team opened two cases and took out a few instruments, chosen completely arbitrarily, it seemed to Blanc. Lafont could have a battle tank in his kitchen and this lot wouldn't find it, he thought, increasingly feeling uncertain. Tonon disappeared through a door, which probably led to a visitors' bathroom or a broom cupboard. Souillard spotted an iMac on a side table and turned it on. At least one of them is a pro, Blanc thought.

Then he heard the noise of a car on the gravel. It was a dark Citroën C5. Blanc closed his eyes for a second. At least I'm not completely on my own, he thought with a touch of relief.

"Marcel, I'm so sorry for all this inconvenience," Aveline Vialaron-Allègre said to the man of the house, proffering her cheek for him to kiss. It sounded as professional as a doctor informing a patient that he had been diagnosed with a fatal illness. Then she nodded perfunctorily to the gendarmes. "Go ahead, *mon Capitaine*." Blanc hoped he had noticed the smallest of smiles toward him, but realized he was probably imagining it, out of lust as much as nervousness.

"This Paris cop has no idea what he's doing," Lafont replied. He sounded relaxed, as if he found the search wearying but something that didn't concern him. But as the search continued he gave Blanc a look that said, *Wait until I'm done with you.*

"Thank you for being so cooperative, Marcel," the *juge d'instruction* said. It was less than clear if she was being reassuring or sarcastic, but one way or another it seemed to shut him up.

Blanc avoided looking at her. She remained in the living room while he went around the rest of the house giving instructions to his men. It was the most lackluster house search he had ever seen. "You could at least open the cupboards and drawers," he badgered one of them, who seemed content with just glancing into the bedroom.

His Nokia rang. A Paris number that he didn't recognize. "Should I post you to Guyana? Or maybe you'd like to become a police training officer in Afghanistan? If you absolutely insist on behaving like an idiot in Provence, then you could at least do me the favor of not involving my wife."

Vialaron-Allègre. How did he get my private cell phone number? Blanc wondered, hurrying through the rooms and out into the garden. The minister was screaming so loudly down the phone that everyone could hear him. How does he know his wife is here? Did Aveline tell him? Once out in the open, Blanc took a deep breath. Suddenly he was overcome with a remarkable light-spiritedness—that of a condemned man standing on the scaffold with a view of the guillotine. It was all over. There was no point in fighting it anymore. He gave the minister the facts in the most relaxed manner. Two of the gendarmes and one of the forensics team had strolled out into the garden and were lighting up cigarettes. They were never going to find a Kalashnikov. *Merde.*

Abruptly Vialaron-Allègre halted his tirade of threats and curses. Maybe his new tone of apparent resignation was really just self-confidence. "Has this whole thing even the slightest trace of credibility?" he asked, unexpectedly calmly.

"It had enough credibility to convince the *juge d'instruction.*"

Blanc thought he could almost hear the wheels of Vialaron-Allègre's brain whirring. As if the politician was rapidly working through possibilities, strategies, alternatives. "Pass me to my wife," he said suddenly.

Blanc located Aveline on the terrace near the pool, standing smoking on her own, and handed her the phone, then retreated so as not to eavesdrop. She seemed relaxed and continued smoking as she talked. Her husband must have been able to hear her inhale. Maybe that would calm him down. One way or another he didn't seem to be saying much, as she was doing nearly all the talking. She seemed hardly to expect him to say anything or reply to any questions. After ten minutes she handed Blanc his phone back. The minister had hung up.

"What did you say to him?" Blanc asked, unable to restrain his curiosity.

"I told him to distance himself from Marcel as quickly as possible. Before this thing makes it into the press."

"We're not going to find the damn Kalashnikov."

"My husband is very grateful to you for advising him in advance."

Blanc stared at Aveline Vialaron-Allègre, tapping the ash from her Gauloise onto the gravel. So cool and calm. I've seen you in a different mood, he thought to himself.

"We are already on a one-way street, *mon Capitaine.* U-turns are not an option." Her dark eyes sparkled fire. He thought back to the upstairs room in her house, to her presence by his side, and the words she had said: Do you love taking risks? She's dancing on a high wire over an abyss, Blanc suddenly realized, and enjoying every moment of it. That's why she's here, making an enemy of the most powerful man in town.

Just at that moment an old green Toyota Corolla came through the gate. As soon as the old crate had come to a stop, out sprang Gérard Paulmier with notebook, pen, and a camera round his neck.

"*Merde,*" Blanc swore, going over to him. "Who told you about this?" he hissed.

"It was an anonymous call, but it sounded so crazy that I had to take a look. In thirty years I've never come across anybody prepared to take on Lafont. You'll be on page one tomorrow. Tell me what it's all about, or should I just work it out as I go along?"

Blanc's mind was whirring. Who could have told him? Somebody who wanted to see the back of Lafont? Or somebody who wanted to see the new boy come down from Paris dragged into a police misconduct scandal? "You can have the story all to yourself," he said reassuringly. "Just give me a few minutes first."

"Is it okay if I take photos in the meantime?"

"Obviously not."

Paulmier laughed, walked back over to his car, and leaned against it. Blanc ordered one of his men to go over and stand by the reporter to make sure he didn't do anything stupid. Then one of the others came over to him, shaking his head. The forensics team were creeping out of the house, putting their kit back in the van. Paulmier took a few photos anyway, and the gendarme standing next to him did nothing. Tonon had somehow made it from the guest bathroom to the patrol car without anybody noticing. Blanc had no idea how long the man had been sitting in the Mégane's passenger seat. It looked as if he was asleep. Fabienne came out onto the terrace and shot a brief glance at the *juge d'instruction.*

"Tell me you found Lafont made an online Amazon order for a Kalashnikov," Blanc joked wearily. "Or made an e-mail request for an assassin from Marseille? Otherwise we may as well pack it all in, in more than one sense."

"Don't give up yet, *mon Capitaine*. About two weeks ago Lafont looked at aerial shots of the garbage dump on Google Earth."

"That's hardly a crime."

"Are you laughing at me?" Fabienne hissed. "We turn the guy's house over and I'm the one giving you proof he was checking out the scene of the murder a few days before it happened."

"The virtual scene of the murder."

"So? What normal person looks at satellite pictures of a garbage heap? Lafont could have worked out the access routes, the layout of the parking lot, even the position of the scrap metal container, all without needing to go down there and without any witnesses."

Blanc glanced at Aveline Vialaron-Allègre. "Is that enough?"

"It's certainly interesting. But no, it's not enough. Not to arrest him. And certainly not to convict him."

"Lafont also used Google Maps to check out the routes to the dump," Fabienne exclaimed, increasingly frustrated. "I can prove that. The shortest route, the route from the town hall to the dump. And an alternative route. Goddamn it, surely that's enough to—" She stopped when she saw the look on Blanc's face.

Doors banged closed. The gendarmes were piling back into the cars, swearing because the hot sun had turned them into ovens. None of them bothered to report to Blanc. The forensics team's van was already on its way out of the gate. Paulmier looked at them in confusion. Lafont was nowhere to be seen. "*Connards*," Blanc muttered. "The operation is just getting started. Come on!" He ran over to the Mégane where Tonon was dozing away. "The three of us will do it on our own."

"Where are you going?" called Fabienne, running after him.

Blanc threw open the driver's door, noticing that Aveline Vialaron-Allègre was hurrying over to her Citroën at the same time. She had got the message, he realized. Okay, now there are four of us. "We're going to produce the Kalashnikov!" he growled triumphantly.

"Are you taking off?" Tonon spluttered, trying in vain to fasten his seat belt as the Mégane swayed across the road. Fabienne, in the backseat, hadn't even bothered to try. They raced over a pothole so fast that the shock absorbers groaned. "This is only a Renault!" the front-seat passenger shouted. "It would fall apart if you shouted too loud. One more pothole like that and—"

He fell silent as with a screech of brakes Blanc swerved out onto the *route départementale*, sending Tonon crashing into the door. Blanc looked in the rearview mirror. Nothing. Then the other Méganes with the gendarmes in them appeared. They all turned right, toward Gadet. Then the dark blue Citroën, which turned left. And Paulmier's old green Toyota. Also left. He was just turning his eyes back to the road ahead, when he saw something white in the mirror. The forensic team's van? Then he recognized it as the big Audi Q7. No sooner had it pulled out of the gate than it soared past the Toyota so close and so fast that Paulmier only just managed to regain control of his swerving vehicle before it nearly crashed into a pine tree. The elderly journalist let himself fall behind them.

"You're heading for Caillouteaux!" shouted Fabienne, who seemed to be enjoying herself.

"I owe you two lunches!" Blanc replied, ramming his foot down on the gas pedal while trying at the same time to turn on the flashing blue lights.

"Just keep at least one hand on the wheel!" screamed Tonon, bending over and turning on the blue lights himself.

"The town hall!" Blanc explained. "Lafont checked out the route from the town hall to the dump. Not from his house. What better hiding place than the town hall. Who's going to search for a Kalashnikov in the office of *Monsieur le maire*?"

"The new steel filing cabinet," Marius said. "That horrible thing he only had installed recently."

"In the same week as Lafont was down in Marseille in his wife's red Mini. To visit his old friends."

Blanc raced up the hill, cutting the corners. It was a good thing that Provence was dead over lunchtimes. From somewhere beneath the hood there came a loud clank. He hoped the old jalopy would make it the last mile or so into the town. They came to a straight stretch, and the Q7 flashed past the Citroën, its monstrous radiator grille now filling the Mégane's rearview mirror—like a shark's maw catching up on a diver. He could hear the heavy diesel engine ramped up on maximum revs even over the noise the Mégane was making and the roar of the mistral. Blanc weaved from side to side to stop it from overtaking.

"*Putain!*" Tonon swore. His forehead was bleeding from where he had hit it against the door frame.

"I'm not going to let him pass us," Blanc hissed through clenched teeth. "Lafont mustn't get to the town hall a single second ahead of us."

"We don't have a search warrant for the town hall," Fabienne reminded him, not that it seemed to bother her.

"We do have a *juge d'instruction* behind us."

"Providing she hasn't ended up in a ditch." Tonon turned round and shook his head. "I can't see her car any longer. Just this goddamn white monster."

Aveline. Blanc no longer looked in the mirror. His T-shirt stuck to his ribs, salty sweat ran down his forehead into his eyes, adrenaline pumped through his veins. He felt as if he were flying a jet fighter through the forest. "We'll show this scumbag!" he growled to let off steam.

The streets of Caillouteaux. The clunking sound under the hood was getting louder by the minute. The police siren reverberated off the walls of the houses. An elderly cyclist on a racing bike appeared out of nowhere. Where did he come from? Blanc swore. The Mégane just managed to swerve past him. A few seconds later, however, the big Q7's right wing mirror hit his elbow and sent him flying. Blanc kept his foot on the gas.

He only brought the vehicle to a screeching halt when they had reached the little square next to the town hall, nearly knocking the headless naked statue off her pedestal. The shutters on one house opened and an elderly woman peered out in curiosity. Blanc didn't even bother to turn the engine off. He sprang out, followed by Fabienne and Marius. They had reached the first steps on the way into the town hall when the white Audi appeared, slowly now. He spotted Lafont behind the wheel, red in the face and glistening with sweat, his sunglasses at an angle. They stared for a few seconds at each other. The mayor had realized he had lost the race, that he wouldn't overtake the cops. The heavy 4×4's engine suddenly resumed its howling as, with tires smoking, he did a U-turn in the one-way street they had just come down.

Blanc suddenly stopped. He's doing a runner, he realized. The Kalashnikov is more important, he told himself. Someone like Lafont can't just disappear. We'll get him.

Then a horrid screeching of metal set his teeth on edge. The Q7 had forced its way down the alley at the same time as the dark Citroën came up it. The massive Audi had scratched a long curve all along the driver's side of the Citroën from the front bumper to the trunk, shattering the side windows. Aveline turned away to avoid the hail of glass. Then the Audi was gone. Blanc heaved a sigh of relief. At least it wasn't a head-on crash. He ran down the steps to help Aveline out of the car. But then the Citroën's motor started up again. The *juge d'instruction* had done a handbrake turn in the alleyway and set out back down the alleyway Lafont had just disappeared from.

"*Merde*," swore Blanc. She's going after him. *Do you do it for the thrill of the risk?* For a moment that seemed to last forever he stood there on the square, uncertain what he should do. Then he turned back to Fabienne and Marius, who were still standing on the steps, numb from shock.

"Into the town hall," he ordered. "Get your hands on this

damn Kalashnikov, even if you have to blow open his steel cabinet. Call the forensics team and the other gendarmes back. And tell Nkoulou. Go on, get on with it."

Then he ran back to the Mégane, jumped in, and put his foot down, just as Paulmier came into the other end of the alley. Blanc braked abruptly and let the journalist past onto the square. "You'll have the story of your life!" he called out to him. Beyond the alley he came across the cyclist Lafont had knocked down. A small crowd had gathered around him and someone waved him to stop. Blanc made a gesture of excuse and turned on the blue lights. Then he put his foot down again, roared down the narrow street ahead, which Aveline and Lafont had to have taken. Neither car was to be seen. The only certain proof that they had come this way was the fresh black tire tracks on the first dangerous corner.

Fire

The siren was howling. Blanc honked his horn whenever he dared take a hand from the steering wheel, which wasn't often. He raced down the hill on the *route départementale*. When he came to a straight stretch, he spotted the two cars for a second or two, maybe five hundred yards in front of him. The white Audi almost filled the width of the road, the Citroën tight on its tail. Lafont had the more powerful car, but Aveline was the more audacious driver. He watched as both cars came to a crossing and swerved onto an even smaller rural road, one he had never taken before. *"Merde!"* he swore. With every second he fell farther behind both of them. By the time they reached the next roundabout, he would have lost sight of them altogether. He was having so much trouble keeping the Mégane on the track that he didn't dare make a grab for the radio to call for backup.

He reached the first roundabout and turned. Suddenly there was a yellow mail van to his right. He spun the wheel at the last moment, sending stones flying on either side of the road. For a fraction of a second he glimpsed a young, blond woman behind the windshield, her mouth wide open in a ghostly silent scream.

She braked so hard that the van slid obliquely across the road, its tires smoking.

Blanc glanced into the rearview mirror to check that the mail van hadn't actually hit a tree. His ears echoed with the howl of the siren, his hooting of the horn, the roaring of the vehicle's overstressed four-cylinder engine, the hammering noise still coming from under the hood. Then there was smoke, thin ochre plumes drifting between the pine branches on either side, at head height above the ground. There was a burning smell in the air. "This old crate's going to blow up on me," Blanc shouted out to nobody.

He stood on the brakes. The tires screamed in protest. Right in front of him on either side of the track were two wrecks. The Audi Q7 had gone nose-first into a ditch by the roadside, its wheels in the air, still spinning. The driver's door hung open. The Citroën had traveled a few yards farther into the undergrowth. Its windshield was shattered. The doors were closed. Blanc had passed the wrecks before the Renault came to a halt. He ran back, jumping over the ditch. "Aveline!" he called out, ripping open the driver's door.

She was conscious, though a little line of blood ran down from her left temple. The deflated airbags covered the steering wheel and door frame. He pushed them out of the way and felt for her seat belt. "I'm fine," she mumbled woozily.

"Yeah, right, you look like you've just returned from vacation." He pulled her out of the seat belt. "What happened?"

"I rammed Lafont."

Blanc didn't reply, thinking he couldn't have heard right. He still had the damn mistral rushing through the trees in his ears. The rustling branches. He felt faint.

"There was no way I could get past that fat crate of his," Aveline continued. She was gradually coming back to reality. "I was afraid Lafont would sooner or later stop hurtling along blindly through the countryside, but would think it through. What would I have done in his position? I would have turned down the next forest track. In that four-by-four of his he could have carried on forever, while my sedan would eventually have got stuck in the ruts. So I just crashed into the rear of the Audi when he braked to take a corner. I rammed him into the ditch."

"And damn near broke your neck in the process," he exclaimed. "It's not far to the patrol car. You can lie down in it. I'll call paramedics and backup. Lafont is on the run on foot. He won't get far."

She shook her head and gave him a pained smile. "This isn't the Jardin de Luxembourg in Paris, *mon Capitaine*."

"The forest isn't that big."

"The forest is on fire," she shouted at him. "Don't you see the smoke? Don't you smell anything? There's a fire raging somewhere out there."

He shrugged. "That'll just cut off Lafont's path."

"And ours. If we aren't lucky. The mistral fans the flames. They'll rush through the undergrowth faster than you can run. A lot faster. We have half an hour at most to find Lafont, then we need to be out of here."

Blanc stood up. He had heard a crackling noise in the forest, almost as loud as gunfire. "We don't have half an hour," he whispered. "The flames are almost here."

The track stopped just a few yards beyond where the two wrecked cars had come to rest. Already the ground started to dip where the Citroën lay. A few paces beyond it fell steeply downward for maybe a hundred feet. The ground was covered with macchia bushes and knee-high thistles, with a few stunted oaks clinging to the slope. The red sandy soil had been blown away in places to reveal gray rock. The valley below was more thickly wooded and dropped away in terraces down to the Étang de Berre. The sky above them was still crystal clear and blue, but down below clouds of smoke were gathering like dirty cotton wool. The center was almost black while the mistral was blowing yellowish plumes into the air. Blanc noticed an old pine burst into flames. Then a bubble of resin exploded into a red ball of fire, the wind bringing the sound like a gunshot up the hill to them.

"There he is," Blanc called out. Standing by the side of the road he had spotted Lafont's massive shape halfway down the hill. He had discarded his linen jacket, and his white shirt stood out like a semaphore flag. The mayor was stumbling down the slope, not bothering to look around him. And ran straight into the cloud of smoke.

"Marcel has a habit of making mistakes under pressure," Aveline Vialaron-Allègre said calmly. "The fire will have him."

"He's still only halfway down the slope."

"The wind will soon blow the flames uphill."

A second tree burst into a flaming torch: an oak, its leaves turning into black, oily smoke. Reddish-yellow flames were now glowing amidst the smoke. The first yellow plumes had risen so high into the air that they now obscured the sunlight above their heads. The bitter stench was getting worse by the moment. Blanc could feel the heat on his skin and a choking sensation in his throat. It was as if someone had opened a giant oven door, closed it, then reopened it and closed it again. And every time the oven remained open for a few seconds longer. He wasn't even sweating anymore—the wind and the heat had dried his skin.

"*Merde,*" he said, pulling out his gun. "I'll get the bastard."

"*We'll* get the bastard."

"Lafont has killed twice."

"All the more reason for there to be two of us."

"But—"

"We're not still living in the 1950s, *mon Capitaine.* I can look after myself."

Blanc just shrugged, grabbed hold of the branch of a stunted oak, and began to make his way down the slope. He had to pause for breath. It was as if all the oxygen was being sucked out of the valley. The heat increased with every step he took. He was in danger of losing consciousness, and then the flames would take him. He shook himself. Keep going! Lafont was older than him, overweight, and clearly already exhausted. Blanc would catch him up before long. Keep going!

The roar of the mistral got worse, or maybe it was a different sort of roar: flames burning wood. Or there again, maybe it was the blood boiling in his head. Keep going. Behind him he heard the crack of a branch, and a suppressed cry from Aveline. Don't turn round. Keep going. Blanc reached the bottom of the slope. The shrubbery was thicker, thornier, and gray trails of smoke billowed among the branches. A scorpion ran across his shoe, fleeing the flames, up the hill he had just come down. A snake as long as his forearm slid down the branch of a rosemary bush and stared at him with dark green eyes for a second. Keep going.

He heard another crack; a pine tree branch next to him broke. Blanc ducked to avoid the splinters. He was afraid the tree's resin would explode any second, but then he realized that the tree had not burst into flames. It had been a gunshot. He threw himself down into the undergrowth. Down, onto the ground. The smell of old wood and pine needles.

"Get down," he shouted to Aveline. He had no idea if she could hear his voice over the noise. The earth trembled. Panicking ants ran around dragging white eggs behind them. He peered through the undergrowth. There was no sign of Lafont amidst the confusion of wood, leaves, and smoke. Don't let him pin you down, the flames are coming this way, he told himself. In any case it was better to have Lafont shooting at him rather than Aveline. He sprang to his feet and made a long dash to the next shrub. Another gunshot, from somewhere out there. Where was the bastard?

Blanc pressed his face to the ground again, trying to breathe more regularly. The earth was trembling more than ever. He could hear a buzzing like that of a swarm of bees. It got louder, deeper. Motors, he thought, confused. Then he recalled an image from his first year of service. Water cannons on their way to deal with a student demonstration in Paris, colossal machines rolling along slowly, making the shop windows and even the asphalt surface of the boulevards vibrate. Were they about to tackle the blaze with water cannons? He looked around nervously, but all he could see was smoke and branches. Pull yourself together!

The buzzing got louder. He could feel the vibrations now not just beneath his feet but throughout his body. Where was Lafont? Where was Aveline? The sky above his head turned dark. A giant shadow obscured the sun, cutting through the plumes of smoke like the wings of some immense pterodactyl. The droning had become so loud his hands were shaking. He looked up in shock: A huge yellowy-orange aircraft was flying just above the treetops, a cumbersome propeller aircraft, its wings bobbing in the rising hot air. All of a sudden a hatch in the rear opened out and he thought that at any moment a hail of bombs would begin to fall, like he had seen in old war films. But instead a great cloud emerged from the aircraft. Blanc pressed his face to the ground. A second later he was soaked. A wall of water descended on him, smashing branches, ripping apart leaves. For one surreal second he saw millions of drops battering down onto the rock-hard dry earth and bouncing up again, little pearls of glass in the air, before falling down again and turning the red soil to mud.

Blanc began coughing. For a few seconds he was shivering with cold until the heat dried out his clothing. Then he heard a fresh rumbling. Fire engines, he thought, when his head finally cleared. He should have got the picture straightaway. The fire-extinguishing aircraft down at Marignane, capable of carrying hundreds of gallons of water in their holds for dumping on flames. He'd seen their spectacular feats of low flying often enough on the television news. He tried to remember how many of the aircraft they had. Five? Six? Seven?

He saw the next shadow approaching. This time he was prepared. He kneeled down, his left arm shielding his head, his right hand holding the Sig-Sauer pistol in an attempt to keep the gun dry. When the droning became almost unbearable just before the water was released he sprang to his feet and looked around him. There was something white visible behind the trunk of a pine tree to his right, just slightly farther down the now gentle slope, no more than twenty yards away. Lafont. Blanc ducked down again and let the wall of water rush over him. He could hear it hissing as it fell on trees that were already alight.

Carefully Blanc crept forward through the undergrowth, hoping Lafont would not have moved, pinned to the ground by a combination of water, fire, and fear. He could hear the third aircraft approaching. This time he didn't dare to try standing up again but got down on his knees and glanced toward the pine tree: Lafont, his face as red as a lobster, his shirt ripped, partly blackened. Behind him a bush was on fire. He could go no farther. He was only ten yards away now. Then the next wall of water hit.

More droning. A fourth aircraft on the way. A movement to his left. Blanc turned in confusion. Aveline! She was still bleeding from her temple, had lost her left shoe, and was limping. She was heading for an old tree to shelter from the next deluge of water, but she was slow. Blanc turned his head quickly and stared ahead of him into the smoke. Something had changed. Suddenly he saw Lafont's huge frame emerge from behind the pine tree: an arm, a hand, a gun.

He sprang to his feet and fired, again and again and again, as the deluge of water poured over him.

Le Midi

The cicadas took up again around 8:30 in the evening. The mistral had suddenly stopped in the middle of the afternoon, as if somebody had turned off a fan up on Mont Blanc where the wind came from. By suppertime the air was pleasantly cool, and the water Blanc gulped down from the plastic bottle deliciously cold. He had showered for what seemed like hours to get the stench of smoke and blood from his pores. He realized he had missed the cicadas.

He had been flying on autopilot for the last few hours. He couldn't remember the noise the Sig-Sauer had made, just the kickback from each shot, a dull punch to the outside of the elbow. He couldn't remember Lafont's screams, just the red splashes that appeared on his shirt growing ever larger until they covered his whole torso. He couldn't remember what Aveline had said to him, only her hands as she grabbed his right arm and pushed it up. He couldn't remember what the mayor yelled at him, just the spittle flying from his mouth.

The first sound Blanc actually recalled hearing was a curse and a deep male voice, curiously muffled. "Goddamn tourists!"

Three *pompiers* in full kit and breathing masks beneath their silver helmets had broken through the undergrowth while Aveline and he were kneeling next to Lafont trying to stem the bleeding with some strips of cotton torn from Blanc's T-shirt. Then the firemen saw the wounded man. Blanc responded by jumping to his feet and showing his police badge, a rather absurd gesture in the middle of a burning forest.

If the firemen hadn't put rubber masks over their faces, from which they greedily sucked in a flow of oxygen, they might well have suffocated. But in the end they made it back up the hill to the roadside where the blue lights of large fire engines, two ambulances, and half a dozen blue Méganes were waiting. Lafont was taken into the back of one of the ambulances. Suddenly Commandant Nkoulou was there and ordered two gendarmes to sit next to the stretcher in the ambulance, which then set off with a patrol car escort.

Eventually Blanc had found himself back at his desk, staring out of the window, waiting for a call from the emergency department from the Hôpital Nord in Marseille, where they had taken Lafont. Aveline was at the court in Aix. Tonon had shown him the Kalashnikov they had found in the steel cabinet in the town hall. Fabienne was writing notes for the file, staring for hours on end at her computer, avoiding looking at him. Then the call from the hospital came and Tonon opened a bottle of rosé and Fabienne had kissed him on both cheeks, and Nkoulou came in and said he could go home.

Amongst the bits and pieces he had brought from his Paris apartment was a radio alarm clock, a promotional gift in a box that Geneviève and he had never even opened. Now Blanc had

set it up to the rear of the house, so its aerial might receive a
signal. While the digital display still showed a blinking 00:00
because he had never bothered to set the time, the nine o'clock
news was droning out of the plastic loudspeaker. The forest fire
had just managed to make the penultimate item on the national
news: almost thirty acres wiped out, the mistral gusting at up
to fifty-five miles an hour, the speedy intervention of the fire-
fighters. The gendarmes in Miramas had arrested a man who
had been too lazy to take an old mattress down to the garbage
dump and instead had set fire to it on the roadside on the *route
départementale*. The very final item was the arrest of Lafont
"in connection with investigations into a murder case and local corruption."

So Lafont will only be charged with the murder of Moréas,
Blanc thought. He was too weak to be interrogated, the doctors
at Marseille's Hôpital Nord had said. Maybe they owed him a
favor or two. One way or the other, it would give Lafont time to
think up a strategy. If he denied having anything to do with
the death of the building contractor, they would be unlikely to
dispute his defense. After all, what did they have to prove he
had killed Fuligni? And then what would happen? At the trial
at the courthouse in Aix, Aveline wouldn't want to get involved
in a charge that had no hope of success. She would let Fuligni's death pass as an accident, if she even mentioned it at all.
None of the lawyers would mention Fuligni, and no verdict would
be pronounced by a judge. Lafont would pass as merely the man
who had taken out a violent guy everybody had been afraid of.
All the old allegations against Moréas would come up again, the
files Tonon had kept up all those years would be opened again.
Who knew, maybe Marius himself would have to take the wit-

ness stand. A clever defense lawyer could do something with that. In the end Lafont could come out as the man who got rid of a thug the police had failed to put away in twenty years. Maybe even the good guy.

He heard the knocking of a diesel engine coming from the little road. A white, modest C3 he had never seen before drove through his gate. Blanc shot to his feet, suddenly nervous. The oblique rays of the evening sun reflected off the windshield so he couldn't make out who was in the driver's seat. Whoever it was drove up to the old olive oil mill so fast that the tires sent up clouds of dust. Instinctively he reached for his belt, but he had left the Sig-Sauer on a shelf in the bedroom. The driver's door opened.

Aveline.

It took him a moment to recognize her. She was wearing a simple white T-shirt and jeans and, despite the late hour, large sunglasses, covering a wide plaster on the side of her forehead. Her hair was hidden by a blue baseball cap with the words NOVA SCOTIA on it.

"What sort of car is that?" he asked, walking toward her.

"It's a rental, from the garage. Until the new C5 is delivered."

"At the state's expense, I assume."

"It was an accident incurred while working."

"It's a good thing our *juges d'instruction* don't have too many accidents while working."

She took off her sunglasses and smiled. "Are you worried about the financial drain on the French taxpayer, *mon Capitaine*?"

"I'm worried about you, *Madame le juge*." He came a few steps closer to her.

"You would have done better to worry about yourself."

"Does your husband intend to send me to the guillotine?"

"He's already sharpened the blade and hoisted it."

"I can already feel a twitching in my neck." He was standing right next to her now, but she didn't seem to have noticed.

"Then my husband realized that the scandal surrounding Lafont was not only unavoidable, but potentially useful. The elections are imminent. The minister will personally make sure the *'Affaire Lafont'* is the basis to launch a campaign against local corruption. *La ville propre.* Clean up the town. A good slogan, don't you think."

"And what role am I expected to play in this?"

"None at all. Commandant Nkoulou will play the leading role in this little comedy. You should be glad your head is still on your shoulders."

"I am indeed," said Blanc, taking her in his arms and kissing her.

She allowed him a long embrace, then she leaned back a bit and looked him in the eyes. It was a look that seemed to be simultaneously cold and passionate. "Let's be quite clear on one thing," she said in a soft voice. "I have no intention of ever leaving my husband." Then she kissed him again.

My life just keeps getting more complicated, Blanc thought.

TURN THE PAGE FOR A SNEAK PEEK AT
CAY RADEMACHER'S NEXT NOVEL

Available November 2018

Blood on the Road

In twenty years of service with the gendarmerie, Captain Roger Blanc had never seen so much blood: a dead black fighting bull blocking the road, a dark colossus with at least two dozen 9mm Parabellum gunshot wounds. A few yards behind it lay the horribly ripped-open corpse of a man. The blood of both man and beast had mingled and dried into a cracked brown crust on the stinking tar surface of the road.

It was late afternoon, but the sun still hung above the horizon like a poisonous flower. A battered white street sign indicated the way to Saint-Gilles down the *route départementale*, a minor road branching off to one side. I know the name of that place from somewhere, Blanc thought, but in the heat there was no way to remember where or when he had heard it. Someone had fired a gun at the sign a long time ago, and the edges of the holes had gone rusty. The winding roads were narrow gray ribbons in a world of sand, salt, and tough grass: the Camargue.

Brackish water pooled like leaden mirrors the size of lakes and as calm as puddles, some of them an almost chemical blue, others bright red like diluted watercolors. Yellowish white bubbles of foam clung to their marshy edges. The grass was knee high, every blade as sharp as a dagger, swaying slightly up and down, up and down, in a gentle westerly breeze that brought no relief from the heat. Dragonflies danced over the surface of the water. Blanc noticed elegant pink silhouettes stalking along the blurred horizon and realized with astonishment that they were flamingos. He had only seen them once before, an eternity ago, in the zoo at Vincennes, when his children were still young and his marriage still intact.

Bright flashes of light boring into his eyes like needles diverted his attention to the macabre piece of theater lying at his feet. Rays of sunlight were being reflected by the steel watch on the wrist of the man who had been tossed by the fighting bull's horns. His body lay some fifteen feet beyond that of the shot animal.

Blanc bent down over the man's body. He was in his midfifties, between 5'7" and 5'8" tall, slim, and suntanned. An ultralight angular pair of sunglasses covered the upper half of his face; long gray hair already turning white spilled out from under a helmet that looked as if a computer-game designer had made it with a 3-D printer. The dead man was wearing black cycling shorts and a sports T-shirt in cobalt blue and neon yellow. Not that there was much of either color visible given that one of the bull's horns had struck the cyclist in the abdomen while the beast itself had thrown up its head, ripping him open as if with a butcher's knife from his navel almost to his throat. The edges of the wound were jagged, and the man's small intestine bulged out of the opening like some pale garden slug. Blanc spotted the end of a broken rib as well as a few other organs he wasn't too keen on identifying. Gorged bluebottles were crawling all over the corpse. The smell of blood and partly digested food mingled with that of the brackish water. Blanc felt faint and got quickly back on his feet.

He looked around, squinting despite his sunglasses. Just a handbreadth higher than his immediate surroundings a luxuriant green meadow glistened, enclosed behind a sturdy fence of square wooden beams and iron posts, with only one access gate, which was made of wood in a massive steel frame. It lay wide open.

Blanc looked back at the dead man. He had been riding an expensive-looking mountain bike that had skidded maybe thirty feet until the front wheel had ended up in the drainage ditch at the side of the road. Then Blanc looked at the bull, its legs stretched out like the imploring arms of a beggar, its heavy lilac-colored tongue hanging from its mouth, the lines scraped in the tarmac by its horns, each one as long as a man's arm, and the side of its massive body ripped open by the bullets.

An older gendarme, sweating profusely, came over to him, the name RONCHARD on his badge.

"Was it you who shot the bull?" Blanc asked.

"Yes, *mon Capitaine.* A witness reported the accident. My colleague and I were the first on-site and found the body." Ronchard nodded toward another uniformed gendarme, who was using a compact camera to take photos of the road and the victim. He was holding the camera at arm's length as if afraid it might explode at any moment. Blanc doubted he would produce a single usable photo of the scene.

"The bull was still standing next to the victim," Ronchard went on. "At first we didn't dare get out of the car. I wasn't keen to tackle that half ton of bone and muscle with just my service pistol. It just so happened we had a UNP-9 in the car because we were on the way back from the shooting range. I'm a hunter in my spare time and . . . *eh bien* . . ." He hesitated, then gave a humorless laugh. "It wasn't exactly a marksman's shot. I rolled down the side window and emptied the magazine."

Blanc glanced back at the bull and nodded. "Maybe you'll get the sawed-off head as a trophy. Bit different from a pheasant."

"I'll be in the papers, that's for sure. I can't remember the last time a tourist in the Camargue was impaled on a bull's horns."

Blanc nodded toward the open fence. "Was that gate already open when you got here?"

"As open as a flasher's fly."

"So the bull was grazing in a meadow that had been left open," Blanc mused. "Why wasn't the gate closed? And how long had it been open? *Bien*, one way or another, a cyclist just happens to be coming down a country road on his mountain bike."

"These animals are bred to fight, *mon Capitaine*. They are extremely aggressive and very fast. Maybe the animal got disturbed and it felt threatened. Or maybe it was just bored and hot with that black pelt in this sun. Maybe the screech of the brakes irritated it. Those things are monstrous beasts. In any case the creature must have seen the cyclist. There was nothing in between them. The bull lowered its head and charged. Hits him straight on. It'll be in the pages of *La Provence* in the morning."

"Maybe the front page," Blanc murmured gloomily, removing the victim's sunglasses. "Have you taken a closer look at him, Ronchard? Do you know him?"

The man coughed. "The helmet and sunglasses covered up most of his face, and in any case I wasn't that close."

"Try to ignore the ludicrous cycling outfit he's wearing. Imagine him in designer jeans and an elegant dark jacket, wearing a shirt so white it hurts your eyes, with always one button too many undone. That's how this gentleman normally appears on his frequent television appearances."

It was Thursday, August 4, the seventh day of a heat wave that felt as if God had dragged the Midi away from Europe and planted it in the Sahara. Every day the radio was predicting temperatures of 95 degrees—a political move, Blanc figured, made not to panic people. If the temperature gauge in his run-down old Renault Espace still worked, he expected the little display would show 100 degrees from morning to late in the evening.

On Wednesday he had given up trying to inspect the roof of the old olive oil mill he had been living in for several weeks. The curved terra-cotta tiles had been heated by the sun to the extent that he had been forced to put on gloves just to touch them. After a few minutes, covered in sweat and dehydrated, he had retreated down the rickety wooden ladder he had found in a Dumpster near the house. But he had been careless enough to go up there with his shirt off and had come back down with sunburned shoulders. He cursed his own stupidity later when the burning from his neck to his upper arms stopped him from falling asleep. Born a northerner, always a northerner.

On Thursday morning he had sat in front of the nearly useless monitor of his antique computer staring at the screen saver. The heat had sapped the destructive energy of even the usual suspects in the criminal fraternity, so there was not much to do. He had tried to move as little as possible, which wasn't easy given that the chair was too small for his nearly six-foot-six frame. The shabby little concrete office block in the center of Gadet had air-conditioning, but it was less than inadequate and hadn't been serviced in years with the result that the whirring metal box emitted nothing more than a few waves of lukewarm air stinking of mildew. To get any fresh air at all the gendarmes had to open the windows from time to time, even if it did feel like they were opening the doors to an oven.

As always Blanc had gone to work in dark jeans and a black T-shirt and felt as if even the light cotton was scraping the sunburned patches of his skin.

His partner wasn't doing any better. Lieutenant Marius Tonon was also sitting staring apathetically at his screen, though at least he wasn't plagued by sunburn. His massive subordinate's olive-colored skin had long since become immune to the rays of the sun. But he blinked continuously, and there were big inflamed rings around his eyes while spiderwebs of tiny burst veins had exploded across his eyeballs.

Blanc had had lunch with his colleague in the shade of the plane trees in Gadet's Le Soleil restaurant, watching Tonon knock back a pastis "to cure my thirst." And then another. Only then did the landlord silently deliver his usual carafe of rosé wine.

When they were just starting to nod off in the office later, Blanc and Tonon jumped at the ring of the telephone. "*Merde*," Blanc muttered when he glanced at the display and saw that it was their boss calling.

Commandant Nicolas Nkoulou as ever lorded it over them in his office at the opposite end of the corridor, his immaculate pale blue uniform contrasting perfectly with his gold-rimmed glasses and chocolate-colored skin, on which there was not a single bead of sweat. He looked at Blanc and Tonon for longer than usual and for a moment it seemed as if he was about to say something totally different than what he was supposed to say to them. But in the end he collected his thoughts and pushed a piece of paper across his desk to them.

"This has just come in. It would appear to be"—the commandant cleared his throat—"a rather bizarre accident. A cyclist, a bull, and a real mess. Go check it out, purely pro forma."

"*Putain*, what does he mean pro forma?" Tonon whispered as they closed the door to the boss's office behind them.

"That he's given the job to us because everybody else thinks it's too hot," Blanc replied, requisitioning a squad car. "How long will it take us to get down to the Camargue?"

His colleague rolled his inflamed eyes. "Have you ever looked at a map?"

"The only map I know remotely well is the street map of Paris."

"Welcome to the real world."

As he walked out into the glaring sunlight, Blanc pulled the cloth armband bearing the word GENDARMERIE onto his left arm. Even that hurt. "I never would have thought that I'd feel better in that moldy hunk of concrete than I would outdoors," he grumbled, looking back at the gendarmerie station and noticing a blind twitch. Almost certainly a gloating colleague. *Merde.*

"You'll feel at home in the Camargue: it's salty, flat, and boring. Just like the north, only a bit hotter."

"I don't recall mad fighting bulls careering down the streets back home," Blanc replied dismissively.

His colleague flopped down into the passenger seat with a groan and fiddled with the dashboard until Radio Nostalgie filled the Renault Mégane, which was a bit of a relic from the past itself. Patricia Kaas. "*Reste sur moi.*"

"I'd like to know whether it is a Provençal or Spanish fighting bull," Tonon said, unconsciously mouthing the words of the melody so it looked as if he was singing along. It annoyed Blanc and he concentrated on looking at the road.

"A bull is a bull," he replied, driving slowly out of the gendarmerie parking lot. There was hardly any need to rush.

Tonon gave him a sympathetic look. "You wouldn't say that if you were a bullfighter. In the Spanish corrida it's a matter of life and death. Usually it's the animal that gets stabbed, but sometimes the bull can win. Spanish bulls are bred so that their horns point lower—that makes it easier for them to get you."

"That's only fair."

"Provençal *cocardiers*, however," Tonon went on, "are smaller

than the Spanish animals, faster, more nervous, more mobile—
and their horns point upward."

"Nice for the *torero*."

"We call them *raseteurs*. Their job is to seize the rosettes
fixed between the bull's horns, tiny little things tied to the base
of the horns, right above the powerful skull. No normal person
would do it of their own free will. A *raseteur* doesn't wave a red
cape or play around with a sword or prance around the arena like
some fancy Spanish fairy. A *raseteur* has no weapon save for the
crochet, which looks a bit like an outsize knuckle-duster with
hooks on it. That's what he uses to snag the rosettes from the
horns if he's skilled enough and can get that close to the bull. A
raseteur is dressed all in white and has to be quick on his feet.
That's why we call it the *course camarguaise*; it's really more like
a race than a fight. It can end in bloodshed, but it doesn't very
often, and if it does, it's the man's blood. Throughout the spring
and again in the autumn the spectacles are held in arenas such
as those at Arles or Istres, sometimes Spanish-style but more often Provençal-style. But even the best bulls end up in the abat-
toir. Their meat has a gamy taste."

"All your thoughts come back to the kitchen," Blanc teased
him. "If there are that many beasts, how come cyclists don't get
gored more often?"

Tonon laughed. "Because there's enough free space to get out
of the way most of the time. The Camargue is nearly eight hundred square miles, full of swamps, meadows, rice fields. The town
of Saintes-Maries-de-la-Mer has a Mediterranean coastline with
beaches, gypsy music, happy tourists. Saint-Gilles is a hick town
with a huge church, Aigues-Mortes is a sort of medieval Disney-
land. But apart from those three towns, the whole area is more
or less deserted. In the middle of the wasteland there are a couple
of places where Parisians and the English come down to bust

their balls on the backs of the famous Camargue white horses. There are the little *cabanes* that used to be lived in by the *gardians*, the cowboys of the Camargue with their black hats and tridents, the guys who look after the bulls but who can't afford the huts anymore. They're lived in by the Parisians and English who cool their balls off in them after they've been out riding. The cattle just wander freely through the wasteland, but the fighting bulls are kept in enclosed meadows behind strong fences. As a cyclist, there's normally just you and a few thousand uninterested flamingos."

"You sound like a great fan of the Camargue."

"You might say that."

Blanc turned onto *route départementale* 113, which ran mile after mile straight ahead between fields and lines of cypress trees. It felt a bit like driving down an endless airport runway without ever taking off. He was glad to see the traffic get a bit heavier as they approached Arles or else he might have fallen asleep at the wheel. His colleague nodded at the road sign that read SAINTES-MARIES and said wearily, "That way, just keep straight ahead. We're bound to come across the whole mess sooner or later."

It only took a few minutes before the patrol car was in a whole different world, driving through an ocean of grass and silvery water. Blanc spotted a *cabane* a few hundred yards away from the road. The straw roof had gone dark, but the walls were whitewashed to the extent that they were almost blinding. The northern end was narrow, rounded, and without windows. Blanc had experienced the mercilessly icy mistral and could imagine why these huts out in this unsheltered expanse presented it with a streamlined, wind-resistant face. There didn't seem to be a track across the marshland to the *cabane* and he wondered how anyone was supposed to get there from the road. A few white horses were tied to a wooden fence near the building. Paulette Aybalen, who lived near Blanc's dilapidated oil mill, also kept Camargue horses on her land. Sometimes she would ride out alone and sometimes with her daughters through the forests that lay on the other side of the mill. A wild, attractive woman. A woman . . . And then his thoughts went back to Geneviève and why she had left him. He wondered if she was still on vacation in the Caribbean with her new lover. Or whether she was back in Paris with him. Looking out the window of *his* apartment, cooking in *his* kitchen, falling into *his* bed in the evening . . . Blanc wasn't paying attention to the road and almost drove into a drainage ditch when a few miles down the road took a sudden turn.

"The Camargue is better than Valium," Tonon commented, as soon as he had gotten over the shock. "As soon as you get here, your thoughts drift off elsewhere. What were you thinking about?"

Blanc was too worked up to give him a bland, inconsequential answer. "My wife," he replied.

"Your ex-wife."

"We're not divorced yet."

"Dream on. Is she still crying her eyes out, or has she found a new guy?"

"She's on vacation with him in the Caribbean."

"I'm sure your ex spends every day lying under the palm trees thinking about you." Tonon punched him so hard on the shoulder that Blanc came dangerously close to driving into the ditch again. "Believe me, I'm speaking from experience. One cop is enough. A woman who's been hitched to a gendarme doesn't make the same mistake twice. Get her out of your head."

"We have two kids."

"Grown up?"

"They're allowed to vote. But at times they act as if they are still in kindergarten."

"*Eh bien.* They chucked you out of Paris and sent you down here to the farthest province. Your wife left you. Your kids don't want anything more from you except a bit of money now and again. Sounds like ideal conditions for a new beginning."

Blanc thumped the steering wheel. "My career is shit and I'm driving through a swamp to see the only cyclist in France stupid enough to get his guts ripped out by an ox. You call that a new beginning?"

"Whenever you reach the bottom, you have to go up again. It's the law of physics."

Blanc looked at his overweight, exhausted colleague who hadn't been promoted in decades and didn't bother with an answer. He put his foot on the brakes because there was a line of a dozen cars in front of him, stuck behind an RV with Dutch license plates. The van's driver was doing under thirty miles per hour through the plains. Every time there was nothing coming from the other direction, two cars would pull out and pass the RV. When it was his turn, Blanc pulled out and roared past the huge white slug, even though there was a group of brightly clad cyclists coming toward him. One of them flipped him the bird.

"Flat land. Good for cyclists," Blanc muttered, pulling out again to overtake another pair of cyclists, an overweight middle-aged couple on mountain bikes.

"All you have to do is watch out for fighting bulls and mad drivers," Tonon replied.

Blanc declined to reply and instead nodded up ahead to where a blue light was flashing rhythmically and a uniformed gendarme was using a paddle to wave traffic around a lane that had been blocked off with tape. "We're there," he announced.